Polinka Saks

—— A N D ——

The Story of
Aleksei Dmitrich

Northwestern
University Press
Series in Russian Literature
and Theory

»»»»»»»»»» ««««««««««

Aleksandr Druzhinin

Polinka Saks *and* The Story of Aleksei Dmitrich

TRANSLATED AND WITH AN INTRODUCTION

BY MICHAEL R. KATZ

NORTHWESTERN UNIVERSITY PRESS

»»»»»»»»»» ««««««««««

Northwestern University Press

Evanston, Illinois 60201–2807

Polinka Saks first published in Russian in *Sovremennik*, 1847. *The Story of Aleksei Dmitrich* first published in Russian in *Sovremennik*, 1848. Translated from the edition published by B. F. Egorov and V. A. Zhdanov in the Literary Monument Series published by Nauka, Leningrad, 1986. English translation and introduction copyright © 1992 by Northwestern University Press. All rights reserved.

Published 1992

Printed in the United States of America

ISBN: cloth 0–8101–1052–0

paper 0–8101–1077–6

Library of Congress Cataloging-in-Publication Data

Druzhinin, A. V. (Aleksandr Vasil'evich), 1824–1864.

[Polin'ka Saks. English]

Polinka Saks ; and, The Story of Aleksei Dmitrich / Aleksandr Druzhinin ; translated and with an introduction by Michael R. Katz.

p. cm.

First English translation of Polin'ka Saks and Rasskaz Alekseĩa Dmitricha.

Includes bibliographical references.

ISBN 0-8101-1052-0 (alk. paper). — ISBN 0-8101-1077-6 (pbk.).

I. Katz, Michael R. II. Druzhinin, A. V. (Aleksandr Vasil'evich), 1824–1864. Rasskaz Alekseĩa Dmitricha. English. 1992. III. Title: Polinka Saks. IV. Title: Story of Aleksei Dmitrich.

PG3330.D7P613 1992

891.73'3—dc20

92-7016

CIP

»»» CONTENTS ««««

»»» «««

Translator's Note

Polinka Saks was first published in the journal *Sovremennik* (The Contemporary) in 1847. *The Story of Aleksei Dmitrich* was published in the same journal in 1848. Both stories were reprinted in an authoritative edition by B. F. Egorov and V. A. Zhdanov in the Literary Monument Series published by Nauka (Leningrad, 1986). It is this text that I have chosen to translate.

The system of transliteration is that used in the *Oxford Slavonic Papers*, with the following exceptions: hard and soft signs have been omitted and conventional spellings of names have been retained.

I wish to express my gratitude to the University Research Institute at the University of Texas at Austin for a Special Research Grant for this project.

Special thanks are due to Saul and Paul: Gary Saul Morson, my colleague at Northwestern University, who encouraged the project from the start; and Paul Ivaschenko, my research assistant at the University of Texas at Austin, who provided help along the way.

»»» «««
Druzhinin's Prose Fiction

AN INTRODUCTION

The last issue of The Contemporary . . . *includes* Polinka Saks, *a story by Mr. Druzhinin, a complete newcomer to Russian literature. There is much in this story that bears the stamp of immature thought and exaggeration, and the figure of Saks is somewhat idealized: in spite of that, the story contains so much truth, so much warmth of soul and faithful, intelligent understanding of reality, so much talent, and so much originality, that it has immediately attracted general attention. The character of the heroine is particularly well drawn— obviously the author has a keen understanding of Russian women. Mr. Druzhinin's second work, which appeared this year* [The Story of Aleksei Dmitrich], *confirms the impression created by his first—that the author possesses original talent—and leads us to expect a great deal from him in the future.*

Vissarion Belinsky
"A View of Russian Literature in 1847"[1]

Aleksandr Vasilievich Druzhinin was born in 1824 at his family estate of Marinskoe in the district of Golov, in the province of St. Petersburg into a well-to-do gentry family. He was educated at home until the age of sixteen and then sent off to military school in Petersburg. There he studied foreign languages and began his literary career, writing humorous verse and generously supplying compositions to other less talented students. He graduated in 1843 and joined the Finland Regiment. As a result of his literary inclinations, he was chosen regimental librarian. In 1846 he retired from the military and took up a post in the civil service, from which he retired five years later to devote his life to literary and journalistic pursuits.

Druzhinin served as literary editor of *The Contemporary* from 1848 to 1855 and gradually moved from his earlier position of moderate liberalism into the conservative camp. He was one of the first Russian critics to deny that literature should be subordinated to social or political ends. After *The Contemporary*, he established a new journal called *The Library for Reading*. Together with Pavel Annenkov and Vasily Botkin, Druzhinin became one of the pillars of the "aesthetic movement" in Russian literary criticism.

Druzhinin was a highly cultured man, well versed in painting and music as well as in the major European literatures. In terms of personal characteristics, he has been described as slightly remote, phlegmatically cool, with an "alien" (i.e., non-Russian) streak: he kept regular hours, was known for his diligence and efficiency, neatness and reliability. Yet there was reported to be something strained and forced about him, and he was constantly surrounded by an air of melancholy.

From 1847 to 1855 his literary output was prodigious: he wrote novellas, stories, and feuilletons. He was a translator of some note and completed versions of several Shakespeare plays. He founded a society to help needy writers; he produced a history of English literature (which paid particular attention to Dr. Johnson, Boswell, Crabbe, and Scott); he wrote a biography of his good friend, the Russian painter P. A. Fedotov; and he became the center of a group of writers and critics who kept alive the tradition of independent thought during the last, bleakest years of the reign of Tsar Nicholas I.

In the late 1850s Druzhinin was afflicted with failing health and a decreasing capacity for work. In January 1864, not yet forty years old, he died of consumption in Petersburg, whose harsh climate helped bring about his early demise.

In 1847 Druzhinin published in *The Contemporary* an epistolary novella entitled *Polinka Saks*. The story was an enormous success and became his best-known contribution to Russian literature. The foremost literary critic of the time, Vissarion Belinsky, praised it not only in the essay quoted above but also in several of his letters. To Vasily Botkin he wrote, in December 1847:

> I'd be curious to know what you'll say about *Polinka Saks*. I liked the story very much. The hero is too idealized and reminds me too much of [George] Sand's Jacques, there are some rather drawn-out situations, at places it reeks of melodrama, it's all very young and immature—yet, in spite of all that, it's good, sensible, very much so! Nekr[asov] gave it to me to read in manuscript. After I read it I said, if it's the work of a young man, one can expect great things from him, but if it's the work of a mature writer—then [one can expect] nothing or almost nothing. It turned out that the man is twenty-five years old, and the story was written by him three years ago; but what made me happiest of all was that the author himself was not at all satisfied by his own work.[2]

Two months later Belinsky wrote to Annenkov expressing his enthusiasm for yet another of Druzhinin's works published in *The Contemporary* in 1848, *The Story of Aleksei Dmitrich*: "What a new story Druzhinin has written—it's splendid! Thirty years of difference from *Polinka Saks*! He'll prove to be as important for women as Herzen was for men."[3]

Polinka Saks began life as a drama rather than a novella. A draft of that work survives that contains both the central idea and an outline of the main characters. Clearly, the work was conceived as a polemic with the popular French novelist George Sand, in particular, with her early novel *Jacques* (1834), which was translated into Russian in 1844 and published in *Notes of the Fatherland* in a somewhat abridged version. There are many similarities between the two works, and Druzhinin has often been accused of imitation; in fact, the differences are quite striking and far more significant.

George Sand's epistolary work became the prototype for a series of novels devoted to the subject of the "amorous triangle." In *Jacques*, the wealthy, noble, wise, mature hero (age thirty-five) behaves selflessly in order to bring happiness to his beautiful, young, naive bride Fernande (age seventeen) and her handsome, romantic young lover, Octave. Although still in love with Fernande, Jacques perceives the selfish but sincere relationship between the young people; accepting the idea that "love is the only thing in life," he contrives to make his suicide look like an accident, thus setting his wife free to follow her heart's desire. The novel ends with the happy couple united in romantic bliss.

Love is clearly the main focus of Sand's novel, the center of her fictional characters' existence. Her principal theme is the vicissitudes of romantic love: its power, fleeting nature, tragic consequences. Love pervades the work: any and all obstacles to it must be overcome. In fact, both Sand's male and female characters have nothing else in their lives: no work, no reading, no interests, no aspirations.

Druzhinin was not the only Russian writer to be so attracted by Sand's treatment of the "amorous triangle." Alexander Herzen, in his first and most important work of fiction, *Who Is To Blame?* (1841–45), borrowed the same theme, but recast it in a Russian setting and engineered an altogether different outcome. The triangle develops into a short-lived ménage à trois until the conflict is finally resolved. But in Herzen's version it is the romantic rival, not the faithful husband, who "quits the scene." The tragic "lost soul" Vladimir Beltov ultimately departs and resigns himself to a life of aimless wandering. However, his decision brings no relief to any of the principal characters: Lyuba's health rapidly declines while her husband, Dmitry, sinks deeper into drunken despair. The novel ends with tragic unhappiness for all three main characters, while the author ponders the question posed by the title, "Who is to blame?"[4]

In *Polinka Saks* Druzhinin returns to this theme and engages in his own polemic with George Sand. The hero, Konstantin Saks (age thirty-one) is not only a husband but also a conscientious civil servant "who undertakes special commissions" and manages "to get involved in struggles, or, as you say, in battles." He is an insomniac who works late into the night, exposing abuses in the tsarist bureaucracy. His name is not Russian; it is probably of German or Baltic origin (there were many such civil servants in St. Petersburg). Needless to say, Saks's wife has no appreciation or understanding of her husband's career or his concept of civic duty.

Not only is Saks devoted to his work, he also tries to take an active role in the reeducation of his young wife. At one point the image of Pygmalion is invoked as the hero struggles to bring his own beautiful Polinka to life. He attempts to develop her aesthetic sensibilities—especially her appreciation of art, music, and literature. He introduces her to some of George Sand's early novels, including, of course, *Jacques*; but his wife is merely bored and disgusted by the content. Saks persists and tries to provide Polinka with his own version of a proper upbringing in place of the one she never received from her parents or at the fashionable girls' boarding school she attended. He strives to develop her capabilities, instill independence and understanding, increase her spiritual strength, and disperse all sentimental nonsense. However, his efforts in these directions seem to be to no avail.

Saks is also depicted both as an intellectual and a progressive landowner. He spends a great deal of time at home "reading and writing"; his wife describes his study as full of "serpents, skeletons, and stones"—that is, revealing evidence of his interest in the physical sciences and the material world. His political liberalism is reflected in his decision to reduce the onerous quitrent for the peasants on his estate,[5] in his concern for conditions in the countryside and the results of the reform program, and in his general views on the role of women. In connection with the last, he cites the examples of Richardson's Clarissa and Rousseau's Julie as modern European heroines[6] and then compares them to the heroines in his own national literature: "Russian writers are more candid: they either politely leave women out and write stories without heroines, or else introduce some pale, downtrodden figure onto the stage. . . ."

Saks's letters to his wife reveal his sincere affection and profound caring for her, his diligence toward his work, his wide-ranging intellect, and his plans for the future. When at long last he returns to Petersburg from his special assignment investigating corruption in the provinces, he already possesses full knowledge of the emotional entanglement back at home. He believes that both his young wife and her handsome admirer are "right" in their feelings of love for one another. After a period of indecision and unhappiness, he allows his wife a month to sort out her feelings and to give himself time to reflect. At the end of the allotted period, he summons his rival, Galitsky, to an interview. Saks reveals that he has arranged for a divorce and nobly declares that he intends to entrust Polinka to Galitsky. He advises them to go abroad and marry and warns Galitsky that he had better make Polinka happy, *or else*. . . . Saks then announces his own intention to go abroad, but before doing so he makes yet another set of progressive arrangements for the management of his estate and peasants.

The heroine, Polinka (age nineteen), is presented at first as an attractive, naive, spoiled child, who "sleeps like a little baby with her hands tucked under her cheek." She has terrible taste in music, no background in literature, and is an extravagant housekeeper. But, according to Druzhinin, all the blame must be ascribed, not to her nature, but to her nurture. All her troubles are due "not to her character, but to the results of the upbringing provided by her parents. . . . And still, her parents were not so much to blame as society which, with all its demands, forces women to become like little children." Polinka's head was stuffed with nonsense; she was locked away with girlfriends and governesses, sent to a foolish boarding school, and denied any "exercise" that might have strengthened either her body or her soul.

Nevertheless, the impact of Saks's devotion and his repeated attempts to reeducate Polinka eventually bear fruit. She witnesses her husband's noble generosity, learns of his warning to Galitsky, and finally comes to acknowledge her own abiding love for Saks. As she sinks deeper into physical illness with death drawing near, she admits, in a heartfelt letter to her confidante, that "she'd always loved" Saks; then she writes directly to him, confessing the error of her ways and demonstrating the power of his reeducation in what she calls her "final examination." The novel ends after Polinka's death, at the very moment this poignant confession is delivered to an unsuspecting Saks.

The last of the three principal characters, Galitsky, is a young and boyishly handsome staff-captain, adjutant, princeling, and social lion. We are told that, although he was born "an empty man," "pride and fame have bestowed intelligence on him." He has no convictions whatsoever—or else so many that it doesn't matter. As he was Polinka's former suitor before her marriage to Saks, Galitsky falls ill when she plights her troth. But when he comes to see Polinka soon after her wedding, he delivers a letter from his sister Annette in which she declares: "You have nothing to fear: it's only in novels that things turn out badly if a young man in love is introduced into the company of a husband and his wife." Galitsky proceeds by the most direct route: he falls madly in love with the "sweet, clever, and charming child." He persuades (bribes) his friend Pisarenko to "make a muddle of the case" that Saks has been sent to investigate, thus delaying his return home and allowing Galitsky time to pursue his romantic interest. At the end of the novel the poor prince is out of his element: haunted by Saks's warning, he is finally forced to admit his own inability to make Polinka happy.

The appearance of Druzhinin's *Polinka Saks* in 1847 was greeted with tremendous enthusiasm. Its progressive "social tendencies," its attempt to acquaint Russian readers with Western literature, its treatment of the "women's question"—all inspired praise from the liberal intelligentsia. Belinsky's views have been quoted above. Turgenev was also greatly impressed by the novel, and the friendship between the two writers grew so strong that for several years Druzhinin was one of the chosen few to whom Turgenev would entrust his own works for comment before they were submitted for publication.

In Dostoevsky's novel *The Adolescent* (or *The Raw Youth* [*Podrostok*], 1875), the narrator describes the vivid recollections of the hero's father, Versilov, concerning the Western liberal values he had held during his own youth in the 1840s: "he told me himself that at that time he was an extremely 'stupid little puppy' and not exactly sentimental, but *just so*, and he had just finished reading *Anton Goremyka*[7] and *Polinka Saks*—two literary works which had an enormous civilizing influence on our developing generation at the time."[8] Even Tolstoy was not unmoved by Druzhinin's novel. In a letter from October 1891 to a Petersburg publisher and minor author, M. M. Lederle, Tolstoy listed those works which had made a significant impression on him as a young man. Along with novels by Sterne, Rousseau, Pushkin, Schiller, Gogol, and Dickens, he cites Druzhinin's *Polinka Saks* and describes its influence on him as "very great."[9] As late as 1906 Tolstoy was still summarizing the content of Druzhinin's story to his family circle and calling the work beautiful.[10]

» «

While Druzhinin's novella was hailed as a major contribution to the discussion of the "women's question" in Russian literature, the significance of its feminist theme has certainly been exaggerated. Although obviously derived from George Sand's *Jacques*, *Polinka Saks* represents a retreat from the position of a woman freed from social constraints and burdensome institutions, able to follow her own emotions. Whereas Sand's lovers Fernande and Octave were united in mutual affection after Jacques's staged suicide, Polinka and Galitsky's happiness is short-lived. Druzhinin advocates a much more conservative position: the heroine is overwhelmed by the nobility of her former husband's sacrifice; both his selflessness and attempts to reeducate her are finally rewarded. She realizes her own true, abiding love for Saks, and this recognition destroys her superficial happiness with Galitsky as well as her physical and spiritual well-being. She dies of consumption, punished for her mistake but in full knowledge of her own character and that of her former husband. This uncompromising resolution was to be echoed in Russian literature in M. V. Avdeev's novel *The Reef* [*Podvodnyi kamen'*] (1861), where the hero, Sokovlin, generously steps aside and yields to his rival, Komlev, only to find that his wife, Natasha, returns to her husband voluntarily and there discovers a love even stronger than the previous one.

It was only in N. G. Chernyshevsky's revolutionary novel *What Is To Be Done?* [*Chto delat'?*] (1863) that a radical solution to the dilemma was proposed. There the husband, Lopukhov, only "pretends" to commit suicide, allowing his wife, Vera Pavlovna, to follow the dictates of her heart and marry their close friend and soul mate, Kirsanov. Lopukhov, as it were, seems to accept the advice offered to George Sand's hero Jacques by his sister Sylvia: she had suggested that her brother forget Fernande and go off to start a new life in America. Chernyshevky's Lopukhov does just that. Several years later he returns to Russia under a new name, reestablishes contact with his former wife and her second husband, and selects an ideologically suitable mate for himself. The two couples then settle down to lead a splendidly rational existence. Mind you, even the relatively liberated Vera Pavlovna had to rely on the efforts of men to liberate her: Lopukhov rescues her from her oppressive family environment; Kirsanov, from a loveless marriage and her unfulfilling work in the sewing cooperative; and Rakhmetov, from her guilt and intellectual error.[11]

But "emancipation" is a relative and gradual concept and must be viewed as stages in a process occurring over time: in that sense, Druzhinin's *Polinka Saks* does indeed represent a significant step forward in acknowledging a woman's right to happiness and fulfillment.

» «

When Belinksy read Druzhinin's second work, *The Story of Aleksei Dmitrich*, he declared that it was even better than his first ("Thirty years of difference from *Polinka Saks!*"). Although many critics declined to follow Belinksy's bold lead, this extraordinary novella deserves to be rescued from obscurity.

First, it presents powerfully drawn portraits of characters quite different from those in Druzhinin's first novel. The narrator himself, though present for only a brief period, the title figure, Aleksei, his close friend, Kostya, his first love, Vera, and even the romantic figure of Baron Rctzell—all are striking in their originality and complex psychology. More than one commentator has noted the similarity between Druzhinin's characters and those created by Dostoevsky. Not only do Druzhinin's characters evoke such comparisons; many of the images and themes in *The Story of Aleksei Dmitrich* also parallel Dostoevsky's.

The narrator can surely be seen as a prototype of the underground man. A recluse who fears any and all entanglements, especially those having to do with family life, he sits in his corner in proud solitude, amid gloomy reflections, conceiving bizarre utopias. His only escape is to visit his friend and soul mate, Aleksei Dmitrich, and to listen to the story of his life.

The title character narrates his autobiography as a series of episodes, detailing first his deprived and stunted childhood in Petersburg, where his family moved when he was only five years old. A precocious child, his heightened sensibilities, sentimentality, and intense emotional attachments resulted in two extraordinary relationships—one with an attractive young boy named

Kostya, the other with his friend's beautiful young sister, Vera. As the narrator warns the reader about Aleksei Dmitrich in advance, "His first friendship resembled love, his first love resembled friendship . . . and both passions ended unhappily."

At boarding school the hero encounters Kostya once again. There he is even more struck by the boy's physical beauty and spiritual sensitivity. A firm bond of friendship is forged, one that lasts until Kostya's sudden death from a battle wound received in the Caucasus. This friendship does indeed resemble love—with its intense erotic and emotional bonds, unquestioning devotion, and profound impact on the hero's entire life.

The other object of Aleksei Dmitrich's affections, Kostya's sister Vera, is the embodiment of feminine beauty, vitality, and love. Aleksei is smitten by both the purity of her soul and the maturity of her intellect. But the hero is fated to be frustrated once again, as Vera falls victim to her own abnormal devotion to her father; she chooses to remain home to protect him from her brutal and selfish stepmother, rather than following her own romantic inclinations by escaping with the hero. Aleksei Dmitrich is finally forced to abandon her to what he terms "family fanaticism."

Dostoevsky's name has already been invoked; indeed, Druzhinin's second tale reveals an intensity of attachment to the beautiful Kostya and the equally beautiful Vera, a complex emotional world inhabited by these children, the psychological aberrations manifested by various characters—Kostya's fatal charm and naive power, Vera's masochistic self-sacrifice, the stepmother's extreme egoism and brutality, Baron Retzell's courage and cynicism—motifs familiar from the fictional world of Dostoevsky's early prose and later developed in his major novels.

Belinsky's prediction that Druzhinin's second story "confirms the impression created by his first—that the author possesses original talent—and leads us to expect a great deal from him in the future"—was not to come true in precisely the way Belinsky had expected. Druzhinin soon turned from literature to criticism and began to refute the views of his former admirer and those of other "civic critics" who followed Belinsky's lead—including N. G. Chernyshevsky, N. G. Dobrolyubov, and D. I. Pisarev. During the 1850s and 1860s Druzhinin took an even stronger antiutilitarian stand and eventually moved into the conservative camp, where he achieved considerable renown.

Belinsky did not live to see Druzhinin's "betrayal" or his celebrity. But, as in so many other cases, he could certainly recognize artistic talent when he saw it. Both of Druzhinin's early literary endeavors, *Polinka Saks* and *The Story of Aleksei Dmitrich*, deserve to be read and enjoyed in their own right as works of imaginative fiction by an original, talented mid-nineteenth-century Russian writer, as well as for the ideas and social currents they reflect.

»»» «««

Polinka Saks

A Prologue in Two Letters

I

From Konstantin Aleksandrovich Saks to
Pavel Aleksandrovich Zaleshin

I haven't heard from you in quite some time, you venerable Pantagruelist;[1] I really should repay you in kind, that is, by not writing to you at all, but in that case I'd suffer even more than you. Were I to be awarded a medal or be expelled from the civil service, you'd be the first to find out about it in the newspapers. Were I to die, they'd probably even write about that, too. Of course, I wouldn't be described as a "high official whose passing is being mourned by his subordinates"; in fact, I must work another five years before I can even deserve to be called a "husband well respected by one and all"; still, you'd learn that a certain person named Saks, a civil servant who undertook special commissions, had been stricken from the register of a certain ministry.

But without your letters I know nothing whatever about you. You're a wealthy landowner, you beat your dogs, and, in the words of our forebears, in the provinces you're described as a father to your peasants, but who among you isn't a father to his peasants? Come on then, let's correspond more regularly.

Besides, today I'm so inclined to candor that I've put a blank sheet of paper in front of me without planning my letter in advance. Who else can I talk to? My wife's sleeping like a little baby, hands tucked under her cheek; but I can't sleep, thanks to my accursed habit of working at night. . . . Besides, I'm not feeling very cheerful.

Meanwhile, the day both began and ended happily. This morning I concluded some business that had been assigned to me at work, and I did so in such a way that not one wealthy gentleman could stand there dumbfounded, scratching the back of his head, without anger or passion—*sine ira et studio*. I exposed all the machinations of a certain committee you know well, and openly challenged all the participants to battle, without ever rejecting the idea that there really was no need for anyone to intervene from above for the good of the treasury or the common property. The Minister read my report several times, agreed with my conclusions, and today expressed his deepest gratitude to me. I returned home with a feeling of joyful excitement; the idea that my efforts had not been in vain provided me with a considerable degree of self-satisfaction.

Polinka was pretty as an angel, cheerful as a little bird—and that's as it should be. I was delighted to find her seated at the piano; her strong mezzo-soprano greeted my ears as I climbed the stairs. You know how our ladies and young women are so barbarously indifferent to music: it grieves me to acknowledge that my wife is worse than many in this regard. She yawns at the opera and likes to play polkas and galops at home. The Sperl-Polka[2] alone has caused us a great deal of bad blood.

This time, however, she was singing Desdemona's famous aria.[3] The splendid piece brought to mind many moments of my childhood and youth. I'm most grateful to fate for my soul's receptivity and its ability to remember: I've lived and suffered enough, and have been angry enough, yet not one bright moment has been forgotten, not one lucid feeling has lost its hold on me.

I didn't hide my pleasure: Polinka's fresh, strong voice moved me deeply. I almost concluded that such energetic singing couldn't possibly emanate from a weak soul; and if she possessed a soul, we'd soon discover it.

Still, Polinka's style of singing in no way conformed to the conventions of the music. She was singing the sad aria "Assisa al piè d'un salice"* just as boldly and spiritedly as one is supposed to sing "Chernyi tsvet"† or "Jeune fille aux yeux noirs."‡ She even introduced her own whimsical variations at the end of each couplet, whereas the repeated endings and the melancholy refrain of the song are supposed to emphasize one and the same idea, persistent and heart-rending.

I concluded that she didn't understand the meaning of the words and probably had never heard the story of Desdemona. They're only planning to stage the opera here, and we still don't read Shakespeare.

Therefore, after she finished, I sat her down next to me and, in a lighthearted manner, pointed out some mistakes in her performance. Then I told her my own version of the story of Othello and his wife. She listened with enjoyment and immediately referred to me by the name of the Venetian Moor. I really don't know whether that indicated a suspicion of jealousy or whether it was an allusion to my story.

Laugh, go on, laugh at our erudite chatter. It doesn't sound so

*"Sitting under the Willow Tree."
†"The Color Black."
‡"The Young Girl with Black Eyes."

good in a letter, but in practice I know of no greater pleasure than following the ideas of a child who's so dear to me, raising her up to one's own level and that of the age, conveying in a comprehensible manner everything that seems both profound and poetic to us—because I must confess to being in love with my wife, in love with her like a little child, like an old man, like a madman. Fate itself has preserved me for this passion. As a result of the abnormal, premature development of my strength, first love carried me away while I was still only a young lad. I was a mere twelve years old at the time—so what kind of passion could it have been? But it survived a long time and then expired painfully; that's why during my entire youth, although I experienced so much on earth, I'd yet to experience genuine love for a woman.

All during the rest of that day Polinka trailed after me like a kitten, flitted around me, and showed off her housekeeping arrangements, which had only one disadvantage, namely, they cost ten times as much as everyone else's. She told me once again how annoyed she felt when I was off working at the office, and on this occasion she uttered a rather original thought about my pursuits. According to her, we closet ourselves up in our rooms and write all sorts of nonsense of our own choosing, the substance of which really doesn't matter: our superiors scrutinize the fruits of our labor and reward those whose work is most splendidly written. You can imagine how frightened Polinka was on account of me, *qui écrit toujours en pattes de mouches.**

Of course, she laughed while recounting all this nonsense, even though her naïveté is not at all to my liking. At first I thought about explaining it to her, but I decided to leave the mysteries of my workplace for another day. Toward evening I too became like a child and almost found myself playing dolls with

*Who always writes in little mouse scribbles.

her. She refused to go to the theater or visit her aunt, and our evening turned out to be the sweetest ideal of family happiness; not only would it have been envied by our local scatterbrained moralists, but it was one in which even you would have found no fodder for your satiric wit.

As usual I didn't go to sleep, and while Polinka slept, I sat on the bed, gazing at her little face, at which I shall probably never tire of looking. It's so enchanting at those moments when, under the influence of sleep, its features cease taking in impressions from surrounding objects. I looked and looked and looked until oppressive thoughts began crowding into my mind.

The distinguishing feature of Polinka's beauty is her childlike appearance. Her lower lip protrudes some measure beyond her upper: her beauty is girlish, not womanly. The whole lower part of her face is so round that not one dimple is visible. This suits Polinka extremely well, but in my opinion a woman nineteen years old could do without such distinction.

And so, these features correspond to Polinka's character . . . no, not to her character, but to the results of the upbringing provided by her exemplary parents . . . the devil take them![5] Still, her parents were not so much to blame as society, which, with all its demands, forces women to become like little children.

I recalled my wife's existence when she was a young girl: she was known for her innocence, her naïveté, her . . . I well remember her group of friends who swooned in ecstasy at her pranks, at her schoolgirlish *bons mots*! And our stupid young people whispered: "Such a wonderful child! What an angel!" They never considered that we needed women, not angels. With what pride on our wedding day did her aging father utter the stock phrase: "Take care of my Polinka—she's still such a child!"

Has it never entered your head, dearest Papa, that for a man who's been around, who's experienced both victory and defeat, who's long since put aside any pastoral notions, labeling her a child is no longer an honored title?

Innocence, child, schoolgirl! These words carry great weight among admirers of women, but does that make it any easier for me? And now for over a year I've been trying to mold a nice, sensible helpmate for my tortured soul, which, all joking aside, is in such need of friendship, genuine gaiety . . . in need of someone to talk to in all honesty.

For over a year I've been trying with all my might to bring this lovely statue to life! My efforts are still far from success, very far. . . .

The first task I set myself was to educate Polinka's aesthetic sensibility. I surrounded her with works of art; her hand didn't come in contact with a single object that wasn't elegant in the best sense of the word. And what happened? My valuable paintings stand covered in dust, flowers wilt from lack of care, the furnishings of our rooms, over which I expended so much effort, don't quite please her, aren't exactly to her liking. . . .

In vain did I attempt to provide her with a taste for music: it's a punishment for her to have to sit down at the piano. In spite of her splendid voice, she's ashamed to sing for other people, even for me. I don't know whether she sings when alone, but today was the first time she played a serious piece of music in my presence. . . .

What can be expected from reading? I must confess I've seen so much harm come from a passion for books that I'm even afraid to rely upon it as a resource. I attempted, however, to supply her with George Sand's early novels:[6] I was completely convinced that one woman would find another's spirit accessible. But it turned out to be just the opposite: she yawned and yawned again—and threw the books aside in disgust.

Practical life is both alien and incomprehensible to her. In society she finds precisely those things strange that come closest to making good sense. She doesn't even want to know the nature of her husband's work in the civil service, or why he has to closet himself up in his office so frequently at night. . . .

But I can see I've really started blabbing and have blurted out far too much. So be it; it's just as stupid to hide one's affairs from others needlessly as it is to proclaim them to anybody and everybody. There's no reason for me to stand on ceremony with you: it was for good reason that you and I studied together, roamed the world together, and fought together in the Caucasus. Of course, these events took place not quite in the order just described: first we roamed, then we studied, and finally, to crown our philosophic theories, we set off to destroy some part of mankind.

Still, we're friends, even though we went our separate ways some time ago. You left for your Arcadia and settled down, *moyennant un peu de pantagruélisme,** far away from the tempests and irritations of society, while I fell in love, married, and clearly saw that I had to begin my romance from the very beginning.

This letter has brought many gloomy reflections to mind and has excited me as if I were a lad of eighteen. I decided to have another look at Polinka to dispel my thoughts; therefore I interrupted my writing and went in to see her. She was asleep, stretched out like a child, with the same angelic, innocent look on her face. I wanted to give her a kiss; afraid to disturb her sleep, I leaned over and almost touched her lips. Her heart was beating so unevenly, first softly, then quickly, as if it were telling some tale with great animation. . . . For a long time I stood there, leaning over, listening to its sound. . . .

During these sweet moments I wasn't fully alive, but rather in

*With the help of a little Pantagruelism.

a kind of delirium. It seemed that this indefatigable heart of hers was relating Polya's entire life to me: how in childhood she'd been turned away from any attempt to strengthen her body and soul, how her head had been stuffed full of all sorts of nonsense, and, finally, how she'd been locked away in a crowded house filled with girlfriends and governesses. This heart of hers told me how it dreamed at times of a broad field, a forest with treetops swaying with a little breeze, a sun that frolicked and was reflected on the smooth surface of a lake. . . . I was told many more similar things, but I'll spare your patience since you're not married, not in love, and probably never will fall in love.

Still, you must have enough imagination to understand the feeling that began to burn within me after hearing all these tales. Without abandoning my sweet position, I renewed my pledge to provide Polinka with my own version of an upbringing, although it would be necessary to break with society once and for all. I made a vow to develop her capabilities fully, to instill both independence and a genuine understanding of society in her way of thinking, and by so doing to remove her from the ranks of pleasant yet vacuous women. I vowed to increase her spiritual strength, to direct it toward everything good, to disperse the cloud of sentimental, nonsensical innocence that oppressed this poor child of mine. . . .

I feel I'm to blame regarding Polinka: during this last year and a half I haven't made of her what I wanted; I haven't done it precisely because at times I behaved like a child with her and became distracted by her sweet shortcomings. In this last year and a half she could have become a woman: I've become convinced of this by her lighthearted sarcasm, her slight irascibility, and her habit of biting her lower lip during any argument. All this is an indication of genuine character.

I haven't done everything I could have. God grant I won't have to pay dearly for these moments of stupid indulgence!

Will I finish my work soon? Will this need to provide Polinka with an upbringing soon pass? If my wish is fulfilled, I'll be so happy! With what abandon will we, she and I, arm in arm, go out to greet life, with its good and bad sides, and then you'll see how clever, bold, and cheerful my little Polinka will be!

II

From Polina Aleksandrovna Saks to
Madame Annette Krasinskaya

The happiest day of my life was when I received your letter, *ma toute belle, mon incomparable Annette.** I imagined myself back in the white hall of our boarding school, the one we used to abuse so much, but where it really was very jolly.

Mama conveyed your letter to me very faithfully; you can be sure no one read it but me. Was it because you didn't know where I was living that you didn't write to me for so long? You'll find my address at the end of this letter.

All this while I've been wondering whether you'd started to dislike me because I didn't marry your brother. My dearest, you must realize that my papa was fast asleep and dreamed up the idea of marrying me off to Saks. All our relatives were against it; they referred to my poor Kostya as an eccentric, a free-thinker, and Lord knows what else—but Papa wouldn't hear a word of it. I must confess that I married him willingly, even though before our engagement I despised him terribly for all his cruel words

*My lovely girl, my incomparable Annette.

about our boarding school. . . . Besides, your brother went off to take a cure . . . obviously, it was God's will, Annette.

You write that my husband is old and ugly. You yourself, *mon ange*,* said something quite different to me two years ago. You'll never find a nobler or bolder face than Saks's. He's somewhat bald, but I'll persuade him to wear a wig. And he'll only turn thirty-two this May.

Then you ask why he isn't serving in the military. "*Vous êtes arriérée, mon enfant*,"† my husband would say. "*Il faut être de son temps.*"‡ Nowadays we prefer civilians. Besides, Kostya was in the military—and even fought in battle.

I don't regret having married him: I've been so happy this past year and haven't been bored for one minute. On occasion we've spent long evenings sitting together all alone—I was happier than if I'd been at a ball. Saks has seen so much and been absolutely everywhere. When you listen to him talk, it seems as if you yourself are traveling through foreign lands and seeing such interesting things you couldn't possibly imagine. We're living very well, but don't host any large gatherings. Saks has divided all our acquaintances into groups: if, for example, my relatives are dining with us, he doesn't invite his friends. Mother gets very annoyed at that. But his friends are all artists, musicians, and young civil servants.

Don't be angry with me, *mon ange*, for defending my Kostya. There's no one to intercede for him, very few people like him, most call him an eccentric, some are even afraid of him. Papa said somehow that Saks was a restless man and that many well-respected people left the civil service as a result of him. I can't

*My angel.
†You've fallen behind, my child.
‡You must keep up with the times.

understand that: you should see how kind and quiet he is at home. He always bows in such a funny way when he meets my maids, and once I found he'd laid out his own clothes because his valet had gone off to have dinner. I scolded him a bit.

It's still rumored that some time ago he fought a duel with someone or other; I've been afraid to ask about it—perhaps he committed some terrible act! What if he's only pretending to be so kind?

There's no keeping track of all his other surprises. Once he spent a large sum of money and bought me a present of some completely discolored pictures. And what pictures they are! Some kind of cows or brigands standing among mountains. And he's bought me some statues that I'm embarrassed to display in my room. He's hung an old portrait of a very lovely woman over my bed and says it's a picture of Saint Cecilia.[7] God only knows where he came up with that saint.

He's very polite to my relatives, although he doesn't like them and prefers not to associate with them. I spoke with him about this not long ago: he was silent for a while and then wanted to change the subject. In order to provoke an argument with him, I began talking once again about my mother and father.

"I owe them a great deal," I said by the way.

"And I'm obliged to them for only one thing," he replied.

"What's that?"

"For managing not to ruin you entirely."

Oh! He's quite an expert at paying compliments. He doesn't like my girlfriends either and calls you a troublemaker. That's because even though you got married, you still like to whisper things to me.

I often think: does this man love anyone? Neither before our wedding nor afterward did he ever tell me honestly that he was the least bit in love with me. "My love is not expressed in words, but in life," he used to say sometimes. If only he'd kiss my hands, fall to his knees! *Fi donc!** His shirt might get wrinkled; his clothes, dirty. He never appears in anything except a frock coat or tails—*tiré à quatre épingles*†—it's the height of boldness if he dares put on a summer jacket instead of tails!

If he's not writing, he reads all night until dawn; Papa used to say that his books were all so harmful. . . . I became concerned about his health and one night I went in to see him in his study. Near him all sorts of serpents, skeletons, and stones were lying about . . . there wasn't a single book in sight.[8] He sat me down on the soft arm of a chair and told me all about his books and some of the objects lying there on the table. . . . Even a deaf person would be spellbound by this man.

I wanted to read myself; in the morning he brought me the novels of George Sand, about whom, you recall, your cousin spoke with such horror. Kostya told me that George Sand was not a man but a woman, and therefore I'd soon come to understand her works and like them. Oh, *mon ange*, if she really is a woman, she's utterly shameless and very boring. In one of her novels a man makes his way into the bedroom of a young lady and spends the whole night standing near her bed! The books you brought to our boarding school had similar episodes, but there it was all so amusing; you knew it was bad and laughed at it. But these books are so boring, I put them aside for another time.

What a cold person Kostya is! Once he brought me to the point of tears. Somehow I brushed against his fingers clumsily and he gave a strange shudder.

"Aha! You're jealous!" I said, joking.

*Heaven forbid!
†Dressed to the nines.

"Jealous indeed!" Kostya replied.

"Tell me, what would you do if I were unfaithful to you?"

"Hey! Who's unfaithful nowadays?"

"Well, what if?"

"How unfaithful? On a whim?"

"On a whim! Isn't it possible to imagine I might fall in love with one of your friends?"

"Deeply in love?"

"Yes, lifelong love, forever, out of my mind, head over heels."

His eyes flashed so frightfully that I became afraid.

"Why would I want a wife who was out of her mind, head over heels? I'd kiss you goodbye and go off somewhere."

"And what about him?"

"How would he be to blame?"

I burst into tears like a little child: such coldness would infuriate anyone else. Kostya managed to calm me down only with difficulty. For what reason would he ever agree to fight a duel?

My husband spends a great deal of money and doesn't worry at all about our income. He's made such changes to the estate given as part of my dowry that we're going to receive only half as much income from it as we did before. Papa is so kind, but he's angry about it. "To reduce the quitrent needlessly," he told my husband, "means setting a bad example for all peasants in the neighborhood, doing away with fear and obedience."[9] But Kostya only laughs and won't listen to him.

He's a terrible gourmand, and God knows how he manages with only one table. He's always urging me to eat more; he pours me a full glass of wine and says his dinner is more delicious than chalk and charcoal . . . all this is in our favor again, my dear. Shall I tell you, Annette? . . . But you'll just abuse me. . . . When he's particularly cheerful, he orders a small bottle of champagne to be served in the evening. He and I drink and drink, *mon ange*; we drink the whole bottle! Living with such an eccentric man soon forces one to do eccentric things. . . .

I wouldn't have written you all this, *mon cher petite ange*,* if I thought my husband would always be the same as he is now. I've been trying to change him for some time and keep wondering what to do to make him more like other people. When I got married, Mama told me: "Remember, Polya, a clever woman can make whatever she wants out of her husband." And Kostya himself has said more than once, "A good woman can remake a man entirely."

Even now Mama sometimes gives me needed advice, and it seems that Kostya's not quite as strange as he was before. I hope that by the time you come he'll dance a polka with you and our *bonnes amies*,† he'll toss aside his stupid books and . . . but his carriage has just driven through our gates.

Farewell, my angel, *ma bien-aimée*.‡ Don't show this letter to anyone . . . what if someone takes it into his head to unseal it along the way? . . .

*My dear little angel.
†Girlfriends.
‡My dearly beloved.

Two Letters Instead of a First Chapter

I

From Pavel Aleksandrovich Zaleshin
to Konstantin Aleksandrovich Saks

Greetings, my good Saks, my dear *jeune premier.** Your affairs are going well: you're sitting up at night next to your young wife's bed? You managed to fall in love in your old age—since, no matter what you think, I can't refer to you as a young man. You and I are old roosters, although we turned thirty only recently; the thing is that in the past we could grab hold of life ahead of us, just as people used to collect their salary in advance from the treasury for one-third of the year.

And whose business is it anyway? Be in love, my friend; I respect people in love, and if, in addition, they're legally married, then I envy them. A man gets married—he's happy for a year, even for a month, a week, still he's totally happy; therefore marriage is an extremely clever invention.

Don't misconstrue my light tone regarding Hymen and his mysteries.[10] If I were still in my early twenties, I wouldn't let slip the chance to abuse you and shower sarcastic remarks on family life in general, since a passion to abuse absolutely everything and

*Young lover.

laugh at everyone is a sure sign of youth. But the time is long past when I consoled myself with such humor and delighted in such misanthropic pranks.

I'm sure your wife is nothing but a dear, gentle, clever angel.

*Frisant un peu le diable par sa malignité.**

You've always had wonderful taste; you're famous for it. "Saks admired this," everyone used to say, and all discussion would cease. Such was the esteem your taste was afforded by the rest of us mere mortals. In addition, there's another circumstance that convinces me of Polinka's merit.

Not long ago Prince Galitsky arrived here from abroad. I don't recall whose adjutant he is; his rank is staff-captain. He was staying at the estate of his sister, my neighbor, a woman . . . well, it's not polite to say anything about her. His sister was educated at the same school as your wife, and she did all she could so Polinka would be married off to this Galitsky. He was so sure of his success that he never sought consent either from her parents or from her; instead he went off to drink seltzer water sold in Petersburg *au prix modèré.*† After drinking a glass, he took a stroll with his fiancée. You've probably heard this little story already.

They say one really had to behold the prince's despair; apparently he'd been successful all his life. Our coastal cliffs and lonely woods were filled with tender names bestowed on his "wife" (in her absence) and terrible curses hurled at his sister and you. He became ill with some kind of *mania furibunda.*‡ Then he quieted down, made peace with his sister, and made the acquaintance of her neighbors, includ-

*Almost a devil with her slyness.
†For a modest price.
‡Violent madness.

ing me. Before he left for Petersburg, he offered to deliver my letter to you.

I decided it was inappropriate for you to hide from him; besides, you're already acquainted and will meet him in society—therefore, his wish could be granted. That's why this letter is being delivered to you by Prince Galitsky, the best dancer of polkas and waltzes in the Russian empire.

I know you, most esteemed friend. After reading all this, you'll laugh, perhaps even show this letter to your wife and think to yourself: "An adjutant! A princeling! A polka dancer? *'Pkhe, puchzat!'** as the mountain men would say." No, my dear Saks, Galitsky isn't scum, but a rather dangerous man because he's as proud as the devil. The dazzling success he's earned so early in society has distinguished him from the ranks of ordinary men.

Take away the fame of any well-known writer: do you think his new works will be as good as his early ones? You should recall your own pronouncement in this regard some ten years ago: "Advance me some fame on credit—and I'll become a famous writer."

Take away the *prestigium* from some statesman: do you think his work will be as bold, free, and swift?

Galitsky was born an empty-headed man; he studied very little and not at all well. Now they award him difficult commissions and he carries them out very capably. Women abroad are cleverer than ours; just ask what marvels he's achieved there! I repeat: pride and fame have bestowed intelligence on him in the same way your intelligence has afforded you honor and wealth. Besides, Galitsky's young and has the face of a very handsome boy.

I must confess, I liked him as a man with incredible diversity in his pleasures. His distinction gives him an advantage over our young people in society who have no idea what to do with them-

*What scum!

selves outside a ballroom or beyond the confines of their cottages on Stone Island.[11]

Galitsky has either no convictions whatever or else so many that even the devil can't keep pace with him. He's capable of sitting in a monastery for a whole month and astonishing everyone by his piety; he can converse with our wise elders about the well-being of the human race—or can eat five times a day and drink two nights in a row. The main thing is he can do all this with a pure heart. Self-deception has become a way of life for him; he embodies it completely, therefore, it constitutes his whole life, not merely deception. He and I used to hunt together, sleep on the bare ground, and feast royally; but in Petersburg he can organize dances, then mock our landowners' way of life. Well, God be with him.

As for me, I'm cheerful and happy, *prêt à boire si vous voulez*;* I'm living primarily on my estate and have bought myself a cottage on the seashore. It's my Tiber,[12] it's true, my local Falernian wine "sour-tasting in all respects," but that's not such a great misfortune. Odessa isn't so far away. The wise man was telling the truth when he said, "Live wherever fate takes you; eat, drink, and don't worry about other people."

But you're an innovator and a reformer . . . you compose masterful hymns to individualism and optimism. I can't stop marveling at how your scholarly brethren beat the air in various European capitals. I could fashion a new theory of happiness for myself, but it's better to stick with the old one.

Happiness, my dear Saks, is extremely difficult to concentrate in oneself alone, in spite of our tendency toward egoism. A happy man is like a gas lamp: he throws out a circle of light all around for a certain distance. In other words, happiness is like good

*Ready to drink, if you wish.

food—you put it in your mouth, thinking only about your stomach, meanwhile all your organs are strengthened, your whole body gets fat and then falls to pieces. Let my household serve as confirmation of my gastronomic aphorism.

I purchased the main part of my estate from a young man who wasted all his money and reduced his peasants to ruin. He loved to play cards: he paid for his losses with his peasants, but when he won, he never got anything back. When the estate was sold to me, I came here knowing I wasn't going to El Dorado,[13] even though I resolved not to worry about anyone or anything.

Even before I managed to view all my holdings, I grew sick to my stomach. Instead of villages, there were only assorted ruins here and there, which, as you know, aren't nearly as picturesque in Russia as they are on the banks of the Rhine. Wherever I went I encountered gaunt, pitiful figures who greeted me with low bows. I lost all my appetite—what can one do?—and for a long time I ate very badly. As soon as I left the house I encountered the same ruins, the same sickly faces. Two years have since passed; now I go everywhere and can walk and eat with pleasure. Instead of ruined huts, there stand nice little houses, without which the Russian landscape has nothing to offer, and everywhere I meet such chubby little mugs! Joy and good cheer! You wouldn't believe how quickly these skinny people put on weight.

And so, I'm completely satisfied with my fate now. It's very pleasant, my dear friend, to eat three meals a day, sleep twice a day, and constantly be surrounded by well-fed figures with shiny noses, fat bellies, and waddling walks. I don't think I'll get to visit your Petersburg very soon, where not one year goes by without influenza, piles, and typhus.

Stop! Stop! . . . I wanted to seal this letter. What an awful, exhausting job it is to write, no matter what. Still, I have to fill a few more pages.

You ask my advice concerning the best way to complete your wife's education—that is, you're not asking my advice, but I know your voracious manner. So the question inevitably arises: Why not seek advice from a good man? All the more so since my advice is as well regarded as your taste. My advice is distinguished by the absolute impossibility of ever carrying it out, that's why it's acquired such renown. At every misfortune people say: "You see, if they hadn't listened to Zaleshin, everything would have been all right." Moreover, in reading your letter I see that giving you advice is a very difficult thing.

Your letter abounds in elegance of style, but doesn't really make clear what kind of education you wish to give your wife— in short, what do you want from her? You hope to remove her from the ranks of ordinary women, to show her life, to provide your soul with a helpmate. Hey, Konstantin! . . . At the age of thirty it's inappropriate to throw around such childish phrases. Facts, give me facts—I'm deaf to all abstract consequences of idealism.

You want to make of her a helpmate for yourself. A helpmate in what? That job hasn't been defined in any special regulations like a secretary's assistant or a bookkeeper's helper. I understand only one thing about your plan: you want to develop your wife's aesthetic taste and a slightly bemused attitude toward life with all its vicissitudes. I approve of both these goals.

But . . . you don't describe anything. Do you know what would be better? Write and tell me how you view the significance of women in this day and age; let me discover what you want your Polinka to be for you. Define your ideal and send it to me in a letter, and don't worry about the fact that I've called it an ideal. Let your ideas be as simple and concrete as facts.

I don't blame you entirely. The demands of our age regarding women are strange, vague, and inconsistent. In the works of our best writers and those of our worst scribblers we search in vain for an answer to the question "What should a woman be in this day and age?" The best European talents either pass over it or take pains to depict a series of improbable figures located outside time and space. Our fathers delighted in Clarissa and Julie[14]— they were ideals who fitted their age. But the nineteenth century doesn't yet have its Clarissa or Julie.

Russian writers are more candid: they either politely leave women out and write stories without heroines, or they introduce some pale, downtrodden figure onto the stage. . . .

I see that your wife has studied very little and has seen even less of life. Having taken a young woman, a spoiled product of a boarding school, you should've thought about all this in advance. Now it's late to educate her from books; continue your didactic conversations: women love it when they're told clever stories. Desdemona fell in love with a black man as she listened to his tales. I've always thought: woe to men if their wives don't listen to them sometimes with delight.

Don't keep her in Petersburg: she won't learn anything good there. Either take her abroad (of course not to Baden-Baden or Ems),[15] or bring her to us in the south of Russia. There nature will act as her teacher: who doesn't understand its lessons, even though they're provided gratis? . . .

Women love nature: I've noticed more than once how an attractive woman gazes at the sunset beyond the forest or at clouds scurrying before a storm. It goes without saying that such activities occur not before a fancy ball or after the fitting of a new gown . . . and that's a good thing.

Undoubtedly you have to go everywhere with your wife. It's time to leave the capital: what are you waiting for? You've polished off two or three officials, now you should step aside. All your misfortunes result from the fact that you've always managed to get involved in struggles or, as you say, in battles. Abandon all that: you've done your bit of work, now live for yourself; not everyone lands such a nice wife. What battles do you still want to fight arm in arm with her, as you say in your letter? What's this passion for launching attacks? What immature raging! . . . Strike up the music, music! Let it play that same march to which in former days we stamped our feet across ploughed fields.

Farewell, your Pantagruelist sends you his regards. If you drop in to see me along the way, I'll have room for both you and your wife: my house is enormous. Really, come, my dear Panurge, we'll visit the oracle of the wondrous bottle and ask its opinion regarding the institution of marriage in the nineteenth century.[16]

From Madame Annette Krasinskaya to Polinka Saks

Thank you for your letter, *ma petite Paulette*.[17] Are you in good health, my little peach? Are you just as chubby and cheerful as you used to be? I can't report much that's good about myself: besides, you can ask my brother how I'm getting on, since he's asked to deliver this letter to you.

Now you're good and angry, I know. You find it repulsive to see my poor Sasha. Polinka, have mercy on him and on me: no pen can describe how much I've suffered of late! And now my heart is full of fear; I can't get my thoughts in order. Forgive me, but you're somewhat to blame for it all.

In Italy my brother found out from some Russians that you were married. At first he didn't believe it; then he came galloping back to Russia like a madman. He had to travel to Odessa on business and came from there to see me, without having written, eaten, or slept.

I was really frightened when he came running in, wasted away, pale, eyes on fire. "Is it true she's married?" were his first words. I didn't know what to say and began to cry. He sank into a chair and was unable to speak for several minutes. Finally I went up to him and kissed him. His head was burning, as if on fire. My husband and I persuaded him to lie down; that same day he fell into a terrible fever.

I spent the night at his side. He wept, tossed about in bed, swore at his own stupidity, and called you none other than his own Polinka. First he wanted to shoot himself, then he recalled with ecstasy how he saw you at our boarding school and spent hours chatting with you. Only when the crisis had passed did he finally get some rest: I took advantage of that time to return to my own bedroom and there fell fast asleep.

Suddenly I felt someone touching me. I awoke; he was standing before me, wearing a frock coat and helmet.

"Sister," he said, "tell them to give me some horses. Am I such a child they won't let me go alone?"

"Why do you want to go?" I asked.

He flared up and began trembling. He said that one of the two of them had to quit the scene, that clearly Saks had been fated since birth to clash with Galitsky. I realized that he was planning to go to Petersburg and fight a duel with your husband.

For a long time I implored him to come to his senses; he wouldn't even listen to me. Fortunately, he spied a portrait of you near my bed that had been painted when you were only twelve years old. At first he grabbed it from the table and threw himself on it with bitterness; but, staring closely at your features, he began kissing it and pressing it to his bosom. These efforts so weakened him that once again we carried him in and placed him on the bed without any difficulty. He finally calmed down, ceased his suffering, and seemed to get used to the idea that you wouldn't ever belong to him. "All I have left," he said to me afterward, "is to see her on occasion and to pray for her happiness."

My God, Polinka, I'm so sad when I think what's become of this young man who used to be chased by our ladies, who lived in such a carefree manner, and who didn't even know there was such a thing as grief in the world. . . .

Before his departure I handed him this letter. My angel, have mercy on him, advise him to seek out new pursuits, be kind to him. He's still so young; all this will pass. He'll change, he'll be your friend . . . otherwise, he'll either shoot himself or sink into despair. Most of all, don't tell your husband all you know about this unhappy love: God forbid they should ever meet. You don't know what kind of man Saks really is: he'll destroy my poor Sasha. Even now I can't sleep at night just thinking about this.

You mentioned a duel in which your husband was once involved—I'll tell you the whole story so you can understand how important it is for you to protect my brother and how any unnecessary candor with your husband might cause him harm.

The episode occurred when I had just completed my studies and you were still in one of the middle grades. At that time, for some reason, there were many Russians living in Paris and, as our young people were prone to doing, they threw their money around and lived just as they pleased. Your husband was also there and told everyone he was busy studying something or other—as if it was impossible to study in Russia.

At one of the local theaters a young and very spoiled actress was much in vogue. She used to play the parts of young men . . . so you can imagine what sort of person she was. For some reason our lads took a liking to her, especially a young man also named Galitsky, not a prince, just Galitsky, Sasha's acquaintance and school friend. The actress, overcome for some reason with an attack of modesty, wouldn't allow this Galitsky to see her, in spite of his many attempts to befriend her. He was a bold lad, clever, rich, and not at all used to such refusals. He assembled a group of her detractors and decided to teach the willful young actress a lesson.

One evening, as soon as she came onstage, there arose such a racket, such an uproar, that every word she spoke was greeted with whistles and laughter. The audience was soon infected by this general attitude and began to make noise and mock her. Someone crowed like a rooster, someone else bleated like a sheep, and Galitsky gave free rein to his indignation and abused her from his seat in the first row. This reception so astonished the actress that she started to behave capriciously; she came out to the footlights, tried to speak, and burst into tears.

Well, of course the young people were simply behaving badly—but what sort of crime had they committed?

At that moment Saks left his seat and, standing near the orchestra, addressed the front rows of the audience.

"Ladies and gentlemen," he said, turning both to those who were making noise and those who weren't, "I'll explain the reason for this scandal. Yesterday one of my acquaintances made a bet that within a quarter of an hour he could succeed in turning the public against one of its favorite actresses."

These words were cleverly conceived; the noise started to abate and soon everyone noticed that only Galitsky was still shouting. His friends decided to support him, and the noise was about to swell once more. Then your husband went up to Galitsky and forced him back into his seat. Embarrassed so mercilessly in front of the entire audience, poor Galitsky cursed and shouted until the police forced him to leave the theater. Before he did, however, he challenged Saks, the actress's estimable admirer, to a duel.

The next day an attempt was made to reconcile them. And

who do you think refused? Your present husband. He demanded all sorts of nonsense—that Galitsky publish a letter in the newspaper apologizing to the young woman who, to complete the effect, had taken sick or else was said to be ill. There's chivalry for you!

Galitsky became even more enraged. They separated the opponents: Galitsky fired first and missed. Saks walked up to him and began speaking to him quietly. This conversation was recounted to me by my neighbor Zaleshin, who served as a second at this unfortunate affair.

"Write the apology and sign it only with the first letter of your name," Saks said.

"I won't," replied Galitsky.

"Don't sign it at all—just go away from here."

"I won't," said Galitsky.

The generous cavalier shook his head, retreated to a distance of fifteen paces and—shot him through the head. He didn't even squeak. That's not all. Do you think he ran over to the fallen man, wept over him, or tore his own hair? Saks walked over to the seconds, who were busy with the corpse, and gazed coldly at Galitsky's face, so distorted with rage and convulsions.

"Gentlemen," he said softly, "don't pity this young man. Believe me, he was merely a heartless monster."

Ma petite Paulette, you owe this little episode to the fact that you listen to such charming stories about the Caucasus and battles in which your husband fought. He wasn't there very long . . . they sent him home after a year.

I wouldn't have told you this sad tale if I hadn't been worrying about how to protect my brother from any misfortune. I have great respect for your husband; in spite of the fact that in his opinion I'm a scandal-monger, I don't want to blacken his reputation in your eyes.

Now you'll understand, my dear Polinka, why I appeal to you so fervently on my brother's behalf. At least let him look at you, even speak with you on occasion. Instill some reason in him and feel sorry for him: in his soul he's worth it; he's still a child, kind and noble. You have nothing to fear: it's only in novels that things turn out badly if a young man in love is introduced into the company of a husband and his wife.

CHAPTER II

While these two letters still remain in Galitsky's pocket and their bearer is considering his plan of attack on the happiness of other people, let's have a look at the life of this young couple that's adopted such a praiseworthy goal—to reeducate each other according to his or her own ideas.

It was after one o'clock and still before dinner. Polina Aleksandrovna Saks was sitting in her whimsically decorated boudoir, her forehead wrinkled, lips pouting, brows furrowed, just like Jupiter on Mount Olympus. She was absentmindedly leafing though a book of caricatures by Granville,[18] whose talent had already begun to manifest itself at that time.

There was reason to be angry and to dwell on her misfortune: a storm of troubles, disappointments, dashed hopes, and disillusionments had descended onto this young lady's pretty little head.

First of all, let it be known that Polya (that was the mean and nasty little dog on whom Madame Saks, in an excess of tenderness, had bestowed her own name), Polya had overeaten and fallen ill. The foul creature, with her dark eyes and wet snout, was lying on the other armchair, on a soft cushion, growling gloomily at her mistress, whom even the meanest dogs would approach and fawn over as they do over a two-year-old child.

Then—the dress that she was supposed to wear to attend a meeting of the Assembly[19] tomorrow still wasn't ready. True,

Madame Barre or Izambarre or Nallparre swore it would be by that evening . . . but what kind of an excuse is that?

Then—Mama had just left after quarreling with Polinka about why she'd allowed her husband to take her to the Russian theater the previous day.[20]

Then—and this really was awful—the courier had arrived very early that morning and summoned Saks to the ministry. Kostya himself had said only yesterday that he planned to take a break from his work for a while, and now suddenly, without any rest, he'd gone galloping off like a madman and had yet to return.

And so it's easy to understand why Polinka's broad, gothic room seemed so dark and empty; why the group of Amor and Psyche,[21] so gracefully emerging from the opposite wall, exhausted her patience by their indecency; why Saint Cecilia, driven out of the bedroom, somewhat craftily regarded Madame Saks, as if mocking her grief.

That's why for the last half-hour Polinka Saks had been perched in her large armchair, which she'd pulled way into the corner, her legs tucked under her, her arms wrapped around her knees. Three dogs, their tails raised, were circling her in vain: she wouldn't sit on the floor with them, wouldn't kiss them, and merely cast a worried glance at her ailing Polya from time to time.

Suddenly the dogs lowered their tails and, as if on command, filed out of the room to the right. Someone's footsteps could be heard in the distance: Polinka frowned even more and drew her armchair farther into the corner . . . in spite of all her efforts, she was unable to maintain her most cheerful, affable smile.

Konstantin Aleksandrovich Saks came into her room; he was wearing a black frock coat and a black velvet vest. Traces of his unloved work still lingered on his face; with a worried expression he went over to the armchair where Polinka was sitting, two-thirds of which was still empty.

Suddenly a smile appeared on his face, he threw himself into the chair, blocking the corner in which Polinka sat, and put his arm around her waist.

"Ah! We're angry," he said, kissing her. "I know that habit of squeezing into corners; I know your feline ways!"

"Be quiet, Kostya, be quiet," Polinka shouted, scratching her husband unceremoniously. "Can't you see Polya's ill . . . ?"

"You're ill? What's wrong with you, my little bird?" he said, looking anxiously into Polinka's face.

"Oh, dear! He can't even tell the difference between his wife and a dog."

"Ah! So it's Polya who's ill," said Saks, shaking his head and looking at the little dog, which was still growling. "'It's a great sin to bestow a Christian name / On such an un-Christian creature.'[22] This was once said about a toad, but there's no great difference."

"Oh, what filth! Listen, Kostya," Polinka went on with a serious expression, "why did you deceive me yesterday?"

"How's that?"

"Where did you go this morning as soon as it became light?"

"Work, my little bird, work, there's no getting away from it." And Saks's face assumed its previous expression of annoyance and worry. "Today doesn't even count; what a terrible thing has happened! . . ."

"What, what is it?"

"I have to be away for three weeks."

Polinka froze; her frightened eyes fixed on her husband and her heart stopped beating.

"Where?" she asked with considerable effort.

"Some four hundred versts from here. Pskov."[23]

"My God, what for?"

"I've been assigned an important investigation."

"Well, I'll go with you."

"My dearest, if only I could take you everywhere with me as if you were my little brother! Some people might find it amusing if I take my wife along when I'm conducting business, but what do I care about them? The thing is, you're such a spoiled child; could you endure a gallop along the likes of our roads nowadays? And when I get there I'll have to raise a ruckus, quarrel with them, interrogate them, travel about here and there . . . you couldn't tolerate that torture."

"Don't go, Kostya, my friend! I'm afraid, so afraid. Refuse, leave your work, what do you need it for?"

"Polinka, my dear," said Saks, holding her tighter and tighter around the waist. "Thank you, my child. You're giving me good advice, and I'm delighted. God knows, I'm willing to do anything for you, but I can't turn down this investigation."

"What does this investigation mean anyway?"

"Listen and decide for yourself. Here in Petersburg there was an old slanderer, a cunning rogue, a certain Counsellor of State named Pisarenko."

"I know . . . I saw him. He used to administer old General Galitsky's affairs."

"The adjutant's father?"

"Yes, yes. Well, what of this Pisarenko then?" She leaned her head on Saks's broad chest.

"I don't know," Konstantin Aleksandrych continued, "how he ran the late prince's affairs, but he administered his work incredibly badly. In spite of his important position in Pskov, he cheated both the treasury and those doing business with it and managed to pocket over a hundred thousand rubles. Using his own accounts, which I've studied, I was able to uncover the theft and make accusations against him and his associates. You know what state monies really are. They're paid by peasants from their own meager incomes; they must be kept safe and spent only on legitimate business. For what heroic feats did these monies come into the possession of this scoundrel Pisarenko? Consequently, the authorities have vigorously intervened in this matter and, as a sign of their trust, have asked me to investigate the entire affair. One has the chance to do some good in this case."

"That's true, Kostya, and I'm not unhappy about the good you could do. . . . Leave it, don't go. . . ."

"Let's say I refuse. Let's say they forgive this blatant infringement of official decorum. But my honor might also suffer. Who would go in my place? How could someone else conclude the affair that I've begun? What if an inexperienced person went and befuddled both himself and me? What if a greedy man were sent and compounded the problem? . . ."

Saks paused. Polinka, having covered her face with her hands, was sobbing, not wanting to listen to his dispassionate arguments.

Saks was irascible, like all high-strung people. He often took out his daily upsets on those who weren't even a party to them. He turned in his armchair with such annoyance that the sick dog began to bark and bolted from its place. Polinka grabbed the arms of her chair in her small, strong hands, leapt up, and rushed after her dog, Polya.

Konstantin Aleksandrych also stood up and began pacing the room.

"Polinka," he said, stopping in front of his wife, who was settling the dog back in its previous place, weeping bitterly all the while. "It's time for us to leave these idylls. How long will you remain a child and refuse to make progress? When will you become a woman? I love you, but I'm not running a boarding school. I'm a simple man, a working man—people upset me frequently: I don't even have time to complain about all of it to you. Let's learn to live better and enjoy ourselves whenever possible. Just think what will become of us in ten years: can it be true that you'll still be the same when you're thirty?"

"Don't go, Konstantin!" was all that Polinka could say, and she shed even more tears.

Let's hasten to forgive this poor child: she was grieving not out of mere caprice. A foreboding of misfortune, some vague sadness had invaded Polinka's heart as soon as she'd begun to think about the three weeks her husband would be away.

But Saks didn't know that: he didn't believe in forebodings. A momentary but bitter anger was stirring in his heart; he paced the room with large strides, and when the frightened dog encountered him along the way, he kicked her into the other corner.

Polinka took the little dog into her arms and retreated to the corner, looking timidly at her husband. Tears as big as large diamonds stood in her eyes. Saks didn't like that either. . . .

"My God!" he said, partly out loud, partly to himself, continuing to pace around the room. "A year of love, a year of effort, a year of hard work has all been for nought. . . . What have we achieved? . . . The same unconscious tears at the least distress, the same endless fussing over that little dog. . . . Am I stupid? Am I really capable of what I've undertaken, is it already too late, or . . ."

He slapped his forehead. A painful idea, doubt in his wife's abilities, entered his mind. . . .

No, she's not stupid. He'd observed so much dazzling intelligence, though still so childish, in what she said!

Perhaps her character lacked will or energy?

"Polinka," Saks began once more, drawing near to her. "I've disturbed your Cerberus,[24] forgive me. Scold me soundly, I'm an absolute bore, unfit for women's company."

But Polinka didn't look at him and made no reply. She felt bitter. For the first time in her life she'd had to listen to a stern reprimand, and for what? All because she was sad that she'd have to part with her husband. Her gentleness, her childlike character, so highly praised by everyone, had become an object of Konstantin's assaults.

She was annoyed. Without saying a word, she sat in the corner and became gloomier and gloomier.

But the impact of this first argument on Konstantin Aleksandrych was terrible. He was a passionate and steadfast man, independent in all his actions. If he didn't get along with someone, then it was for life, without acknowledging any need to accommodate himself to the other person, whatever his character. Familism[25] and its trivial, destructive dramas had never occurred to his far-ranging, free-thinking mind, even in its dreams. A wandering life in his youth, wealth and love in maturity, had spared him from the seamier sides of family life.

And suddenly, like a snake in a rosebush, family life threw itself upon him and surrounded him, replete with tears and nasty little dogs, disorder, and quarrels. . . .

Saks sat down in his former place and hung his head gloomily.

Meanwhile, Polinka's anger subsided. The nice child was once again ready to throw herself onto her husband's neck. Let him begin, speak, even though his shame is false. . . .

She went to the piano: she sang Desdemona's aria and played a Sperl-polka. The poor dear, she had no idea how unpleasant Saks found this Sperl-polka.

She began walking around the room. The little flirt knew that her husband loved her rapid walk and would soon start looking at her tiny little feet.

Saks's heart leapt in his chest. Where had his anger gone? Where had the effect of these family horrors vanished?

He gained control of himself, remained silent, looked even gloomier, but glanced over to where Polinka was walking. . . . He wanted to make her suffer.

Don't blame Konstantin Aleksandrych: you may not know what morbid, intoxicating enjoyment comes from tormenting children, even though we're ready to sacrifice half our life for one hair of their head or one smile. How we torment them!

In this connection I'll tell you another story soon . . . a sad story, a strange one.

Saks sat there in silence, hanging his head despondently.

Polinka went to fetch some books from her bedroom and brought them to her husband.

"Look, Kostya," she said, "here's what Tanya Zapolskaya sent me today. Are they worth reading? You know everything."

Konstantin Aleksandrych glanced at one of the books: it was an endlessly long French novel.

"Leave it alone," he said. "It's better to read nothing than to spoil your taste with such rubbish."

"But I want to read something," Polinka said, taking from the shelf a copy of George Sand's novel *Mauprats*.[26] "Is this any good?"

"It's very good, Polinka, but you've thoroughly reviled George Sand before."

"Well, I was wrong. I'm going to read it."

"You've also complained that you didn't understand anything in it."

"I was reading it unwillingly; now I'll make an effort. If you like, Kostya," Polinka said with the cheerful look with which she delivered her most naive pronouncements, "if you like I'll even study this book. You see," here she folded down the corners of the first two pages, "I'll memorize this much, just as we used to do in school: *Il est temps de lever nos yeux vers le ciel. . . . Calypso ne pouvait se consoler départ. . . .* Calypso couldn't be consoled with the departure. . . ."

"Oh, devil take it!" cried Saks, who lost his patience as a result of Polinka's last, excessively naive prank. "Are you pretending or what? Will this never cease?"

"Why are you angry?" Once more she showed him the first two pages of the book.

"Do people really memorize things? Are you really going to learn something by heart at your age? Where will I ever find the patience?"

And, summoning patience to his aid, the hot-tempered Saks tore the novel written by his favorite author from Polinka's hands.

"Give me that book, I want to read it!" Polinka shouted, now also losing her patience.

"*Mais que diable, madame!*"*

"*Mais que diable, monsieur!*" and Polinka stamped her feet, first one and then the other.

"*Que diable, que diable!*"† Saks shouted with joy, drawing his wife toward him with both hands. "More, my friend! Abuse me, get really angry! *Morbleu! parbleu! sacrebleu!*‡. . . . Tell me to go to hell."

"*Morbleu! . . . parbleu! . . .* Kostya, Kostya, you want me to behave like a little schoolboy."

*What the devil, madame!
†Devil take it, devil take it!
‡Damn! Damn! Damn!

Konstantin Aleksandrych was vanquished. All these scenes both exhausted him and appealed to his tender feelings, as happens with people head over heels in love. He seated Polinka on the sofa and sat down next to her. Now it was Madame Saks's turn to recite an admonition.

"Konstantin Aleksandrych," she said impressively, while her husband, who heard nothing at all, kissed her little round cheek: "How long will you play the fool, clown around, make a fuss about nothing? . . . Why, you live in society, my friend . . . you live among people, my dear. . . ."

"I beg you!" Saks couldn't refrain from laughing. "Now she's started giving me moral lessons! She's taking me to task! Well, go on, go on; what's it to me? But don't change your tone. . . ."

Polinka would have gone on for some time repeating this advice gleaned from conversations with her mother, had the sound of someone's approach not caused her to lose the thread of her moral instruction.

The valet came in and announced that Prince Galitsky was asking to see Konstantin Aleksandrych and Polina Aleksandrovna.

"What on earth for?" the words burst forth from Saks.

"He has a letter to deliver," the valet said in reply to his master's thought.

"Ah, from his sister! From Annette!" Polinka cried joyfully. "Ask him in, ask him in!"

The servant left.

"Isn't this a bit awkward?" Saks asked his wife. "After all, he was hoping to marry you."

"He was hoping to. What do I care about that? He missed his chance. Do you know him?"

"I knew him in the Caucasus and have met him here. Apparently we're going to resume our acquaintance, but what shall we do with him? Your relatives don't get along with him, and he's both too young and too princely for my friends. Perhaps we should put him entirely at your disposal?"

Polinka blushed and her heart began to pound.

CHAPTER III

A handsome young officer entered and, after the initial greetings and questions, delivered two letters, the contents of which we already know, to the appropriate parties.

"This task is not particularly onerous," he said, handing Zaleshin's letter to Saks. "On the other hand, I claim a special debt of gratitude from Polina Aleksandrovna. The mail is too slow for letters such as this, and I came much faster than the mail."

"How is Annette? Is she well? Give me her letter." And Polinka began reading her friend's note without even considering the fact that an outsider was present in the room and that this young man's eyes were carefully following her every move.

Saks placed his letter some distance away and began chatting with Prince Galitsky about past military affairs, during which fate had brought the two of them together; during the conversation he regarded the prince with curiosity and not without a certain pleasure.

Prince Aleksandr Nikolaevich had one of those rare faces that appeal to both men and women at first glance. His features seemed even finer and cleverer as a result of his dull, somewhat sickly pallor, further set off by a little black mustache turned upward. His mouth held a tender, childishly affectionate expression, one that is retained for a long time on the faces of men who had been particularly handsome boys.

He was tall and thin, but his weak figure seemed to have been arrested in its development. The uniform with a silver braid made the prince look even younger. . . .

"What's my good friend Zaleshin up to these days?" Saks asked, to continue their conversation. "Is he still reading his Pantagruel as before? Have you become good friends with him?"

"It's been some time since I've had such a pleasant acquaintance," replied the prince. "Your friend could go far, if it weren't for his laziness."

"His goodwill," Saks observed. "But why should we feel sorry? I'm sure he's totally happy."

"He'd also be happy here. Give him an entire ministry: he'd be just as calm and cheerful, and he'd eat, drink, and work diligently. Only hypochondriacs have a hard time in the civil service."

"That is, you think a civil servant. . . ."

"Must be an epicurean. Therefore, more than most other people, Zaleshin should be in the civil service."

"That's almost true. . . . The more I look at you," said Saks, "the more changes I notice. You're much thinner than you were before your cure."

"I had a bout of nervous fever . . . after taking the waters."

"Well, do as you like, but I think taking the waters is stupid. Is there anything in the world more vulgar and more boring than that endless Karlsbad and all similar spas?"

"For me they're even more repulsive," said the prince with a smile. "It was to no avail that I was practically born in a mineral bath. . . . I didn't stay in Germany long; in the spring I went to Italy. . . ."

Polinka finished reading her letter and sat in silence, biting her lips.

"I'll leave you alone with my wife for a little while," said Saks, picking up Zaleshin's letter again. "She's very impatient . . . she wants to ask you all about her friend. It's a pity I have to leave Petersburg so soon . . . though not for long, it's true. If you're free, why don't you stay and have dinner with us?"

The prince bowed.

"Zapolsky, whom you know, will also be here, and an artist from Italy. It should be of some interest to you. We'll talk about Rome with him, and with you: 'About turbulent days in the Caucasus. . . .'"[27]

Saks left with the letter in his hands.

Slowly, with a sad expression that was well suited to his interesting face, the prince approached Polinka.

"Will you forgive me, Polina Aleksandrovna?" he asked softly, stopping in front of her and folding his arms across his chest.

Polinka blushed, then turned white as a sheet. She felt sorry, frightened, and guilty.

"*Monsieur Alexandre*," she said according to her old habits from boarding school, "for what? . . . I was right and you were right. . . . You've probably read the letter?" she suddenly cried and blushed once again.

Without either a smile or a frown, Prince Aleksandr Nikolaevich met this unbearable innocence.

"Do you know what it's about?" Polinka asked again to correct her mistake.

"I can guess," Galitsky replied sadly. "What business is it of mine? I must confess to you openly what I can't hide from anyone. . . . These letters were a pretext—I just wanted to see you."

Polinka, frightened out of her wits, was too scared to look into the prince's face.

"Are you afraid of me?" he continued. "In this day and age, can love result in . . . or, in this day and age, can any passion develop?"

Polinka was terribly confused and didn't know what to say.

"I'll tell you directly, as we used to say in the old days, I myself don't know whether I love you now. I never entertained the possibility of speaking to you . . . all the way here I never dreamed that I might kiss your hand. . . . I have only one inexplicable need—to see you, Polinka Aleksandrovna. Perhaps it's not right to do this . . . tell me to my face. . . ."

The prince was proceeding by the most direct route. His plan of attack was extremely simple. Sentimental scholastic debate could have no place when dealing with Polinka.

When she heard these words, Polinka became a bit bolder and raised her eyes to meet the prince's own blue eyes.

"This is all so strange!" she said. "You think a great deal, *Monsieur Alexandre* . . . you've probably read many books. You ought to attend balls more frequently . . . you have so many friends. . . ."

"I've thought about the reasons for this sadness," the prince continued. "I've thought about my pressing need to see you . . . shall I say it? . . . Once I even consulted doctors, naturally without ever mentioning your name. It's a kind of illness . . . fatal only for me . . . and it may still pass. Your single glance has afforded me relief; I'm feeling calmer already."

"But all this is nonsense," said Polinka, already bolder than before. "You must cheer up, play cards. . . . I'd be glad to help you, but it's still impossible for us to look at one another."

"Oh, you sweet deceiver!" the prince thought to himself. "How skilfully, albeit unconsciously, you noticed the amusing side of my Platonism! Forward! Spare no effort!"

"Does my sadness seem amusing to you?" he wondered aloud. "I thank you for your concern. People are entitled to laugh at me . . . what do I care? As long as I can see you. My situation doesn't come under any general rules. . . . I'm so convinced of the strange, exclusive nature of my illness that I'm ready to go to your husband, tell him everything . . . and he himself. . . ."

"What are you saying? My God! Be still! Don't tell him. . . . If you ever say so much as one word to him . . . I'll never speak to you again. . . ." The poor child turned pale once more: the bloody scene of the duel as described by her obliging friend arose clearly before her eyes.

Not one muscle stirred on the prince's pale face.

"I have no reason to fear him," he said sadly. "I have no rights at all, and I respect his rights deeply. My demands are not great, and he's a generous man."

"I told you, Prince, if you feel any love for your sister at all, say not one word to Konstantin Aleksandrych . . . I'll tell him myself, later. . . ."

"Ah! That's sensible!" the prince thought with satisfaction. "To the attack! Well, Marlinsky,[28] help me out of this one!"

"It's strange!" he began aloud. "A wonderful man! I'd never have expected it from him. In Dresden I saw a painting of the Madonna that was impossible to approach without tears and trembling.[29] No one stood near that wonderful painting, no one chased spectators away, no one spoke to them: I could look at it all alone. . . ."

Galitsky fell silent. Polinka sat there, her head lowered, fidgeting with the ends of her shawl. Tears must have been forming in the corners of her eyes because she was constantly trying to blink them back.

The timid silence was broken by the arrival of Saks and two of his friends.

"You're invited to dinner, *mon prince*!" he cried, upon entering the room. "I'll introduce you . . . but we'll all get acquainted at the dinner table. Pauline," he said, turning to his wife, "my trip's been postponed for two days."

Konstantin Aleksandrych was very pleased with this delay; Polinka was pleased that the poor prince turned out to be so quiet; was Aleksandr Nikolaevich pleased? That, making use of the narrator's prerogative, I won't tell you.

CHAPTER IV

From A. N. Galitsky to State Counsellor Pisarenko

My dear Stepan Dmitrich! What horrible things I've heard about you! You've fallen into a pretty legal mess? Our disinterested Alguazillas[30] have undermined your well-being? I feel very sorry for you, sorry from the bottom of my heart. You remember what your late father once told you: "Hey, Stepan Dmitrich, don't take that post! Nowadays it's hard to work for old men: the younger generation rots and breaks—but it doesn't understand a thing."

I think the same way: woe to him in this struggle who's lived least of all. Our young people have come galloping up from somewhere, shouting all about sublime honesty, even weeping. . . . Well, that still doesn't mean anything: they know nothing.

But worst of all are those upstarts like your friend Saks. Where have they come from? Who gave birth to them? What did they do before? No one knows; yet they know everything, fit in everywhere, keep silent, don't carry on about sublime honesty—they just climb over others to occupy the best posts. God only knows when these people will ever quit the scene.

I'd dearly like to help you, Stepan Dmitrich, but our credit is so muddled . . . you know, the whole Galitsky family has always been distinguished by its ability to maintain itself in important affairs without understanding them at all or doing anything. I'm sending you a few thousand excuses . . . don't feel sorry for me, an aunt of mine died recently (a remarkable woman!) . . . and left me a considerable sum of money.

Govern your Pskov peasants as before: delay the quitrent if you need money. Don't leave me the only old landowner in our whole family. I have a request to make of you, Stepan Dmitrich, a strange request, but an important one nonetheless. I'd like to be of some use to a person with whom, unfortunately, you're well acquainted—namely, Saks. I have no time to describe what my actions will be; later I'll tell you everything. I hope the system of justice doesn't devour you.

In order for me to carry out my plan it's necessary that Saks be delayed for some time longer where he is now, in the investigation of your case. He left about a week ago, but he works quickly.

Besides, I've looked through everything that's been written here about your case. The work won't take him very long: he'll check over the accounts on the spot and interrogate the contractors; then the matter will be concluded and he'll return to Petersburg, which would be most unfortunate for me.

I know your sensible train of thought, Stepan Dmitrich. You're frightened not so much by the inquiry, but by its consequences. "Who cares about honor, as long as there's something to eat," as our clever proverb has it.

But in this case you can rely on me as on a stone wall. All your expenses, all your losses will be repaid with interest, I give you my word, which I've never given to anyone in vain. Only do as I've asked.

Keep Saks in Pskov as long as possible. At least let your case drag on another two months. Confuse him, make things up about yourself and don't worry about a thing. Remember that I have a pile of money lying in a chest and nothing to do with it. If at all possible, don't involve any outsiders in this matter: let all this remain *inter nos*, as we used to say at the seminary.

But why did I say two months? I know your precision: you'll bring the matter to a conclusion exactly sixty-one days from now, counting from today. It would be better if I didn't give you a specific date; make a muddle of the case, drag it out until the last possible moment. When my own business is finished, I'll send you one word: "Enough." Then extricate yourself, as best you can. Do you need any money now?

But don't think it's necessary to drag out the investigation too long: perhaps my "enough" will arrive sooner than two months time.

Now I've remembered that they were supposed to ask my uncle, Count ****,[31] for his conclusions. They value his opinion highly. Then, after I've done some work for myself, I'll think about you, too.

Well, we've struck a bargain, Stepan Dmitrich! Isn't that right? Apply yourself to this matter and rely upon me. Perhaps we'll even find a way to extricate you!

Sincerely yours,
A. Galitsky

II

From Prince A. N. Galitsky
to Madame A. Krasinskaya

When we parted, dear sister, there wasn't a spark of good sense left in me. True, I was suffering from a fever, but God only knows what caused it. Was it love, annoyance, or the exhausting trip? . . . Who can explain it?

But now you can congratulate me on having a persistent fever. It's not love, but madness, insanity. It's a plague that must be contagious. You know my opinion of love: no one can ever disabuse me of the idea that love, once it's flared up in the extreme, must be communicated to the woman we love, if only it's within our power to see her and talk to her.

If a hypnotist can twirl us around his little finger just as he wishes by means of ridiculous movements made by his hands, then what must passion be capable of, if our entire organism trembles and explodes as a result of it?

Is a woman that much weaker than a man, is that why both sexes feel a mutual attraction for one another, so that these destructive outbursts can occur in vain, without producing any effect or arousing sympathy?

I'm in love to an extreme degree. My torments are further intensified by the fact that I have to control myself every moment; I have to pretend. One thing alone gives me support: I'm not suffering from insomnia. When day passes, I'm so exhausted that I sleep like the dead. Of course, I dream of her all the time; what else could I dream of? Still, sleep fortifies me.

I found your Polinka even sweeter than she was when she finished school. She's still very small, although she's grown considerably. Her figure has become even more graceful. Conversations with her husband have been of great use to her because Saks is such a clever and energetic man.

Nevertheless, I still rack my brain thinking about her all the time. She's unlike any other woman I've known, yet at the same time she's like all of them. Understand this as you will: I myself don't understand it. More and more I've become convinced that Polinka is a moral phenomenon.

She was always the favorite in your boarding school, the spoiled child. There she acquired all the innocence and strangeness you were known for in the first few years after leaving school. She was adored at home: they regarded her as a charming little toy, a butterfly that shouldn't be touched because it might destroy its beautiful wings. In society she was much fussed over; old and young men crowded around to say all sorts of silly things to her and hear her childish utterances.

This triple indulgence couldn't help but have an impact on her character. It didn't spoil her or make her capricious, but it did something far worse: it arrested the development of her moral capacities once and for all. I'll leave it to others to describe how this happened.

That's why at the age of nineteen she's just as sweet, clever, and charming as a child of twelve.

My God! Isn't that why I love her so desperately and passionately? My early successes among women turned me long ago into nothing more than a cold connoisseur of women's beauty. An extraordinary passion, almost absurd in its origin, was required to wrench me out of this apathetic condition. Then this passion arrived: I fell in love not with a woman, but a child.

This passion isn't love for a woman: it's love for an angel who's overcome me with her childish charm, an angel who knows our life well enough to be able to speak to us.

That old comparison of women with angels! I've used it often and repent of it, as of a sacrilege. Women are pleasant in and of themselves, but I call and will call only one of them an angel.

No one can possibly question Polinka's right to be called an angel. Everything about her is angelic: her face, which a sculptor could use as a model for a statue of Amor, the daintiness of her figure, the wonderful kindness of her heart, her capacity for devotion, and an ability to love suffused throughout her being.

But woe is me! This ability to love, the source of all woman's virtues, is neither fully developed in her nor acknowledged by her. It appears in everything: her devotion to her melancholy husband, her love for her worthless parents, her passion for birds and dogs, and in part for me, when I lie weeping at her feet.

If I managed to concentrate this need to love, to focus it on myself . . . I don't know whether I could survive, or whether I'd die from ecstasy before her very eyes. . . .

Apparently my relations with her have gone quite far: I see her every day, kiss her hands, talk with her openly about my love, embrace and kiss her. When she wants to stop me, I need only give her a sad look, place her little hand on my burning head . . . and the dear child forgets everything, lets me kiss her, and shares my sadness. Anyone would say I should rejoice, give myself up to ecstasy; but arriving home, I suffer in the depths of my soul, I tear my hair.

What good is it if she constantly dances with me at balls, if she allows me to kiss her at home, if she tells me how nice it is to look at me, that I'm "so very handsome"? She would say and do all that in her husband's presence.

But she says not a word about love; there's not the least sign of the passion that has so tormented my soul in the last month!

Only once—blessed be that day—did I arouse in her something resembling a feeling that has no name. Without that, dear sister, I wouldn't be writing you letters: another week of this kind of life—I'm telling you simply and frankly—and I'd lay hands on myself.

But now, thanks to this sweet recollection, serenity enters my soul at times. I can write you calmly and clearly.

You've guessed that Saks isn't in Petersburg. Before his departure, he asked his friend Zapolsky, whose works you sometimes read, to amuse his Polinka on occasion and keep her from becoming bored. Zapolsky is also on good terms with me and knows that Madame Saks was always close to our family; therefore, I was able to arrange things so that he, a busy man and a married one, took me on as his assistant. We've accompanied Polinka to the theater, reported all sorts of news to her at home, brought her new toys from the English store, read her journals, and sung her the eternal "Fra poco" and "Stabat mater."[32]

Three days ago, in the evening, Zapolsky brought her a packet of music and pictures, and then went off to collect tickets to the theater for that same evening. I was left alone with Polinka. She asked me to sing; I looked over the music and we talked about you; I told her about my pranks in the corps; all during this sensible conversation my hands and feet were cold and blood was seething in my heart.

A few of the tenor's lines before me were so vulgar, strewn with such frills . . . but I wanted to sing; music always comforts me at such moments.

Then among the sheets of music I located a prayer I knew well. . . . I don't recall whose it was, nor did I really care.

I sang this prayer and thought about Polinka. I prayed to my angel and, no doubt, my prayer was not received with indifference.

She stopped behind me and placed her hand on my shoulder.

"*Merci, Monsieur Alexandre,*" she said, her voice trembling. "I'll write to your sister and tell her you're spoiling me. . . ."

I looked around at her. The reddish Petersburg twilight was shining through the window, its pink light flooding the whole room. The figure of my charming little child was etched against this strange background. Polinka was wearing a white dress; her hair wasn't combed like a woman's, but was arranged in a ring around her head; her moist eyes were fixed warmly on me.

Angel, angel! . . .

Unaware of what I was doing, I fell to the floor and pressed my lips to her little feet. Buckets of tears flowed from my eyes, convulsive sobs rent my chest.

My passion reached its extreme limit and burst forth in a paroxysm of unbelievable force. I wept—for the first time in front of another person. And, in spite of these tears, something within me said: at this moment you're high and mighty.

She raised her head, sat me down next to her on the sofa, and pressed her little hands against my burning forehead.

"Sashenka, my friend," she said, taking care of me as if I were a baby at her breast, "stop behaving so childishly. What's the matter with you? You know I love you. Why are you crying? What will Annette say about us?"

But the contagious disease had begun to work: her cheeks were flushed, her bosom agitated.

She moved closer to me and began begging me to leave her alone, to stop loving her.

"My friend," she said meanwhile, "I don't understand why you've taken such a liking to me. Look at me more closely, I'm not all that pretty. . . ."

She went on at great length as to why she wasn't really attractive! You can imagine how all this failed to calm me. My weak chest was rent, but in the face of this graceful move by Polinka, it couldn't endure. . . . I nearly choked from a terrible coughing spell.

Polinka was frightened, but didn't lose control even for a moment. You had to see her then to understand to what levels of ineffable beauty a woman's soul can ascend. She forgot all about me, herself, her husband—she saw in me only a sick friend.

She drew my head to her chest and put her arms around me.

"My God, enough, enough of this, Sashenka," she said, herself weeping. "God is forgiving, it will all pass, everything will be forgotten . . . stop grieving, take care of yourself . . . you know, I'd die myself . . . if anything ever happened. . . ."

Zapolsky was supposed to be back by this time and was bringing his wife with him.

Thanks to Polinka's efforts, I soon recovered, and our day ended at the theater.

You can imagine how little I was able to absorb there! But Polinka laughed and listened to the play with great interest!

You know I came to Petersburg without any definite intentions concerning Polinka. To look at her, to make her regret her marriage, perhaps to have an affair with her—that's all I had in mind. But now my plan has been decided definitively and I won't retreat from it even one step.

Polinka isn't the sort of woman with whom one has an affair and then ceases to care about her. Whereas we can see the outcome of our passion with other women, with Polinka it's only the beginning of love. What does a month mean to me, a year of possessing her, even though that possession may be indissoluble? I need her totally, forever, entirely.

Women—excuse me, my dear sister, women are like expensive, colorful gemstones: it's nice to play with them and sometimes even to wear them. Polinka is a large diamond among them; one needs to possess her forever, conceal her from all eyes, so this priceless diamond will never be deprived of life.

She's nineteen years old and not an unfeeling woman—let's suppose I take advantage of a moment of passion and possess her . . . think only about this . . . my blood's on fire . . . will I ever be satisfied? I've already declared that the place where things end with other women is only the beginning of love with Polinka.

No, there's nothing to ponder, conjecture, or reach a compromise about. Either she'll be mine, forever, inseparably mine, or else I'll live on earth no longer. Saks's return will resolve this entire matter, but until then . . . what will be, will be.

What do I care about this man who stands so proudly in my way? Does he love her? I love her. Is he grateful? What business is it of mine? I love her. Is he bold and strong? What do I care? I love her.

CHAPTER V

I

From Polinka Saks to Madame Krasinskaya

Ah, Annette, Annette! My dearest Annette! What have you done to me? If you could see your little Polinka, you'd be very frightened and burst into tears. No woman has ever experienced such grief as I have. And if God is our judge, I want to take all the blame on myself . . . or else you'll have a great deal to answer for before Him.

Why did you send your brother here? Why did you send your letter to me through him? You thought you could calm him, but you've made it a hundred times worse. If I die, he'll die, too. If I don't come to love him, he'll destroy himself—if I do come to love him, he'll fight a duel with my husband. He keeps saying, "There isn't enough room on earth for the three of us."

If only they could both remain alive . . . if I could be the only one to die! Last night I had a bad headache and a fever . . . I wept and prayed to God that I might die. Then I felt afraid and miserable . . . I don't want to die; besides, he wouldn't go on living after me.

In the morning it all passed and I felt better . . . then I became even more frightened.

There, my Annette, that's what has become of me . . . that's the point I've reached! . . . Ah, if only you hadn't sent your brother here, if only you'd kept searching there for a young woman he could come to love! Why is he so in love with me? It all would have passed: there are so many women better than me . . . I've told him this a dozen times . . . it's only a whim that people think I'm pretty.

I'm not too tall, I look like a young boy . . . if only you saw how thin my arms are, how skinny I've become lately! My eyes aren't at all blue like your Sasha's.

I'm surprised he doesn't find it boring to sit with me: what has he discovered in me? I don't know anything and can't talk about much. Only Konstantin Aleksandrych has the patience to teach me.

My friend, this is my most terrible grief: for some time now I haven't known how to greet my husband—to run to meet him, throw myself on his neck, console him with my chatter. But now I'm afraid to think about him, afraid to write him even a few words because I don't know how to lie. In the evening I'm afraid to walk past his portrait.

It's all because I've betrayed him; I exchange kisses with another man, and I've told your brother that I love him. What is there left for me? In my soul I'm a traitress and a despicable woman.

In the meantime, my husband is correct in all things before me. In your letter you describe him as a wild beast: I haven't slept nights; the terrible story of the duel keeps haunting me. Still, you're not right, Annette; I'm not as smart as you are, I've seen less of the world, but I understand that not everything was wrong in Konstantin Aleksandrych's response.

Wasn't the poor actress whom Galitsky and his friends attacked a woman? Didn't her fame and the public's love mean everything to her: both a consolation and her livelihood, perhaps?

My husband is terrible and fearsome. . . . My God, he's shed human blood! But he isn't cruel. Still, a terrible conclusion to all this is in the making. . . . Lord, deliver us! . . . It's better not to think about it. . . .

When you sent your brother here you asked me to calm him, to feel sorry for him. My dearest, you didn't consider the fact that I'm not made of stone, that I still have to be watched! . . . It's one thing if he'd appeared as he had before: a cheerful, carefree young man. I'd have dealt with him and remained safe. But when I saw his sad eyes, his pale, tired face . . . what became of me!

He's so good-looking! A hundred times better than before. That marble pallor suits him so well! His chest has sunk, his waist has become even nobler, more graceful . . . and his eyes. . . . God, forgive me . . . is it me saying all this?

Yesterday he paraded past my window wearing a helmet with a white plume and riding a black horse that strained and jumped. His thin figure bent so skillfully at each of the horse's movements, and the horse obeyed him so well! . . . His rightful place is in front of soldiers, facing the enemy . . . yet he pines and weeps here together with me! . . .

If I were nice to him simply to console him, if I kissed him just to keep him from falling into despair, I'd still be right, at least as far as my own conscience is concerned. But, no, my friend! I'm a traitress in my soul; I love these caresses: my head often burns, my heart pounds, and I only feel better when I press myself against his chest. . . . Eternal shame, eternal punishment isn't enough for me! . . .

To whom can I turn? From whom can I seek advice and salvation? I can't write to my husband: I've begun to be afraid of him. How can I write to him when one word might result in a terrible encounter and death?

I thought about asking Sasha himself, telling him once more to leave me . . . but wouldn't that be a direct admission of my weakness? Besides, he wouldn't listen to me . . . or even worse: he would, and I'd destroy him. . . .

I've confessed all this to my mother; I've knelt before her and wept a great deal. . . . I made her promise not to say a word about it to anyone. At first she rebuked me for my carelessness and my tears seemed so ridiculous to her. "Go, my little one," she said to me, "sins like that are still forgiven. It'll all be forgotten. Remember one thing: don't see the prince any more; if you do, don't let him do anything more. You'll still be happy . . . keep watch on yourself more carefully. . . ."

As if I could keep watch on myself, control myself when he weeps at my feet and kisses my knees.

Lord! What will become of me? Or don't you pity poor Polinka and won't you send her any help?

II

From Konstantin Aleksandrych Saks to Polinka

Oh, you frivolous girl, you! Oh, you lazy, good-for-nothing little bird! Is this the way you correspond with your aged husband? One letter in almost two months! When I get back, I'll certainly take you to task!

Are you afraid of making mistakes, or what? You could write in French. No, it's all your worries about the house and our affairs! I know, I know! Here are your worries about the house: in the morning you sit in one corner of the armchair and conduct a review of the dogs. At that time you think: what a deceiver that Kostya is! So this is what three weeks means the way he counts!

After your worries about the house come your own affairs: you ride about town, making the poor horses sweat. "Faster, Anton, get a move on, faster . . . to Aunt Julie, to Mama." There you're met by a whole course of lectures on human wisdom, an unquenchable source of morality . . . how fares your Goettingen, your Berlin?[33]

And in the evening, *ma chère*, in the evening. . . . Your girlfriends arrive, little angels, all of them, unforgettable friends. There's Juliette and Pashette and Annette . . . but Annette isn't in Petersburg. Last of all, there's Nadine and Alexandrine.

Then the talk begins, brimming with practical philosophy, imbued with profound knowledge of life and the human heart! Oh, Allah, my ears wilt; as an outsider, it's frightening. "I fear for man!"[34] You remember how Karatygin used to wail that line in the Aleksandrinsky Theater.[35]

But, go on, be lazy. I don't like people who write letters unwillingly. Rarely do moments of spiritual openness come upon us and, without that, what need is there to make such a big fuss? Zapolsky writes me about your health and activities—and I'm content. By the way, about Zapolsky. He writes that Prince Galitsky visits you frequently and, it seems, has fallen in love with you in earnest. The latter is to be expected: Zaleshin informed me about it two months ago.

Shall I confess to you, Polinka? I like it when others find you attractive. It even tickles me when I find out that other men are sighing over you in earnest. It's not good, but it's my weakness, my pride. The time will still come when you and I will live and learn the science of how to exist on earth! As far as Galitsky is concerned, I ask you seriously to see him less frequently; but don't trifle with him, don't ignore him, and don't torment him. Your flirtation isn't wrong; there's no reason to be afraid of it. I like that young man, even though he's a bit proud and frivolous. Nowadays the breed of quiet, modest men has become too numerous; you can't get anything out of them, either for life or society.

I won't say any more. To ask you not to forget your old husband would be an insult. Keep an eye on Galitsky: if he becomes too entangled in lies, let me know and we'll take care of it without offending him.

I've been here for a long time, thanks to that damned Pisarenko. He's either a madman or a brilliant swindler. I've seen a great deal of nettle seed, but I've never encountered such a rascal and can't understand him. He whirls around like a demon before dawn, slanders himself with all sorts of unrealizable schemes, invents the most unlikely excuses, which, however, one has to believe—but in actual fact it all turns out to be nonsense and results in his own shame. But the business drags on longer and longer: I'm straining all my intelligence to forestall the machinations of this wicked official.

It's a genuine little war and—to complete the picture—also involves my love for you; but the desire to see you sooner gives me the strength and cleverness necessary for this litigious struggle.

So, my dear Polya, all sorts of things happen on this earth. Another man might laugh at this battle, but I'm deeply convinced that if the matter is illuminated by love and an understanding of life, no one will think it insignificant. Who gave us the right to demand of life lofty and unrealizable passions? Instead let's learn how to do something useful around us, laugh at what's really funny, and make peace with life in return for what it's given to us.

The longer I stay here, the more I regret that I didn't bring you along with me. You would have liked the quiet life in this little town, the forest through which the sun shines in the evening, and the distant lake with its deserted shores.

You'd make such fun of all of them: we'd chuckle about stuffy local meetings, their hopelessly exaggerated styles. In the group of boring landowners we'd complain about our circle of friends who, never having left Petersburg, think they know exactly what's going on in all corners of the universe, why people dance and make merry in some places, while in others they starve to death or slit their throats.

Then we'd get close to these simple people, search their tanned faces for traces of their past sorrows or present passions: among them we'd find wonderful people, practical people—and good philosophers. Every one of them would interest us: not in his present affairs, but in his past life, because—who among us has not been engaging, in the full sense of that word, at least once in his life?

You and I have lived in the capital long enough. When I return, I'll take a long vacation or retire from the service. Then we'll roam the world for a while, or else I'll begin to think that you and I have stayed in one place too long. At first, if you like, we'll travel around Russia, have a look at her towns and villages, her broad rivers; we'll wander across sands above which tall pine trees creak. We'll see the Caucasus: we may be fed up with all those stories about it—but it's really worth seeing.

From Odessa we'll travel to southern France and begin our tour where travelers usually squander their last kopecks and go no farther. We won't go very far. Italy, France, Switzerland, southern Germany—that'll be enough for us. And for the crowning touch, we'll settle on our own country estate; only then, after all our travels and conversations about everything we've seen, will you stop asking me, "But what will we do in the Russian countryside?"

Is there anything new about all this? Am I building castles in the air, looking two years ahead into the future? That's your doing, Polya: you've given me vitality and youth; otherwise I'd have started to grow old in turn. Wait a bit—I'll pay you back for all this.

I must tell you in more detail about my pursuits; fortunately, today I can relate one story that's not altogether frivolous.

As you know, there's an official working here with me who resembles a funny sort of bird. You'd really be amused by him—I know you, you imp!—when he sits down next to me in the carriage. You'd make fun of the way he hobbles and speaks in such a thin voice.

But he's an ambitious man, even though in his soul he's not very deserving. He has a horrible name: Feefe. I really don't know where his family comes from, but he's Russian. I brought him here with me out of a curious whim: all I have to do is glance at him—then I remember you so vividly, as if I were seeing you in a mirror. Is that because you laughed at Feefe when I saw you last, or because he looks like a bird, and I call you my little bird? . . . In brief, it's a strange juxtaposition of thoughts.

Moreover, Feefe is a quiet man and quite capable. At first he hung around Pisarenko and provided him with information, then he spoke to me about my excessive severity. To that I replied with the polite request that he refrain from meddling in this matter.

But Feefe continued to fawn. Yesterday he announced that Pisarenko's wife wished to see me, and on that occasion told me, according to his own understanding, this woman's sad tale.

Just like you, she was educated at an outstanding women's boarding school. She was always first in all her subjects, and her abilities so astounded everyone that one charitable soul even gave her Italian lessons at his own expense—an extremely useful skill for the daughter of an invalid lieutenant.

She was a girl with a soul, a strong character, and aristocratic instincts that were horribly offended by anything squalid and poor.

You can imagine the poor girl's position when, upon completion of her course, she left the lofty halls of her school to return to her parents' humble dwelling. It's hard to find positions these days, so she had to live at home. Believe me, however much the poor girl held out, her parents' home soon began to seem like hell to her.

Their family was honest and generous. The father, a distinguished, brave soldier, had only one fault: he loved to go on sprees. Her mother, a kind, gentle woman, constantly grieved, wept, and bemoaned their poverty.

Polinka, Polinka! You don't know the whole horror of this poor, impure life, its stifling and crowded conditions, amid hardships and bitter complaints. Your parents aren't known for their moral qualities; on the other hand, at least they're wealthy. You should be thankful to fate for that.

Let's return to this poor girl. I don't know if you'll understand, Polya, why in energetic souls, especially among women, the gloomy side of family life has such great impact. The quiet girl could've been miserable and then grown used to it—but our heroine was miserable and grew bitter: she grew bitter against fate and her own family. This squalid life and endless need filled her soul with unbearable sorrow.

She was passionately devoted to her parents but loved them apart from or outside the house. When her old father returned home in an abject state, when her mother's cries and complaints provoked him to quarrels and reproaches, the poor girl would stop loving them. Her heart was broken; she suffered and was terrified, but at these times she would hardly ever see her parents.

Is it surprising that she threw herself on the neck of the first seducer who blinded her with his wealth and promise to carry her away from this purgatory? As is the case among the best of our illustrious ladies' men, the lover transformed her, with a substantial dowry, into the wife of Pisarenko, when he was still a low-ranking civil servant.

At this time Pisarenko was even worse than now. He was a petty, squalid bribe-taker, and a drunkard as well. Do you think the poor girl I'm talking about grew to hate him? That she dreamt only about leaving him?

Not in the least. For her there began a period of reconciliation with life—to tell the truth, a bitter reconciliation. She did for Pisarenko what she had previously been unable to do for her own father. She weaned him away from his incontinence and introduced order into his household; she treated her husband as if he were morally infirm, dressed their children like little dolls, and brought them up herself. I think that love for her children was the reason for the transformation of her character.

I don't understand how she didn't manage to break her husband of his excessive fondness for state funds. He both fears and respects her and does everything she wants him to. Perhaps she didn't investigate that sphere of her husband's activities; perhaps the remains of her blind hatred for society, the indelible trace of her bitter youth, prevented her from opposing it.

I'll continue my story.

This morning Feefe brought in a tall, pallid woman with two little boys, both aged around twelve. This was none other than Mrs. Pisarenko. She bowed to me deeply and timidly, but looked me over carefully. I asked Feefe to escort the children to the garden and I sat down in an armchair.

She appreciated my concern that her children not overhear any unpleasant conversation; she came up to me and took my hand in hers. There were tears in her eyes. I'd scarcely convinced her to sit down when she conveyed her request to me.

She wasn't asking on her husband's account: she knew of his guilt and the scope of his punishment. The thing that distressed her even more was the thought of her children's fate. They'd witnessed the painful affair; every day they'd seen their father becoming more irritated and embittered. When the case was concluded, what means would there be to provide for their education? What would become of them?

I listened with attention and a noble idea entered my mind. God knows whether I'd have brought this idea to fruition if my own interests hadn't been involved. Listen and see how good deeds can be done on this earth.

Here's what occurred to me: if I did a good turn for this woman, perhaps she could convince her husband to confess more quickly and not to muddle the affair unnecessarily.

"Olga Ivanovna!" I said to her. "Our government doesn't make children answer for the mistakes or faults of their father. However, I understand your difficulty in part: your husband has no time and no one to ask about his children, and he's afraid of a refusal. Tomorrow send both of your boys off to Petersburg without delay; I'll give you a letter to our minister and will explain all the circumstances to him."

The poor woman wept and wanted to kiss my hands.

"When they enter the civil service," I continued, "remember me. I have both credit and acquaintances; we'll provide them with opportunities according to their abilities. It would be better to raise your other children at home, at least until your situation becomes clearer."

She understood the hint very well and appreciated my sympathy even more than the services rendered.

Now my own interest entered into the matter.

"Olga Ivanovna!" I said again. "Give your husband some friendly advice from me. Why is he delaying this case and hindering the investigation? I give you my word of honor: he won't gain anything by it. It'd be better for him to confess and untie my hands. I'll tell you a secret: I'd like to get back to Petersburg as soon as possible. I've left my wife there, and I think about her every hour and every minute."

Then we parted.

There, Polinka, see how people go against their own conscience, how they do good out of egoism,[36] how they enter into negotiations with the enemy, and all because they want to gaze more quickly into your cunning little eyes.

Farewell, my child, *ma petite rose blanche*;* if anything happens, write to me.

*My little white rose.

»»» CHAPTER VI «««

A day after sending this letter Konstantin Aleksandrych was getting dressed in his bedroom. The red morning sun still hadn't started to grow warm, but Saks was in the habit of getting up late. His efforts led one to suppose some unusual event.

In the little room that served as his study sat Feefe, whom we already know, waiting for Saks, and one other person, who has a major influence on the course of our story.

He was an old man of respectable appearance with gray hair; a pair of blue glasses rested on his nose. His entire figure was noteworthy for its astonishing mobility. He was unable to sit still without shaking his head from time to time, twitching his arms, or jerking his leg. This unpleasant restlessness was in strange contrast with his old face, pure, cold, and blue as ice. This time, however, his restlessness was quite understandable. The old man was in a state of great spiritual agitation. From time to time he sighed and then groped about in his side pocket.

"And so, my dear Stepan Dmitrich," Feefe said in his thin voice, "you've tormented us so! How many horses have we worn out, how many pieces of paper have we wasted?"

"So what," replied Pisarenko in a slow bass voice, "if the result was still the same? Who returns evil for good? As you yourself know, my wife was here . . . she wept and sobbed. Go on, she says . . . and my heart skipped a beat. . . ."

"Well, God is merciful," Feefe began once again. "It'll all come out right in the end. And you don't have to worry about your children: you can rely on Konstantin Aleksandrych (here he raised his voice). He's an angel, not a mere mortal."

"I know, kind sir, I've known since yesterday. . . . Why hasn't he come in?"

"He's still getting dressed. He's a dandy: he'll come in wearing a new frock coat."

"Olga Ivanovna told me," Pisarenko inquired carefully, "that his wife stayed behind in Petersburg?"

"Yes, he has a wife. She's flighty, like a little five-year-old boy. But she's very pretty, like a lovely rose." Feefe uttered these words much more softly than he did his opinion of Saks's angelic nature.

"That's what I thought," Stepan Dmitrich replied, his face revealing painful anxiety. At this moment the door opened and in came Saks.

"Oh, my benefactor, my father-protector!" cried Pisarenko, throwing himself at Saks so emotionally that the latter was embarrassed. "May God reward you. . . ."

"That's a private matter," Konstantin Aleksandrych replied politely, "and it doesn't interfere with our main goal. They tell me you've finished your business?"

"It's all finished," said Feefe and handed Saks several papers.

"Well, thank God," replied Konstantin Aleksandrych, after examinining them. "Tell me, Stepan Dmitrich, in all good conscience, what caused you to drag out this matter to your own disadvantage?"

Stepan Dmitrich came closer to him. Something like tears shone beneath his glasses.

"Konstantin Aleksandrych," he said, "my benefactor, be kind until the end. I'll confess everything to you: God grant that no more time should pass."

Pisarenko cast a sidelong glance at the door into the next room. Saks guessed he wanted to have a private conversation, and led him into his bedroom, to the great disappointment of the curious Feefe. Making his way behind Saks, Pisarenko took from his side pocket a piece of paper.

It was the letter from Prince Aleksandr Nikolaich Galitsky, which you can locate in the fourth chapter of my story.

Stepan Dmitrich's repentence was complete. He even wiped away a few tears as he left the room.

Saks concluded several formalities, signed the report, and departed from Pskov before evening. He didn't feel any special anxiety.

But a terrible sorrow was in the offing for him. In society it happens that joy comes to people either at the wrong time, without any sense, or very slowly. You can't put it into a novel or a tale without embellishing it in some way. But wickedness moves so evenly, so smoothly, in such a way that it thrusts itself into print or onto the stage.

On the same day Saks was on his way to Petersburg, mail from Petersburg arrived in Pskov. One of the packets was addressed to State Councillor Pisarenko.

Stepan Dmitrich opened it in the middle of the street, his hands trembling. It contained a lottery ticket worth thirty-five thousand rubles and a crumpled scrap of paper. On this paper one word was written by a hasty hand: "Enough."

Stepan Dmitrich shook and, in a burst of noble disgust, threw the lottery ticket on the ground. He tore the note into little pieces.

Then he stood there, thought for a little while, picked up the ticket, and put it into his pocket.

"If not me, someone else will get it," he muttered through his teeth and started on his way home.

»»» CHAPTER VII «.««

Three letters follow, two of which are inappropriate for publication because of several details and one note with the following content:

"With the greatest of displeasure I observed you, Prince Aleksandr Nikolaevich, under my study windows last night as a result of some changes I made in the arrangement of my apartment. Not feeling any sympathy for enterprising hidalgos, I must confess that a meeting with you would not afford me even the slightest bit of pleasure. Tomorrow I will be moving to my dacha, which I leave it to you to search out if you so choose. It wouldn't be a bad idea for you to leave Petersburg as well, where your least indiscretion could cause harm to us both.

You can guess that this is not my last word. I repeat, I'll be seeing you in one month's time. In the middle of next month you'll receive a note from me; there you'll find my address and a time indicated for our meeting. Until then keep silent, absolutely silent.

K. Saks."

Here is one of the letters:

From K. A. Saks to P. A. Zaleshin

Two weeks have already passed, two terrible weeks, and I still haven't decided. . . . I have no plan in mind; I'm ready to consider myself a madman.

Thank you for your speedy reply, your sympathy and attention. I have no more to thank you for: your advice won't do me any good.

I unsealed your letter greedily; the vacillation in my soul is so great that good advice, or so I thought, could tip the whole matter toward either the bad or the good; unfortunately, I was sorely mistaken.

I can still understand your conclusions. You justify my wife and attempt to turn all my anger against Galitsky. My friend, my wife is in no need of justification. I'll say even more: Galitsky is also right.

But what does all this mean to me? In my position can the idea of justice really have any meaning, any practical application? Without you I know that *she* is right and *he* is right, and that I will be right if I take cruel revenge on them both.

The wounded soldier crawls furiously toward the enemy lines: does he ever really consider that he might kill someone other than the man who wounded him? Or that even the man who wounded him isn't really to blame?

I'm in despair; I want revenge. Does it even occur to me to think about the results of my revenge?

But what am I saying: I want revenge! The point is, I don't have the resolve even to carry out this wicked intention. If I did, I still wouldn't have the means to do it. What do I do with a child who doesn't even understand the mess he's made! I'm not some Armenian who stalks the "villain" and the "traitress," dagger in hand; I don't possess the skill with which an important gentleman knows how to torment his unfortunate wife constantly, forcing her to pay for her hour of errant pleasure by years of suffering; and was it even errant?

You say I should summon reason to my assistance and direct it against passion. You advise me to call upon philosophy for help, the remains of idealistic emotions, and attachment to some previously favorite theories of mine. It's as if you've forgotten that I too am a man, and a man in love—that to assume a doctrinaire attitude and construct theories may be easy in a literary salon or a novel, but not in life. . . . Summon reason! But against whom? Not against passion? It would be all right if things went along so smoothly, and reason knew how to struggle only against passion. But in me reason struggles with reason, passion goes against passion. I've broken apart into two kinds of reason, my passion has divided in two. This terrible civil war has yet to end, and I don't even know how it will finish.

I can resolve on some shameful act, in spite of my aversion to evil deeds; I can conclude my love with a pitiful tragedy, but amid universal hatred I know that you alone won't condemn me. I've revealed the condition of my spirit to you.

I can't even answer for the next day; perhaps I'll appear as a noble hero; stupid people will call me the Count of Monte Cristo,[37] enraptured youths will revere me as a new Jacques,[38] and only you will know that in my actions there can be neither villainy nor nobility. . . .

I'm powerless before fate: let circumstances determine my lot, hers, and his. I wash my hands of it; I have no strength left to act!

You end your letter with sarcastic barbs directed against Hymen, you sing the praises of proud solitude, you say that women's rights are sacred, that no one can prescribe the laws of a woman's love. . . .

Splendid words, effective words, though rather hackneyed phrases; and once again the word *right*, again abstractions, again cold truths! . . .

What need do I have for women's rights? Why do I have to know the theory of woman's love, discover its fundamental laws? It's nothing but words and more words.

At the present time neither society with its prejudices nor women with their unacknowledged rights exist for me. Society can abuse me or admire me, women can disappear from the face of the earth or rebel against men—my situation won't change in the least as a result.

I'll make efforts, grow faint, vacillate, and weep at night; I'll weep, I will, even though my head is growing bald!

All because there are only three of us in the whole world: Polinka, Galitsky, and me. I'd like to value society's opinion; I'd like to stand up for my so-called slandered name; perhaps this prejudice could provide me with the strength to act.

That's enough analysis of your letter; I feel this temporary spell of composure is dissipating: hot blood has risen to my heart; it's climbing higher, crowding into my throat; my fingers have grown cold as ice . . . anguish is about to consume me.

. . . .

How shameful, how shameful it is to be so dejected! I'm summoning my strength once again.

I've just returned from her room. In accordance with my instructions, she's letting it be known that she's indisposed; none of her friends knows whether I've returned to Petersburg or where I'm living. It's impossible to behave any differently; however this story plays itself out, the strictest secrecy is essential, nor is it difficult to maintain.

Only now, having pondered the past, have I understood how large is the abyss separating Polinka's character from my own. I deceived myself in happiness, and now, at the first misfortune, everything's been revealed to me. It's enough to regard my wife's present situation to understand that everything's finished between us; we'll never be together again.

Her grief is touching, pitiful, but it's very far from rational!

She weeps daily; if I speak to her she responds as those con-demned used to answer the grand inquisitor. Sometimes she's overcome by a desire to pray for a long time, a very long time. . . . She's absolutely convinced that her crime is so terrible that there won't even be a place in hell for her!

Try to imagine all this and feel sorry for me. There's no hope of reuniting, no hope of *forgetting* . . . for me love has ended; the piece has been played out and won't be revived. . . .

One question torments me: what does her love for Galitsky mean? Is it the legitimate striving of two passionate young na-tures one for the other? Is it genuine, enduring passion?

Or is it one careless outburst, "resulting in a fall," as our novelists would say? Oh, if only it were that! I'd be able to recover the past, to shut Galitsky's mouth! Love like mine doesn't col-lapse all at once.

With this thought in mind I went into Polinka's room last evening. She was sitting there weeping. I began speaking to her firmly, but with affection.

"My child," I said to her, "are you grieving over trifles? Let's forget the past for half an hour: imagine I'm your doctor and you really are ill."

She looked at me in horror. I was certain that her disordered imagination recalled the story of the man who, on the pretext of illness, confined his "perfidious traitress" to the madhouse.

I continued, trying hard to maintain my serenity. "Our conver-sation will be somewhat painful. What's to be done, my friend? We must look misfortune squarely in the eye, refuse to hide from it, refrain from weeping. . . . Tell me simply and honestly: are you in love with Galitsky?"

She began to cry, begged me to spare her, not to talk to her; she declared her willingness to die in order to wipe the terrible stain from my name. . . .

I clenched my teeth and started to lose control of myself. But I realized that my last question had been too painful for her: gradually I began to direct the conversation to her friendship with Galitsky. I asked her about his behavior, the course of his passion. Suddenly Polinka fell on her knees before me and grabbed my hands.

"He's not to blame," she said. "I'm the one who's destroyed you both; I'm the cause of it all. He's still young, a mere child, you'll forgive him . . . let me be the one to perish alone. . . ."

So that's where my solicitude had led! That's the direction in which my interrogation had pushed her. . . . You hear, she's destroyed him! Oh, women, women! Oh, sweet self-sacrifice!

Rage took away my breath; my heart was pounding. Enmity, unconscious, groundless enmity filled my entire soul. I wanted to tear to pieces this dear creature weeping before me, whose only fault was that she couldn't understand me. . . . I'd give my whole life to make a woman of this child even for one hour, to arouse in her soul some passion for me, to make her beg for my love, and then, with perverse joy, to reject her outbursts, all the treasures of her newly awakened soul.

I'd never fallen so low as I had at that moment; but I regained control of myself and walked out of the room. I attempted to see Galitsky and interrogate him. From his very first words he started babbling such terrible nonsense. I almost drove him out; he spent his nights standing under Polinka's window; so, to avoid any scandal, I moved out to the dacha.

Now you understand my situation, dear Pavel Aleksandrych. My grief isn't enough for me: all my efforts to act fail and come to nought. No one understands me; I'm like a man who's arrived in an unknown land on some important business—struggling and making efforts in vain: everyone hides from him, everyone fears him as an enemy, and if he speaks to them, it's in some incomprehensible language. . . .

Therefore, it's time to end my letter. I've described my situation and can't add a word to it. In any case, whatever I decide, you'll certainly be kept informed.

It's high time to resolve this whole matter in one way or another. . . .

»»» CHAPTER VIII «««

From Polinka Saks to Madame A. Krasinskaya

What shall I write you, my dear friend? I'm alive and well; at least my body is well. My friends and relatives think I'm ill. I sit at home alone all day, surrounded by pillows. That's what he ordered me to do—Saks, that is.

Thank you, my angel, for not despising me, for replying to my unhappy letter, and for letting me write you. Without that I'd have fallen into despair: everything recoils from me, terrible anonymity oppresses me.

What will become of me? When will my offended husband's vengeance come crashing down on me? What will become of him? Oh God, preserve him alone!

He's alive. I received a note from him through my maid Masha. He's also tormented by the terrible waiting, and he's afraid for me. . . . Saks told him what he told me: "In exactly one month's time I'll see him and resolve the entire matter."

What strange words! What sort of fatal meaning do they hold? What did his look indicate, that strange, implacable, cold look of his? What meaning does this life have that he's begun living, with all these curious efforts and preparations?

Your brother wrote that he looks for Saks every day all over town, hoping to discover his intentions; that he's asking for a speedy end to this matter, proposing a means of gaining satisfaction, and beseeching him for me.

All that effort is in vain! No one in the whole town knows where Saks is or what's happening in his house.

Thank God, no one yet knows about me, no one condemns me and despises me!

My closest friends are all convinced I'm ill and that we're living at the dacha.

We really are at the dacha, but what a dacha it is! This huge, old, empty house stands on a remote bank of the Neva in a sleepy forest. The only ones in it are me and my maid, Saks and his old servant. He leaves at dawn and returns late at night. His horses snort beneath my windows; his footsteps can be heard along the corridors. He comes to see me only if Masha is with me; he inquires solicitously about my health, as if I really were ill. They brought me to the dacha this evening in a carriage stuffed with pillows. Masha isn't prevented from fulfilling my requests, even from carrying messages, but she's strictly forbidden to tell anyone where we are. I myself have asked her to keep silent: why destroy that poor girl along with me?

But the fateful date approaches. The month will be up one week from now. . . . Fear has deprived me of all recollection of my guilt; I can't cry or repent. . . . What awaits us after this week? What will become of Aleksandr? I can't think about anything else. . . .

Horrible dreams haunt me both awake and asleep. You recall the song about the black shawl,[39] which we learned to sing as children? I had good reason for fearing that song in which it constantly talks about blood. . . . And then, do you remember that horrible book about the husband who found a lover with his wife and ordered the door to their room to be blocked with stones?[40] I keep thinking and dreaming about all this. . . .

Who can comprehend this awe-inspiring and unfathomable man? I haven't been able to understand him in a year and a half of marriage. . . . God only knows what he has in mind. . . .

But the insult was so painful. . . . My God, my God!

What are my parents doing? Do they remember me at all? Do they condemn me? I've received no answer to any of my letters to my mother. Can it be she doesn't feel sorry for me? I wouldn't treat my own daughter like that.

Did I really neglect my duty on purpose merely to offend my mother? Did I struggle too feebly or suffer too little in the course of my downfall? Did I not kneel before her, begging her protection? Mama, may God forgive you.

Last night some people with grim faces came into my room. The oldest of them sat down and talked to me about marital obligation . . . and he asked me something. I didn't understand anything as a result of my embarrassment and fear.

Suddenly Saks came in, looking even sterner, gloomier than he had all that day. . . . He made a sign to those terrible people and took them away from me. For a long time I heard their voices over my head: they were arguing about something and then fell silent. I was shaking.

The door opened once again and Saks came in with a piece of paper in his hand.

"Polina Aleksandrovna," he said, "will you carry out my request? I swear it will be my last. Sign this document without reading it: it concerns the matter of your honor . . . I won't say any more about it."

Once again, that same cold, incomprehensible look of his. Who could resist it? I signed the paper; he bowed and went out.

It was night and I went over to the window. The Neva was restless and splashing up against the house; old willows with their long branches were leaning down to the water. Branches of some gray, prickly trees were beating against the window. Pine trees extended along the whole bank of the river; not too far away a white cross stood among them. Something terrible had once taken place at that spot. What other thing is now being planned?

My God, I hope this horrible week will pass quickly. What will be, will be. Preserve only him, my Sasha. . . .

What right does this cruel man have to torment me? To say I'm ill, to separate me from my relatives, from all help? Why does he surround me with secrecy, why has he given us such a long, painful time to wait? . . . Am I his slave, am I not a human being, am I not his equal? My blood's seething, bold thoughts enter my head; but, with God as my witness, I'm not thinking about myself . . . I'm the criminal . . . I'm indignant only when I think about *his* fate. Oh! Masha's bringing me a note. It's from him! I'll tell you what he writes.

"Rest assured, my Polinka, I'm well and brave. I'm ready for anything and have considered all possibilities. In a week everything will come to a head. But don't expect greater misfortune: in this day and age terrible outcomes don't occur."

In this day and age! . . . Can it be that in our day and age there are people like Saks? In our day and age are there criminals like his wife?

II

From Prince A. N. Galitsky to
Madame Annette Krasinskaya

(One week after the last letter)

5 o'clock in the morning.

.   .   .   .

.   .   .   .

You're surprised by all these instructions: they smell distinctly like a spiritual testament. One must be ready for anything. You've probably guessed what's going on.

Tonight I received a note from Saks. It contained an address and directions to his dacha. My goodness, he's certainly gone off to the backwoods! Then there was the following postscript: "At seven o'clock in the morning. Prince Al. Nik. will have the good sense to leave his horses, not approaching closer than one verst." The time set had elapsed: this was an invitation to the promised meeting.

After considering the insult, this man's love for his wife, and his iron character, tell me, dear sister, what can I expect from this meeting that's been called? Saks won't be able to commit a crime, but what does it mean—this strange invitation to come so early, to such backwoods, completely alone? I confess to you honestly that I expect either a duel at a distance of only two paces or some similar escapade, intended to remove the taint that nothing except blood can wash away.

I've been in dangerous situations before; more than once have I taken risks, singing the songs of my dear Béranger,[41] but now I feel not entirely at ease. War is a different matter: there's commotion, animation, and the awe-inspiring nature of the Caucasus. But here the whole town is sound asleep all around me, murky dawn peeks in my windows, everything's very simple and quiet.

Of all the many local residents surrounding me, my imagination paints a picture of the irritated enemy with his implacable look that no human gaze can endure without wincing.

I didn't sleep much last night: I wrote a little, burned some of it, thought about Polinka . . . to tell the truth, when don't I think about her? I got up easily and in good spirits, as happens on those occasions when sleep doesn't bring us serenity.

Only the gray morning made an unfavorable impression on my good spirits: it was dark, even though the sun must have stood fairly high. A light rain and fog spoiled the weather completely. In spite of the fact that it's now August, it's hard to know whether it's spring, summer, or fall.

The horses are ready. Farewell, sister, if I don't return, my servant Ivan will deliver this letter to you. Don't forget my instructions.

12 o'clock at night.

Sister, I'm losing my mind . . . I'm ill, I don't know how to write to you, where to start, how to explain it all. . . . I . . .

No, I'll get ahold of myself, I'll summon composure to my assistance; my story will be long and steady; may you experience just a small part of what I've experienced today. . . .

Without any further preparations I left the house and set out for Schlüsselburg.[42] After covering a fair distance, we turned off the road and headed toward the Neva. Calculating the distance and making sure of the place, I left the carriage and ordered my coachman to return to the main road. I proceeded along the left to an old English garden that was hardly distinguishable from the forest.

I didn't expect to find such total, gloomy desolation so close to Petersburg. Old trees had fallen to earth and were decaying serenely; no one was concerned about them; groves of young birch trees grew in between. Paths were all overgrown, and it was only possible to make them out because the grass there was lower and grew more slowly.

Soon the Neva appeared before me. A thick pine forest grew along the entire bank, as if left over from the time Petersburg was founded. The other shore wasn't visible: the fog hadn't yet begun to lift, and the Neva, out of kindness, although still narrow at that point, appeared like a boundless ocean.

The place was so desolate, so sinister, that I confess I checked to see if my blunt rapier could be drawn easily.

After looking all around, I noticed that on my right, near the riverbank, stood a large manor house that scarcely peeked out from behind a stand of spruce and pines. This is where my Polinka lived, where my angel was languishing and praying for me. My blood was boiling; I imagined myself as Amadis, Roland,[43] or a Spanish gallant under the windows of his beloved, in full view of her jealous husband.

The house was beautiful, but dark and old. The outbuildings had fallen into disrepair; there were no curtains at any windows: their place was taken by pine trees and spruces whose branches reached higher than this enormous house.

I approached on one side: there was no gate, no door, no one in sight. It was the same on the other side. I became angry. I found a door on the third side of the house, knocked, and straightened my clothes.

An old servant opened the door and bowed deeply. His gloomy figure was in keeping with the place. Without allowing me to say one word, he led me through a suite of lofty, empty rooms.

It was old and covered in dust, furnished in the style of Catherine the Great. Portraits of men in wigs and powdered ladies gazed down mysteriously from darkened walls long unaccustomed to seeing guests.

We passed through a long hall where, during bygone days, wealthy noblewomen with fans and dandies in embroidered caftans would stroll; then we emerged into a long, dark corridor.

"The first door on the left," the old man said to me, and then disappeared, as if falling through the floor. *"Diable! C'est un coupegeorge!"** I thought to myself.

Don't be surprised at my patience in describing all these details: now I understand their great importance, their necessity. Through the rest of my life today's events will remain as vivid as they are at this very moment.

I opened the first door on my left. I was met by Saks. He was paler than usual but just as composed, with the same impenetrable, dispassionate look on his face.

We bowed to one another.

"Prince," he asked, "did you follow my advice and leave your horses? Vigilance is essential."

"I came on foot for the last verst and a half."

"Good. Sit down. As a result of your discretion I've been satisfied with you this last month. Not a living soul knows about this affair. Now we can chat at our leisure."

He rang. The old man who'd led me here entered the room. Saks whispered an order to him.

I glanced around this gloomy, high-ceilinged room with its decorated walls, black wardrobes for which the baron, a great collector of antiquities, had paid a terrible price. Aside from a table piled high with papers, a leather-covered sofa, and two armchairs, there was no other furniture in the room. On the wardrobes stood busts of people with iron features and neatly combed flowing hair.

A gentle sound could be heard at the door. I could have recognized this divine walk from a full verst away. It was she—my angel, Polinka.

The door opened; it was she, my beauty, my child, my trea-

*What the devil! It's a den of thieves!

sure. She cried out warmly when she saw me; color came into her pale face.

She had grown thin, but only slightly. The healthy scent of the pine trees and proximity of the river had not allowed the burden of grief to weaken her. Praise be to Saks, eternal praise to this great man!

He motioned for her to be seated on a chair next to me and he sat down on the sofa. Polinka exchanged glances with me; we pulled our chairs closer to each other at exactly the same moment. . . . Who could take her away from me now?

Saks noticed this and smiled gloomily.

"Aleksandr Nikolaich," he said, addressing me with a look of reproach. "I didn't expect you would be frightened, Polina Aleksandrovna. Why did you keep on sending her notes? What's all this about the fateful time, the horrible meeting? Are we living in Mexico or under a feudal regime?"

I wanted to reply. "You'll get a chance to speak," he said with some annoyance. "I needed that month to observe you and to finish some business. Polina Aleksandrovna," he said and got up from his chair. "You're completely free. You're no longer married."

He handed me a piece of paper. You must understand what this is all about. . . . Where could one possibly find the gratitude this generous man deserves! . . .

"And now," he said to Polinka, "you'll go to your mother's dacha. I've already informed her, and tomorrow you'll go abroad. Prince Aleksandr Nikolaich will take a vacation and join you there."

"I'll retire . . . ," I said, with a stupid look on my face.

"Splendid," replied Saks. "Thousands of eyes will be looking at you in the hope of enjoying some scandal. Get married without any fanfare and live as far as possible from the capital."

Only then did Polinka comprehend the full majesty of her husband's act. Deathly pale, she fell at his feet and wept before him, as I'd wept that previous evening . . . you may recall.

I stood there like a fool, my feet didn't stir, my tongue didn't move. Saks wanted to lift Polinka up, but she wouldn't get off the floor; she resisted him the way stubborn children do. This scene was too painful for Konstantin Aleksandrych: he walked away from Polinka.

He approached me; his voice, shrill, rapid, abrupt, rang out solemnly in that empty room like the command of a skillful superior before his motionless battalions.

"Prince," he said, "you've taken both my wife and my daughter from me simultaneously. You've taken away my life. Don't think this child has been given to you gratis: I'm not relying on you alone! Remember, whatever you do, two eyes will be watching you; wherever you are, I'll be following you step by step. You're taking away a child—not a woman. Woe unto you if my child isn't happy."

One could hear him choking over these words; he hastened to utter this painful farewell.

"I tell you simply and openly: I'll be watching you all your life. At her first tear, her first sigh, her first sorrow—you're done for."

He turned and wanted to leave. But Polinka wouldn't let him go; she blocked the door, sobbed, shook, but was unable to utter a word. Joy and remorse had a terrible effect on the poor child . . . at that moment I was jealous of Polinka's regard for Saks.

We lifted her up. All this time I didn't dare give the dear child one caress, didn't dare kiss her.

And Polinka understood me.

I saw from the window how Saks and his old servant led her to the carriage, sat her in it, or, better to say, laid her in it.

I waited for Saks a few minutes longer in a strange stupor. I saw his droshky racing ahead of the carriage, but I still couldn't tear myself away from the window.

If only—not now, but five years from now—I could die for that man!

.   .   .   .

That evening I visited Polinka. She had a fever and a head-ache. We wept and exchanged kisses . . . people don't die from joy. . . . Soon, very soon! I hope that my damned retirement won't take too long to arrange!

III
From K. A. Saks to P. A. Zaleshin

My dear Pavel Aleksandrych, there's one more bachelor in the world. I'm alone again, as I used to be in days gone by. There's no more little Polinka Saks; now there's only Princess Polina Aleksandrovna Galitskaya. The shorter name suited her better: Polinka Saks.

I like you because after reading this letter you won't begin to sigh or cry: an extraordinary event, what unexpected news. You'll probably say: apparently, that's the way it had to be; this man's ideas don't entirely coincide with his actions.

I'm going abroad: some business has come up. I think I'll have to remain there for some time. As a bachelor I'm reducing my budget by half, and consequently I want to ask you a favor. Let me know if you don't want to do it, if it's impossible, or if you just don't feel like it.

In my absence assume primary control of my bailiffs: trans-form them in a philanthropic-Pantagruelist fashion. I need less money; you can curtail the collections.

Release the little estate I inherited from my father to the obligated peasants, in agreement with the new regulations.[44] Investigate the laws yourself, since I have no time to do so.

I used to be careful, but I've served my time. Under your supervision, I've let my subjects' stomachs grow and their bodies fatten, like those of your Crimean settlers. This will be sufficient for the first time.

If I return to Russia soon, I'll visit you first of all. We'll also visit the oracle *de la Dive Bouteille*,* but I don't really know what I'd ask him about.

*Of the wonderful bottle.

CHAPTER IX

I

From Princess P. A. Galitskaya to Madame Annette Krasinskaya
Nice, November, 184–

I rarely write to you, Annette . . . but I know you'll forgive me.
You know very well from your brother how and where we're
living. We've been married for some time now, and I'm happy;
but my health has improved only slightly. After my last illness in
Petersburg, it seems I was in a great hurry to leave, and have
remained ill up to now, but in a strange way. . . . I have a pain in
my chest and at times a fever. That's not too important . . . but
sometimes I fall into a stupor, walk around all day as if in a
fog. . . . Certain fragments of thoughts run through my mind
night and day; sometimes I sit for hours at a time staring at one
and the same place, thinking about nothing at all.

Most often I remember something: I recall my own childhood.
Then I think about my first marriage and imagine all this in a
rather strange way, without meaning . . . without sadness . . .
without gladness.

Sometimes only words whirl around in my head; I don't know
why, but they oppress my heart with their significance. Your
brother wrote and described how Saks bade farewell to us. . . .
Oh! . . . My heart's pounding again, pounding, and once more
there's a ringing in my ears: "Remember, Prince, at her first tear,

her first sigh—you're done for." Why do I keep hearing those words?

I don't know why but I keep weeping. My bosom wants to cleave . . . but I have to hide these tears. Two relentless eyes follow us around: their gaze is so gentle, so serene. Once again I hear those words all around me: "at her first tear—you're done for."

My husband never tires of looking at me; he's abandoned his whole family, he adores me. . . . I love him just as much. Do you believe that to this day I still find it strange to see him: apparently I'm still ill and can't regain my strength. It's odd, but when he sits near my feet, kissing my hands, I'm still afraid to kiss him; I imagine something unfamiliar, someone saying something that has nothing to do with the matter at hand. Then all of a sudden a voice rings in my ears: "You're taking my life away . . . I'm not relying on you alone . . . I'll be following you step by step . . . woe unto you if my child isn't happy."

My God! Why do these strange words haunt me so relentlessly? When I go to bed . . . I fall asleep late, my thoughts are so confused . . . I remember something, I remember—and suddenly I hear that voice once again piercing my soul: "Remember, at her first tear. . . ."

I hear it, I hear it . . . this voice speaks in my own heart; someone's eyes shine before me, and quiet, firm footsteps resound as if coming across the rug in my room.

Saks! . . . his name seems so strange to me. . . . Saks is here. He's left Petersburg . . . he's following us . . . step by step he's pursuing us . . . he's looking for me . . . Oh, my God, comfort him . . . grant him happiness . . . he's a great man. . . .

Again these words . . . again his eyes. . . . The pen falls from my hand, a fog descends on my thoughts. . . . "Remember, Prince, this child has not been given to you gratis!"

From Princess P. A. Galitskaya to Madame Annette Krasinskaya
Florence, February 184–

My dear friend Annette, I see that I will die soon, and I have so much to tell you, to make such important requests of you. . . . I know my illness . . . you remember the strange words that tormented me all that time. They explained a great deal to me, a very great deal; they gave me life, but at the same time, I'm dying from them, but now I know why. Now everything in life has opened up for me; I've experienced so much in these last two months. . . .

My friend, you don't know that I love him with all the strength of my soul. I found this out only recently: I love my husband—not the one I have now: him I feel sorry for—but I love him, Konstantin Saks. Do you know what divine pleasure it is to express one's love for the first time, to write this beloved name, to cover it with kisses and shed warm tears over it!

I love him and have always loved him. Previously I understood neither him, nor myself, nor life, nor my love. Ten words of his tore away the curtain from my whole life, clarified everything toward which my soul was groping in the darkness. May God bless that man who even in our separation gives me life, revives me, completes the upbringing he began. . . .

I've always loved him: I loved him when I married him, loved him when I was kissing your brother, loved him when I was betraying him. I loved him when those parting words of his were uttered to us . . . but all that time I loved him unconsciously; only now have I become conscious of all my love. On the edge of the grave I've become happy with that love and wouldn't trade it for anything in the world.

. . . .

In the north of Italy the air did me more harm than good. My chest has begun to ache even more; in addition, my heart pounds almost all the time. We decided to move farther south; the prince has wept for nights on end next to my bed and is completely distraught. I've comforted him, devised a plan for a trip to Naples, and persuaded him to stop for a while in Florence, knowing his fondness for such populated places.

We've been living here for more than a week. I've begun to feel a curious change in myself. Up to now I've been completely indifferent to nature: it didn't matter to me whether I was in Italy or Russia; but since my illness has worsened, I've become somehow wiser, more understanding of everything, especially nature.

My health has improved somewhat, and my thoughts have become less confused. Only at night are things the same as before: the same insomnia, the same confusing recollections, the same awful longing. . . .

Once I left my husband at a court ball and went home earlier than usual. It seemed to me that my tiredness and the fresh air would soon put me to sleep. But as soon as I entered my bedroom, that same longing and fever overcame me. I sat down to write letters. Everything around me was fast asleep.

At that time I heard a slight rustle outside the door: the curtain was pulled aside, and a tall figure appeared in the distance. His quiet, firm footsteps, his footsteps could be heard in the room. My hands and feet grew cold and blood rushed to my face. All the while, I was smiling: it was he, and I began to understand him.

Saks stood there before me in his elegant frock coat; his eyes were just as bright, his chest as broad.

He approached and looked at me gently.

"My child," he said softly, "why are you sick and so deep in thought? Isn't it that you feel some grief?"

I heard my own blood approaching my heart and shaking it with its uneven beats.

I grasped his hand, pressed it to my heart, my lips, my warm eyes that were unable to cry. . . .

"Forgive me . . . ," I whispered indistinctly.

He thought I was thanking him and asking his forgiveness.

"For what, my child, what for?" he said with a smile. "Farewell, I'm glad I was mistaken."

He leaned over and kissed my hand.

Long ago I wrote you that this man, neither before our marriage nor after, had ever kissed my hand. Was this some coincidence, or was there some meaning in it? . . .

And when, for the first time, his lips touched my hand, I shuddered and something inside me tore apart. I saw how he turned and left the room; only when I locked the door after him did the blood drain from my throat, and I fell down unconscious. It was the first time in my life I've ever fainted.

And it was for good reason: that kiss . . . his gentle words . . . his sympathy . . . from that moment I understood both him and myself.

In vain does your brother sleep at my feet and try to divine from my eyes my every desire. I can't love him, can't understand him; he's not a man, but a child: I'm too old for his love. But *he* is a human being, he is a man in every sense of the word: his soul is great and serene . . . I love him, I won't stop loving him.

I've destroyed myself and don't understand him . . . but I'm not to blame. God will forgive me because I didn't know what I was doing. And I'm innocent before Saks as well; I destroyed myself without awareness, as a butterfly destroys itself in a flame, as a child left alone will drown in a lovely lake.

I'm far from repentance, and of what would I repent? "What's happened, happened," Konstantin used to say, and now I fully understand the meaning of his words. I've recalled with love, with passion, my entire life with him, pondered all his words as a scholar reflects on the works of a favorite author.

My Creator! I thank you for everything: life, his love, my love! I know neither grief nor fear of death: at those moments so terrible for other people, I think about him; hours of tedious sleeplessness have become hours of enjoyment for me. They're hours of love, hours of remembrance! I'm afraid to fall asleep; I summon this sleeplessness greedily. . . .

.   .   .   .

I stopped at my fainting: it was the first attack of that terrible illness; that's as much as I could understand from what the doctors were whispering around me. It was the beginning of evil consumption.

The strange thing is that I was overcome with joy when I found out that I'd die soon. That means he'll survive me. During my life I won't tell him anything: you can't bring back the past. But after my death he can look into my heart; I'll arrange it so he can see the conclusion of my upbringing; he'll find out that I appreciated him, paid him back for his greatest sacrifice in the only way a woman can: with boundless, ardent love.

As soon as night fell, I lay in bed thinking of him, recalling all his deeds, his words. . . . After thinking about him, I sat down at my table and wrote a letter that he'll receive only after my death.

In this letter he'll find my confession, my passionate acknowledgment, my gratitude to him, my final examination. It will be my first and last love letter.

After finishing this dear letter, I put it under my pillow. My maid knows what to do with it. She's been given an envelope with Saks's name on it and his address in Russia. In the event of my unexpected death, she's supposed to take the letter from under my pillow and send it through the post.

The next night I took out the letter and read it through . . . how weak its expressions were, how terribly much my love for him had grown in that one day! I wrote a new letter, a whole page of paper his eyes will fall upon. . . . Then I prayed to God for him; on my knees I asked Him to grant Konstantin peace, to send him love. . . . No, no, no! He doesn't need any new love!

One thought troubles me: what if my Masha forgets to send the letter or if it gets lost in the mail? I ask you, my angel, to do one last favor for your Polinka. After my death, find out for certain whether Masha sent the letter I've told you about. Remind her, write, make sure yourself. If the letter gets lost, then you go to see him—make a trip to Petersburg—and show him this letter to you. Perhaps through it he'll be able to glance into my soul; he'll discover that I loved him and he'll find his Polya once again.

To think he might never see my letter: this thought is killing me. In it I used language only he can understand; only there will he see that just before death his child became a woman. . . .

It was written with tears and blood; my whole soul is contained within it.

Don't tell your brother I didn't love him. A common error has bound us together to the end of my life, and to the end I'll remain his obedient wife. I feel sorry for him: he loves me . . . may the implacable eyes of my Konstantin cease to follow me; they'll see nothing until my death. . . .

Once more these eyes are looking at me, his voice rings again in my ears, but this time I understand it . . . I adore that voice. . . .

My God! . . . Blood rushes to my head, my heart is breaking . . . death, death is approaching. . . . Lord, one more day . . . one more hour of life . . . so that I can think about him once more . . . read over my letter to him . . . I still haven't said everything I want to say. . . .

I'm feeling worse, much worse. . . . Konstantin, remember me . . . I love you. . . .

Two months passed. Springtime revived Princess Galitskaya. Her husband wept from joy, pampered her, didn't leave her side. The entire town couldn't keep their eyes off the young couple.

Whether Saks guessed something or whether he was content with Polinka's life—in either case he left Florence. For almost a year he had followed the prince and his wife, step by step, as he had said he would when he bequeathed his Polinka to Galitsky.

He had to get some rest. He left for Russia and settled on Zaleshin's Crimean estate. In vain did the good Pantagruelist attempt to fatten up his emaciated friend: Saks's stomach didn't grow and his face didn't take on the extra fullness that so pleased this esteemed admirer of Rabelais.

On one of those quiet June evenings Saks was sitting, lost in thought, on a steep hill, resembling a narrow little green separated from the constantly roaring sea. Behind him, as if on a theater curtain, stretched a long expanse of meadows crisscrossed by groves; a semicircular forest completed this splendid scene. Umbrella-shaped poplars seemed to swim in the transparent pink air.

Beneath his feet the sea splashed quietly, running up on the sandy shore under the cliffs. Smoke from a passing steamer hung in the distance, and somewhere the gentle song of a fisher-man died away.

Zaleshin's heavy valet approached Saks and handed him a letter with a black seal and a foreign postmark.

Polinka was no longer alive. This was the last letter she'd written and read through at night. Only God, Saks, and Polinka herself know what it contained. . . .

The Story of Aleksei Dmitrich

»»» «««

The First Evening

Truly pernicious, even irreverent, thoughts can creep into a person's mind, if, after squandering all his money, he sits alone in a cramped room during the evening, when all Petersburg is out dancing or at the opera. The unfortunate recluse regards both society and all its laws with passion and enmity and invents utopia after utopia, either nasty or gentle, depending on the inclination of his character. Inventing utopias is an extremely useful thing to do: little by little gloomy thoughts begin to disperse, the dreary room livens up, graceful images begin to dart past the dreamer involuntarily, affecting him, flirting with him, urging him to confront bitterness with sarcasm, to endure hardship with the carefree attitude of a young man in love.

For a lack of anything better to do, one may still sit alone in a room sometimes, but it's very difficult for someone whom fate has failed to endow with a deep love for family life, who constantly encounters people, perhaps even those dear to him, but weak people, disagreeable and unbearable people. This unfortunate dreamer won't be able to sit home alone and won't be allowed to invent utopias! Where does such tiresome sympathy come from, such a crowd of patriarchal physiognomies with their eternally sour smiles and unbearable, silent morality!

That's just when an outburst of gloomy dreams ensues—on

the theme of proud solitude and the useless, senseless nature of family relationships! Yes, it's sometimes very difficult indeed for a person who's squandered all his money.

Thus I thought, putting on my overcoat and setting off to see my friend Aleksei Dmitrich, a man possessing one great advantage as a friend: namely, he was almost always at home. Now I'll explain why he was almost always at home.

Aleksei Dmitrich was a military man—true, the only military thing about him was his uniform. His way of life was somewhat strange and too orderly for a military man. He usually awoke at eight o'clock in the morning, drank his tea with incredible resolve, set off to train his company, did so with great care and effort, and continued this pursuit until such time as his stomach began to demand food. Once he became aware of his appetite, my friend would immediately conclude his business and, unimpeded by circumstances, would hurry home with the speed of a hurricane, where his dinner awaited him at any time after eleven o'clock. No one in the world could stop Aleksei Dmitrich on his way home for dinner—one could only catch up with him on horseback.

After a long dinner, Aleksei Dmitrich would have his shutters closed and lie down to rest; he would sleep for an astonishingly long time and then go for a walk along the street. If the weather was clear and the road dry, his face was serene; if the opposite was true, the walk had an injurious effect on his nerves. He would regard those he passed gloomily and would sing quietly to himself *basso* arias from operas that, as is well known, are distinguished by the ferocity of both their tone and content.

Afterward he would have tea at home; then the fate of the rest of his day would be determined. If friends came to call, he would allow them to stay until late at night; he would sing, argue about the theater, relate scandalous anecdotes, and his cheerfulness would soon enliven the whole party. But Aleksei Dmitrich belonged to that small group of people who, according to their own whim, can be both cheerful and boring; such people, if you examine them more carefully, often induce melancholy reflections in others by their own good cheer.

Aleksei Dmitrich's conversation partners didn't belong to that class of young people who hang about by the dozens at circuses and other public gatherings, or who, at the opera, boisterously arrange meetings with one another at some apocryphal countess's residence, or who astonish modest people by their expansive chests and belligerent bearing. The people who assembled at my friend's house in the evening were all skinny, bilious, and pale, lazy and capricious, sometimes enthusiastic to the point of childishness, sometimes sarcastic and cynical. Their youthfulness wasn't fostered by ambitious hopes or encyclopedic knowledge: constant idleness and an unfettered life had endowed them with a practical cast of mind, acquainted them with both higher and lower layers of society, compelled them to love fervently people from those classes who were most in need of compassion and care.

If the evening was spent without interlocutors, Aleksei Dmitrich would read newspapers for an hour and a half and, at ten o'clock, "set out on a voyage to embrace Neptune," as one of my very learned friends puts it, one who is not too knowledgeable about mythology.[1]

One may ask: where did sleep come from? In reply I can report from experience that the slumber of someone who sleeps a great deal is neither sound nor interrupted, but filled with the most entertaining dreams and sweet sensations upon awakening and falling asleep again. These qualities are highly valued by people to whom fate has granted careless motives, those of a Russian.

But Aleksei Dmitrich didn't always get enough sleep. Sometimes, after having his tea, he would set off without haste to one of our theaters; he would arrive mercilessly late, steal his way humbly into the hall, plop himself down in the first row, and sit there with appropriate decorum. Even during intermissions, at times of movement, greetings, and voluptuous glances at the dress circle, my friend would never leave his seat, never rest his elbows on the partition, never scrutinize the local beauties. No one ever struck up a conversation with this peaceful theatergoer; he never exchanged greetings with anyone, even though he knew by name the entire motley crowd seated in the stalls. He recognized many of his childhood friends; from their hardened faces and imposing bearing he recalled their previously attractive, childlike features, but he didn't like renewing old ties. He observed coolly how people who used to sit in the last row had dressed themselves up in splendid apparel and were now seated in the first row, wearing their hair parted and distinguished by their immaculate gloves. Aleksei Dmitrich observed coolly how other social lions, the glory of the first row, would suddenly disappear, without returning to the theater, most likely having become involved in some enigmatic episode, and were wiped off the face of the earth. . . .

It was all the same to Aleksei Dmitrich what show was being presented in the theater: he loved opera, heard *Closerie des genêts*,[2] and was unopposed to *The Bigamist*,[3] that adornment of Sundays and holidays. Our friend didn't like German plays, however, although he once came to the Mikhailovsky Theater[4] with the firm intention of seeing *Zopf und Schwerdt*,[5] or something of the sort.

But the theater's emptiness and the spectators' humble faces filled Aleksei Dmitrich with a cold chill. And when the first lover uttered with fervor, "*O, warum hast du mich . . .* ,"* my friend grabbed his hat, headed home in disgust, and there fell fast asleep.

Such a way of life was rather strange for an educated man. Aleksei Dmitrich didn't conceal it and was ready to share a laugh with other people at his own expense. Nor did he claim that such a life was original: my friend had no such pretensions. Besides, he was just as far from pathetic self-satisfaction as from vulgar disenchantment.

I liked visiting Aleksei Dmitrich; I used to encounter people there whom I had gotten to know in earlier days through military life, and sometimes even through impecuniousness—that Petersburg vampire who always sucks the blood of our young people, enfolding it in the flapping of its dirty wings.

But on this particular evening there wasn't a soul at Aleksei Dmitrich's. He was lying on a bed covered with a blanket, reading, apparently to help him fall asleep. Sadness overwhelmed me as I entered his enormous room, as big as a barn, in which a small candle was burning dimly. I felt uncomfortable.

"God be with you, Aleksei Dmitrich!" I shouted, grabbing hold of his blanket. "If only you'd waited until ten o'clock! Enough, get dressed, let's go out somewhere and have a talk."

"Must we?" he asked with reluctance. "But why can't we talk here?"

"But who can talk if there're only two of us? It's even more boring with two than alone. I have to tell you the truth: fine, you can go to sleep, but then what will I do?"

"But, you see, I got up so early this morning . . . ," my friend said apathetically.

*Oh, why have you done me . . .

"Well, I won't let you sleep," I said, objecting stubbornly. "I'm an absolute gypsy: I have no money and I'm too lazy to go very far. Besides, you need some diversion. Have you been living like this for long?"

"About two years, since I returned from the Caucasus."

"And will you go on living like this much longer?"

"Until I'm tired of it."

In order to rouse Aleksei Dmitrich I decided to make him angry. Besides, I was angry at the unceremonious laconism of my friend's replies.

"Now here's a person who's affecting an attitude!" I said, as if getting ready to leave. "And he blames the Caucasus! There one can find battles, stormy passions, and disenchantment! How could our pathetic, materialist Petersburg ever measure up to that? Create a new way of life for yourself: you Pechorins are all masters at that. . . ."[6]

I'd skillfully managed to wound my host. Aleksei Dmitrich strongly disliked any pretensions of disenchantment, which had previously been so amusing but now were completely ridiculous.

"Way of life!" he cried with dissatisfaction, sitting up in bed. "Why have you become so obsessed with *my* way of life? How is your life any different from mine? . . . "

"I frequent society and watch the human comedy as it's played out on the grand stage. I know women, become involved with them, gratify my vanity. . . ."

"Well, but you're a . . . special case!" my angry host observed, spreading his arms wide in a gesture of deepest respect. "Why, you're a master at 'sitting on exquisite loveseats,' and flitting about 'under intoxicating sounds,'[7] as it says in those books of yours. But we are darker folk, pleased to have supper in our bedroom after the bed's been cleared away, to dance in a crowded hall, bumping into chairs. . . ."

"Oh! Byron! Oh, hero of our time!" I cried without any pangs of conscience. "Now see what he's come up with! Indeed. What is a woman without brilliant surroundings? What is mankind? What is love? What sort of nonsense is vanity? . . . "

Aleksei Dmitrich was now very angry; he got up from his bed, put on his dressing gown, and paced the room from corner to corner. I was triumphant.

"Women!" my friend said thoughtfully. "I love them and would often like to see them. But is it easy to get to know them? He who wants to get involved with women must get involved with family. And who knows, maybe family life is so little to my liking that I'm afraid even to encounter it?"

"I also recognize that kind of familism!"[8] I replied, imitating my friend's misanthropic tone. "It knows how to penetrate our soul, get us involved with pitiful creatures, reward us with *their* suffering, remove all energy and independence from our actions. . . . I can see you've paid a substantial sum of interest to family misfortune."

"Not to misfortune, simply to family life," my host replied, rejoicing in the similarity of our thinking. "Say simply: 'family life.' With this phrase everyone will imagine hundreds of such dramas that destroy thousands of people."

I went on provoking Aleksei Dmitrich; he continued pacing the room, uttering strange philippics against family life. He finally stopped in front of me.

"You've grievously offended me by your attacks on my life," he said politely. "I would have berated anyone else, but I remain silent before you and even seek to justify myself; my foolish nature's ready to indulge you. I see you have no money now and, as a result of having nothing better to do, wander from friend to friend, annoying good people and inciting them to argument. I don't know how to argue, but I'm ready to chat with you. Listen and judge me. I'll tell you a story," Aleksei Dmitrich continued, "that I've never told anyone before, the story of my childhood and youth. There's no need to warn you that in my story there won't be any terrible catastrophes or monstrous villains. On the contrary, those close to me were all splendid people, deserving the best of fates, loving and honest people. Nevertheless, they did me more harm than my most evil enemy. I don't blame them; they've all died, and I remember them with painful emotion and am ready to give everything on earth to bring them back to life, to grant them happiness. In my opinion or in theirs, let there only be happiness.

"Have a cigar, my story's beginning."

I was born in the Crimea where my father was serving at the time. Here's all I remember about that: as a child I was once carried up a hill and for a long time gazed down from there. Little hills, meadows, and streams stretched faraway into the distance. Near us stood straight, tall trees, both in groves and singly; strong gusts of wind shook their pyramidal tops. Far away from me, very far, the sea was visible.

In the old Bolshoi Theater there used to be an outer curtain depicting a vista, with mountains and sea.[9] Each time I saw it, I recalled the early years of my childhood; I very much regret that instead of this curtain there now hangs a view of some stairway showing two vessels of classical form protruding in an awkward manner.

When I was five years old, our family moved to Petersburg. My father hoped to secure a post there; but the main reason for this relocation lay in his muddled financial affairs, which were threatening to deprive him of his last means of support. He rented an apartment on Voznesensky Street. Very early on I got to know this cramped street, with its carriage barns and its heavy odor of the blacksmith's forge. I also remember our building; it was tall, made of yellow stone, with orange wooden corridors on both sides. The walls and outbuildings had been completely blackened by smoke from a fire that had occurred a long time ago; nothing had ever been repainted. The roof was covered with broken tiles—it's a good thing we don't see tile roofs any longer. In the courtyard, between the firewood and a hideous barn, there stood a puny little birch tree. You know the gentleness of a child's soul; therefore you'll believe me when I say that this unfortunate little tree provided me with hundreds of bitter minutes, even hours. Melancholy Petersburg nature and my parents' depressing life fostered in me the growth of a strange and pensive longing. During this time I frequently awoke at night and wept, thinking about the cold and wind in the courtyard, the branches on the sickly little tree that had dried up, the leaves that had fallen off, and how difficult it was for the poor birch tree to grow in our filthy little courtyard. It would have been better if that little birch had never existed.

Now I'll acquaint you with my parents. My father enjoyed unlimited, enthusiastic respect from those close to him. He was known as a man of exemplary goodness and honesty; even now I still hear testimonials to him where his impartiality is praised as the eighth wonder of the world. But it was hard for him to live in this world, especially in times of bribery and corruption. He didn't get along with many people; the bribetakers' code of conduct was unknown to him. No means of escape existed for him: not I, nor anyone else, nor a cozy post, nor a harmless income.

Whether he was embittered by failure or gloomy by disposition, my father made a bad family man. Recalling the events of that time, I see that he loved his children with a rare tenderness, but he never showed us any affection and took no part in our upbringing, since he had so little time. But his greatest mistake was that he let his children become witnesses to the problems of his business and his family.

He participated in some enterprise where the capital was lost in bankruptcy and he was forced into debt. Deformed people wearing spectacles and uniforms and carrying documents frequently visited our crowded apartment. They were appallingly serene, while Father was often angry and would argue with them. It was unbearably painful to see him after they'd left. He'd begin to pace the room, lost in gloomy thought, writing things down on pieces of paper, and would abandon his work with a wave of his hand. These scenes tormented me terribly; my love and concern for my father forced me to listen eagerly to his every word, read quietly what was written on every scrap of paper that dropped to the floor, and invent my own interpretation from these fragmentary materials. My mind so excelled at this work that by the age of ten I understood almost all the details of my father's difficult predicament. I arrived at these gloomy discoveries with the help of my eyes and ears, since I never dared ask anyone directly.

I recall how much work it was for me to make these bitter discoveries. When I happened to hear my father complaining about the term of a promissory note, I would make sly inquiries from afar to find out exactly what a promissory note was. Two days later, so as not to arouse suspicion, I tried in the same way to discover what a term meant. And in all this I was guided not by greed, of course—can greed really exist in a child?—but by genuine, profound concern for my father's grief and by my sufferings over the ensuing disagreements between him and my mother.

I loved my mother less than my father, in spite of her unlimited tenderness for her children. I loved my father's firmness, his rare moments of joy—but I observed neither of these in my mother.

She was a woman who would have been described as exemplary in other circumstances; but she was absolutely incapable of enduring our cramped conditions. She had previously lived in affluence; memories of that time tormented her; but her primary defects were excessive suspiciousness and irritability of character. She witnessed the destruction of our wealth, the increase in our family—and hoped to improve our affairs, not through a radical change in our life, but through small household economies. Naturally, each passing hour demonstrated the absurdity of her plan, but she suffered deeply as a result of each insignificant unpleasantness.

Between my father and mother, from the first years of their marriage, there had existed some secret or, perhaps better to say, some oppressive recollection shared by both, which they were afraid to discuss. In spite of that, the whole house knew their secret, and I, perhaps to my own misfortune, knew it as well . . . but, you know, I really don't want to talk about that. . . . I'm a man of prejudices . . . I can't even think about this subject.

Meanwhile this circumstance sheds considerable light on my character and upbringing. It's sufficient for you to know the following: my parents didn't get along well; they often hurt each other, insulted each other in my presence . . . frequently some terrible, painful reproach would escape my father's lips . . . these words were obscure and strange and would soon cut short any conversation. . . . But this didn't prevent me from suffering in my soul, losing sleep, weeping at night, while my parents slept soundly after they'd abused each other and then managed to settle their own quarrel. . . .

Our whole house was organized around this series of disagreements and complaints. Our servants were devoted to their masters, but as a result of these petty troubles in this petty household, dissatisfaction persisted between masters and servants. As usual, the servants got along very poorly among themselves. Our cramped quarters constantly forced them to confront one another, and every morning there was a steady stream of abuse, scoldings, reproaches, and complaints at such a bitter life; all this uproar hardly died down with the appearance of the master or the mistress. Nor did our servants stand on ceremony in the presence of the children.

I remember that it was this destructive confinement that hindered my full physical development. A great deal of free space is required to bring up a child: it isn't good for him to sit at home alone all the time or to live amid constant turmoil. Our nursery was situated in a small passageway; often, when I went to bed, the stream of traffic had only just begun—especially if there were guests in our apartment. Nothing could accustom me to disturbances and interruptions to my sleep: for hours I would wait for the movement to cease and would fall asleep only when the last maid, having helped my mother into bed, had returned to her own room through our passageway. As a result, I would wake up in the morning tired and for the whole day would feel limp and be in a bad mood.

My father sometimes gave parties in the evening: for what purpose, from what need, God only knows. He would gather some awkward men, not very well acquainted with one another, and they would stand around near the doors, far from the women; some of them would disappear quickly, as soon as they heard a dance being pounded out on the piano. These fears were almost always unfounded: dancing rarely took place, and if it did, it was always very limp, clumsy, and lifeless. The younger men said nothing at all to the women; because they had nothing else to do, and for appearance's sake, they would approach the children, pat us on the head, and say such incoherent things that at times I too suffered as a result of these poor storytellers.

My physical strength developed in a slow and lethargic manner; I was frequently taken out for walks, but would try to avoid these strolls. Somehow the blackened, brick houses glared at me with such hostility, and the people I encountered looked so dark and gloomy, that I soon grew afraid of them, and at night I sometimes saw their sallow, frowning faces in my dreams. We never went to the country, and consequently the lack of fresh air had a detrimental effect on my physical development.

On the other hand, my intellectual abilities were flourishing under the yoke of this grim life; but my development was incomplete and painful. Just like dough squeezed by a press, my intellect was broadened, though it suffered losses in all other regards. I frequently became pensive, and pensiveness—as you know—is a sharp knife for a child. The unnatural exercise of my abilities, in all their innocent receptiveness, imbued me with both suspiciousness and dreaminess. Upon hearing some children's story, I would immediately begin building castles in the air and applying its characteristics to myself and my family. Thus, during one period, which lasted over a year by the way, I had imagined that fate had endowed me with the strength of a bogatyr;[10] another time I pondered how splendid it would be to stumble across a large sum of money on the street. Pleasant dreams! Tender recollections! *"O mein Jugend! meine Jugend!"** I say, together with the German anthology.

Terrible sentimentality and a high degree of intensity were manifested in my attachments. At the age of ten I became passionately attached to a boy two years younger than I, who sometimes came to play with my brothers. I never played at all, because such childish propensities had long since disappeared in me. This child was related to one of our neighbors and was in all

*Oh my youth! my youth!

regards my complete opposite. I was irritable and dull—he was gentle as a maid and, in spite of that, quite a troublemaker. He often came to visit us sporting bumps and bruises on his face, which, moreover, were very becoming to him. Soon after his arrival, one would hear noise and commotion in all our rooms, and sometimes things ended in a fight in which the combatants themselves scarcely knew who was fighting against whom and for what. Kostya couldn't stand me precisely because I would never hit him for any reason. In his presence I seemed even more timid and listened despondently as my infrequent overtures of friendship were met with sarcasm, abuse, and promises to nail me up someday until it really hurt.

Still, his presence was a source of great joy for me: I gazed at him, listened to his voice, and thought about him with inexpressible pleasure.

Kostya's father, a general who'd squandered all his money, slept and dreamt of a way to get rid of his children and have the state assume their guardianship. As a result of such Spartan reflections, he left his estate in Voronezh[11] and entrusted his six-year-old son to his brother's care, with the suggestion that he consign the child to the state for his upbringing at the first possible opportunity. But Kostya's uncle was opposed to all upbringing whatsoever, both public and private. Without paying any attention to his brother's wishes, he kept the child at his estate in the Petersburg province and brought him up along with his own children in such a way that his friends and relatives could only gasp and shrug their shoulders.

Indeed, Kostya's uncle was a strange fellow. He expressed incomprehensible contempt toward Petersburg, visited it with loathing, yet brought both Kostya and his own children along with him. Both in the country and in town, he followed their every step unnoticed, often referring to the difficulty of dealing with children—but the children didn't even know how to count to ten, and they were unfamiliar with the history of important events or any moral teaching. The eccentric old man spent his days digging in the field and the garden; the children assisted him. He told them about grasses, stones, and flowers, taught them how to draw these items, and neither praised nor condemned their observations and pranks. He never gave them any books to read; instead of geography, he taught them how to draw plans of the house, garden, and surrounding woods; he took them out without their hats during hard frosts and cruel heat. It's not surprising that his neighbors, including my own father and mother, chuckled over this old pedagogue; they nicknamed him the Englishman, the eccentric, regarded Kostya as a poor victim, and felt sorry for him. None of them noticed that the poor victim enjoyed good health, that in all his actions one could observe both strength and agility, that the victim's little eyes were always shining as bright as stars—while the children of those adults who were laughing were monsters in all respects.

Chance came to the poor victim's aid and prevented him from becoming a complete Emile.[12] Cholera was paying a visit to Petersburg, and Kostya's uncle, having consumed too many fruits of the earth provided by nature for man's enjoyment, passed away. Thanks to help from his strong family, the children were all supported by charity; Kostya, according to his father's wishes, was sent off to a boarding school where three years later I too became a student. For a while I lost sight of my childhood friend, but I had no time for him. My own father died from cholera as well, leaving our whole family in the most dire straits.

The size of our family decreased by one, but our living space became even more crowded. We moved from the second to the third floor, right under the roof; the walls of our new rooms were marked and patched, never having been painted. My mother lost her head as she regarded our tangled affairs; she hoped to correct them and would trust the first person she met; but this charitable soul usually robbed her and complicated our affairs even further.

A great source of bitterness was my older brother, who had died recently. At the time he was serving in Petersburg, squandering his money and constantly getting involved in scandalous episodes. He was a strange person: listening to him speak and following his adventures, one could take him for some kind of *Landsknecht*[13] or a brawler at the time of the Regency.[14] To provoke a fight, get involved in a quarrel with his supervisor or even with the police, was a most ordinary occurrence for him. About his actions, which deserved the strictest retribution, he spoke as simply and innocently as people in society do about opera, dinner in a new restaurant, or a stroll along the Nevsky Prospect. In a word, my brother was a ruffian, something like the troublemaker Burtsov.[15]

As soon as night came, if he had yet to return home, we all waited for him with trepidation. Our premonitions were well-founded: rare was the day when we didn't have to extricate him from some misfortune, intervene on his behalf. You can imagine what grief this man caused us all. My father's iron severity had kept him in fear of God; but after his death, my brother yielded to his feudal inclinations. Fortunately, he soon got himself sent off to the army, where in time he became an excellent soldier. Nevertheless, his departure calmed the rest of us and demonstrated the truth of the Italian proverb: *lontano degli occhi, lontano del cuore.**

A new misfortune was in the making and I myself was the innocent cause of it. I was getting on in age, but my turn to enroll

*Out of sight, out of mind.

in an institution still hadn't come.[16] My mother grieved and concealed it from me, but I was fully aware of my position. I was being prepared at home as well as possible. My German teacher also provided instruction in church history; my arithmetic tutor taught me history.

I didn't like any subject at all; I found them all equally repugnant. I never had even the slightest inkling of curiosity and didn't study my lessons willingly. This circumstance was made stranger by the fact that children, in spite of all the harm done by our present system of education, almost always get attached to one subject or another, most often to mathematics or history. And well they deserve children's attachment! But I didn't experience anything like that.

A final blow was being prepared for my moral system. As a sorrowful witness to poverty and constant family distress, I longed for some kind of entertainment. I was glad when the arrival of outsiders interrupted the pathetic silence of our daily existence, glad when time for lessons came, even though I so hated to study. My father had a bookcase filled with old books: previously no one had read them, at least they had been locked away; but at the time I'm describing, the lock was broken and the books were at my disposal. There stood the works of old Russian authors: a translation of *Candide* in the most cynical terms (remember the theory: the cynicism of expression indicates the morality of the generation), a translation of *The Passions of Young Werther*, a translation of *The Sufferings of the Ortenburg Family*,[17] a translation of *Visions in a Pyrenean Castle*,[18] and a translation of *The Secrets of Nature* by Eckartshausen.[19]

Up to now I've described for you the course of my thoughts and upbringing in a rather logical way, but from the time of *Candide* and Eckartshausen I'm silent and don't know what to say. After making a considerable effort, perhaps I could come up with something, but there are limits to everything, most of all to an analysis of a gloomy, insignificant life.

I'll tell you only that I became passionately attached to the most harmful pursuit of childhood—reading. Once again, the origin of this attachment wasn't my own curiosity: neither the shadow of science nor the spirit of truth disturbed my soul. In reading books I could tickle my imagination and be happy because I thought neither about the tearful faces of our domestic servants, nor my mother's gloomy glances, nor the distress threatening us from all sides. . . .

Aleksei Dmitrich fell silent for a moment. His artless tale had penetrated the depths of my soul. But idealistic emotions had yet to forsake me; I was still unable to approve of Aleksei Dmitrich's conduct with his own family.

"I've understood your story," I said to Aleksei Dmitrich, "and you know, it seems to me that you were not only a victim, but that you yourself added to your family's woes. How is it that you, a child, should feel such antipathy for hardship and cramped conditions? Where did you acquire such a hostile attitude to your parents? Did it ever occur to you to console your mother, to tell her you had no fear of poverty, that you only wanted her to stop grieving and take care of herself. . . ."

"Hey, most honored friend!" said my host. "It's fine to say such things at your age, and fine to do them at mine. Remember that at the time I was only fifteen years old."

"Well then . . . ," I replied, vaguely understanding Aleksei Dmitrich's drift.

"The point is that every child is a most implacable egoist. Concord, harmony, joy—all these things are fresh air for a child, and if they don't surround him, it's not the child's fault; he's angry at everyone, without understanding who's responsible for destroying the harmony. Hardship irritates him: can he grasp its causes? That's why the majority of marriages are unhappy— women are just like children, and for marriage, wealth is a token of harmony.

"You won't believe how terrible the effects of an unhappy family upbringing can be all during the remainder of one's life, how vividly, in the minutest actions, one can observe the unconscious hostility implanted so long ago in the soul of a child. I'm reputed to be a wicked man; this reputation doesn't afford me any pleasure, and that's why I'm seeking to justify myself to you.

"You must understand the one strange feature in my character. Another person's grief doesn't affect my soul; instead, it hardens it. Moans and complaints, whoever's they are, affect me in some incomprehensible way.

"It may happen to you, in spite of your propitious character, to experience some bitter event in life. Your beloved may deceive you or you may be beaten in a game of cards: but don't come to me for advice or friendly sympathy. I strongly believe that in times of misfortune a man can temporarily become like a woman, even a child, and I know this may even be useful; all the same, I ask you, don't ever grieve in my presence, don't complain of your fate. I care for you deeply and therefore will remain silent when faced with your grief; I'll even utter some noble phrase, but in my soul I'll be angry; I'll despise you . . . at least for a while.

"In my position I sometimes have to discipline my subordinates. In the face of this arduous responsibility, I'm glad if the guilty person accepts his misfortune with equanimity and forbearance. But any entreaty, any weeping under such circumstances just hardens me. I become a monster, at least in my soul, because, thank God, I'm aware of my own strangeness and don't allow it to gain power over me.

"But, my God, what becomes of me if I happen to witness a bitter family scene! An entire book couldn't convey my feelings at the time. My bile wells up so high that I become ill. My pointless rage, however terrible it may be, can still be restrained within limits. And then the most biting, bitter sarcasm squeezes my lips and tries hard to burst forth, and I'm definitely unable to overcome it. . . ."

Aleksei Dmitrich fell silent. This painful confession evoked a multitude of thoughts in me; my friend's character was vividly portrayed, and I understood why Aleksei Dmitrich had cursed his own childhood. . . .

We both remained silent and looked at each other.

"The devil only knows what to make of it!" my host continued, tossing his cigar down on the table. "You begin telling a story and end up with anthropology. . . . But my tale is as worthy as Scheherazade's stories and will last more than one evening. Next time the events will be more interesting—I'll begin with my time at school."

"Who's not been to school?" I inquired. "I'll expect much that's good, although I can foresee terrible attacks on various methods of education."

We said our farewells and I left.

The Second Evening

Only chatterboxes take such pleasure in tête-à-têtes; a decent man almost always considers them oppressive. I find visits from a best friend difficult if there isn't a third person present, even a stupid one, to enliven the discussion. In private conversation a person may behave like a terrible scoundrel: he can retreat from his convictions, argue without enthusiasm, and indulge the sort of person he would be sure to mock if there were three or four people present.

But my last conversation with Aleksei Dmitrich constituted an exception to this general rule. I wanted to renew our discussion as soon as possible, but Aleksei Dmitrich was a difficult man. It meant nothing for him to abandon a book one page before the dénouement or to interrupt a conversation at the most interesting juncture. However, I had inadvertently touched his weakest point; the result was that he himself offered to continue his story.

Somehow, during our conversation about educating children, I'd asked him what had ever become of little Kostya, whose Emile-like education had been in such contradiction to the demands of our society. Aleksei Dmitrich smiled, sighed, and frowned all at once.

"Yes, I'm obliged to you," he said. "Kostya is the most exquisite and distressing chapter of my story and, accordingly, of my whole life. In addition, this episode is extremely instructive, especially in our time, when everyone is so concerned with education. Come visit me this evening and I'll tell you everything in due course."

It was obvious that Aleksei Dmitrich enjoyed talking about this subject. As you'll discover from the story, Kostya was his first friend, and Kostya's sister was the first object of his passion. Our hero manifested these affections in a strange way; to use his own expression, his nature was dislocated in all its joints. His first friendship resembled love, his first love resembled friendship, and, to crown it all, both passions ended unhappily. That evening we sat down on the sofa and he resumed his story.

"When I turned sixteen," Aleksei Dmitrich began, "a council of relatives and friends gathered in my mother's apartment. Opinions were expressed about me; my God, how long-winded and incoherent this conference was! My main teacher, *maître Jacques* among pedagogues, praised my success but declared that for my further education it would be best to send me to boarding school. My mother dedicated a portion of her meager income and my relatives helped as best they could; to do them justice, their help was kind and generous. But they were poor people, and the sacrifice they made was so uncomfortable that my heart sank whenever I thought about it. In the annual expenditure for my education every ruble represented a deprivation or was extracted from a secret fund for a rainy day; rainy days occur rather frequently in the lives of impoverished families.

At that time a preparatory school run by a Frenchman named Charlé was held in high regard; he had been taken prisoner in 1812 and since then had remained in Petersburg.[20] In that memorable year for Russia, Charlé was neither a barber nor a drummer, like so many of our foreign tutors: he served as a lieutenant in the emperor's young guard and was taken prisoner, not as he was bringing up the rear, but with a weapon in his hands, on the parapet of the Shevardinsky redoubt.[21] However, in spite of such a romantic life, Charlé was a nasty fellow.

I haven't the least sympathy for veterans *de la grande armée.* Those blue uniforms marching through half of Europe, *Ces habits bleus par la victoire usés,*[22] are acceptable only in Béranger's songs. Wandering through the world I've seen only two or three such heroes. It's bizarre for a contemporary man to hear ecstatic stories of how some thirty years ago some thirty thousand men perished on a broad field at Wagram.[23] "Why did they perish? For whom did they die?" one wants to ask these old men, but they only laugh at such questions. Many of them consider Napoleon an astonishing philanthropist and, in support of this view, will tell you how he used to visit hospitals after the battle of Austerlitz. . . .[24]

Besides, all those veterans are pedants, and pathetic ones at that. If it were possible to transport some admirer of Frederick the Great back to the changing of old Fritz's guard in front of the Potsdam Palace,[25] if it were possible to put another of Napoleon's worshippers into the skin of a poor conscript being readied for battle . . . then our future Jominis would never have composed verses like that.[26]

Charlé was a pedant, implacable and dry. He lost his good common sense over systems of education and treated his enormous boarding school as he used to treat his regiment in the young guard in former days. He oppressed poor children and suppressed all human emotion out of the purity of his heart; "strictness and discipline"—he used to say at every occasion, at every step.

His institution could aptly be called a moral slaughterhouse. As a result of its reputation, each year children from the best families would enroll in significant numbers. In spite of the inevitable tears on entering the school, it was nice to see this line of new victims, this group of lively lads. There were rambunctious dark-eyed boys who looked around boldly, craning their necks like little eaglets; there were skinny little fair-haired boys with large heads and bright, pensive little eyes, tender, wonderful creatures, whose every step would be watched with maternal affection.

Among them were rosy little children, full of aristocratic *calinerie** for which there is no word in Russian; rarely did any ugly children, whose future energy would be displayed in their awkward, clearly marked features, turn up among them.

But Charlé wasn't very interested in the physical aspects of his pupils; he didn't gaze affectionately into these little faces, nor did he adjust each pupil's studies to suit his character. The teachers were excellent; on that score, one must give him his due; the children ate well, got sufficient exercise, but all the same, it was terrible to see what he managed to produce a year after the arrival of the new recruits.

The eaglets' eyes dimmed, their wings dipped, and they began to look more like ravens or jackdaws. The thin, fair lads grew even thinner, their mouths hung open in a most ridiculous manner, and imbecility began to show in their large eyes. The rosy young aristocrats fared the best of all, because Charlé wasn't a man of stone and loved to get presents from their parents; but even these boys became wild and stupid.

Charlé regarded every boy whose insubordination threatened the general order as a personal enemy. Punishment followed punishment, and espionage surrounded the recalcitrant on all sides. Charlé constantly roamed through the rooms of the institution telling the older boys to keep an eye on the younger, instructing ten-year-olds in abstract morality, at which lectures

*Tenderness.

the listeners merely shook their heads and cursed their solicitous tutor. Owing to the clever politics of the institution's landlord, constant disagreements prevailed among the pupils; and as a result of these disagreements, not one prank ever remained a secret.

News of my enrollment in the boarding school frightened me: I'd never seen children my own age. Therefore, in spite of all my pride, I still had an extremely low opinion of myself as a result of having had no grounds for comparison. I was also horrified by the idea of discipline, the expectation of making new friends, and the notion of studying itself. I had a great deal of information in my head, but I'd given up in the face of any branch of knowledge based on a logical progression of facts. Every form of speculation served to confuse me. Therefore, I never learned any mathematics, which demanded both a firm foundation and the ability to deduce the unknown from the known.

My physical powers were very weak; the fact that I was tall and more developed than my years was to no avail. I was ungainly and sickly; some incomprehensible sluggishness predominated in my organism. I resembled a person who had slept for twelve hours straight without stirring and who was too lazy to get out of bed, not because he hadn't gotten enough sleep, but because he'd gotten too much.

And so, one fine morning I approached my new residence, filled with fear. But as soon as I'd passed through the gates, I was filled with boldness, God knows from where. The spacious old building surrounded me with its semicircular wings; old trees towered above the roof, having long since outgrown the building. A broad white staircase led up to it.

I asked where Mr. Charlé was to be found and entered his apartment with fear. I was met by a dried-up, unctuous man whose age was impossible to guess. Instead of a mustache, some tufts of hair trimmed in a most unusual way stuck out from under his nose; side-whiskers in the shape of commas both began and ended near his ears. It seemed that the only thing on his face were these tufts of hair and some side-whiskers; his nose, mouth, and eyes had somehow disappeared or were entirely invisible.

You can imagine my astonishment when this cold creature approached me in a friendly manner, put his right arm around me, and began walking around the room with me. Affectionate words poured from Mr. Charlé's mouth; I listened to all these compliments, blushed, and considered myself the happiest person on earth.

"I see you not as a pupil, but as my assistant," the clever Frenchman said. "Your age and dependability warrant that you won't refuse to share a part of my work with me."

I bowed and thanked him.

"You'll be enrolling in the upper class," said the proprietor of the boarding school. "Anything else would be impossible. You'll exert great influence on your fellow classmates; anything else would be impossible. Try to preserve this influence, use it for the good, and help to maintain order."

He sat down in an armchair and sighed deeply.

"Children from the best families," he continued, "are spoiled and become more so with every passing day. The younger generation is concocting great misfortune for itself; God forbid I should live to see that difficult time.

"In my boarding school morality declines with each passing day; immorality, unheard of in former times, is taking firmer root among the children. I'm telling you this quite frankly: among all children in this school you won't find even two worthy of your affection. Keep your distance from them, avoid their acquaintance or any schoolboy friendships. I'll give you a list of the worst offenders, even though they're all worthless—keep an eye on them, for their own sake; their fathers, if not the children themselves, will appreciate your nobility. . . ."

I'll spare you any further lofty phrases uttered by the farsighted proprietor of this boarding school.

After my conversation with Charlé, I proceeded to the recreation hall with a group of my new school chums. We soon became acquainted and talked about things with great enthusiasm; but suddenly all my interlocutors, without any apparent reason, lapsed into silence and dispersed in all directions with looks of dissatisfaction.

One of the young pupils was heading straight toward me. He was being followed by five or six older pupils, all dirty, with indolent and forbidding faces. When the younger boy drew near, I recognized my old friend, Kostya.

Our meeting was very strange. Kostya looked me over from head to foot with the most audacious, impudent expression.

"Hello," he said to me in a rude voice. "What an ugly monster you've become! Do you remember how I beat you up?"

I was infuriated by his cold-blooded rudeness. My vanity had been so pampered earlier that day that the first unpleasant shock affected me more than it should have.

"Oh, you mangy little dog, you!" I shouted at Kostya. "Now I'll get back at you. . . ."

I didn't even have time to finish my sentence before I went flying onto the floor as a result of a blow to my legs delivered by my opponent with extraordinary agility. I would have broken my skull if Kostya hadn't supported my head with his arm.

"It's not a good idea for you to fight with me," he said, helping me up from the floor. "It might be all right if you learned how to fight. Let's go over to the window."

He made a sign to the group accompanying him, and they obediently headed off to one side.

Kostya hadn't grown at all in the three years since he'd enrolled in the school. One might have concluded that some serious illness had arrested his development, if this impression had not been contradicted by his healthy appearance and the graceful proportions of his miniature limbs. His beauty exceeded all probability; it was to no avail that he did everything to detract from it. His jacket was missing several buttons and was torn; his face was scratched and dirty, but it still retained its former attractiveness. In all my life I had never seen anything more elegant than his round yet boldly chiseled features, his small mouth protruding proudly and impudently. His eyes shone with a gentle glimmer, like stars on a dark night. In a word, neither his untidiness nor his furrowed brow, nor the constantly impudent, even wicked, expression on his face, could prevent Kostya from being a most beautiful child.

"Why've you come here?" he asked me, after hopping up onto the windowsill and dangling his legs. "You'd be better off getting out of here, asking to go home again."

"I wasn't happy at home either," I said with a questioning expression.

"I remember, you poor fellow, I remember," said Kostya, recalling our past life. "Nasty things happened to you there, but at least the people were . . . "

"As if you didn't have the same!" I ventured, and then grew frightened.

Kostya's little eyes flared up, like phosphorous matches catching fire.

"But . . . here!" he said, clenching his crooked teeth with a childishly hostile expression. "There aren't any real people here! . . . I'd like to trounce them all . . . " he continued with emotion.

"Enough, Kostya," I said in reply. "Your uncle spoiled you. What's to be done? Apparently everyone suffers. . . ."

"They're all dogs here," he continued his strange evaluation. "Everyone either bites or crawls. I'd run away, but there's no place to run. . . ."

I looked at him in surprise.

"We'll be friends," he said again. "Look here, you can be with us and for us, though if you decide to sneak . . . but I know you, you wouldn't dare!"

He extended his tiny little hand, dirty and hard as wood.

Just then the German tutor came up to us; he had reddish side-whiskers, rosy cheeks, and glasses, and wore a dissatisfied expression.

"What's this, Herr Nadeschin?" he said sternly, addressing Kostya. "Your jacket's covered with inkspots again? I've told you so many times . . . and Mr. Charlé has given you orders! You're a pathetic child, done for!"

This time Kostya's eyes blazed with their constant fire. Nervous anger arose in his chest; all his limbs trembled and suddenly fell still. The tutor himself grew instinctively afraid, became embarrassed, and almost retreated when faced by the powerful impact of this boy's gaze. I don't know what would have happened if, taking advantage of the fact that I still had hold of his hand, I hadn't jerked him toward me with all my strength. The tutor, without finishing his reprimand, fearing too violent a scene, left us alone.

It took considerable effort to calm Kostya down. It was at least a quarter of an hour before his eyes began to dim and his body returned to its normal state. Then he came to appreciate my role.

"Thank you, Aleksei," he said to me, placing his hand on my shoulder. "Thank you for taking care of me. Sometime I'll return the favor. Good-bye."

A group of pupils stood around us.

"Away, lads!" Kostya shouted to them, and the crowd respectfully dispersed. He went into another room, followed by his dreary bodyguards.

"What a strange fellow!" I said to one of my new friends.

"Watch out for him," he replied. "He'll latch on to you and bring you down. No wonder no one can stand him. No one in the whole class's speaking to him."

"Ah! Are you talking about Nadezhin?" asked one of the teachers, butting into our conversation. "Indeed, watch out for him: he's a terrible brat."

This double warning confused me. It was quite impossible that his elders would abuse the same pupil who was so disliked by his comrades; and boys usually don't abuse one of their own who engages in open struggle with the tutors.

The result of all this was that I desperately wanted to become closer to Kostya and succeeded in doing so. My former friend was so unaccustomed to sympathy and friendship that he responded wholeheartedly. To tell the truth, all disadvantages were incurred by me: the clever lad made me write compositions for him, borrow books from other pupils, and more than once he attempted to involve me in one of the adventures that characterized his stormy life at school. In vain did I attempt to get the better of this incomprehensible being: I tried to refuse all his requests, didn't talk to him for days at a time, and even took the most vulgar steps: I lectured him. . . . Kostya turned out to be a most worthless fellow.

He had been born with a gentle, timid character, the remains of which produced an astonishing, incredibly amusing contrast with his usual impudence and arrogance. They say that previously he wasn't like that at all, but obviously he'd enrolled in our institution at a bad time. I still remember him as a very nice, lively child. But in boarding school it happened, as is often the case, that the child's liveliness was seen as impertinence, his frankness as unruliness, his cheerfulness as sarcasm, and so on.

After so defining the nature of the poor child, Charlé considered he had the right to take various steps to oppress him. Humiliating punishments were showered upon Kostya. Charlé wasn't above inciting other pupils against him or spreading absurd, immoral rumors about him. But while it might have been possible to kill Kostya, only God himself could have broken his spirit.

It's striking, but this energetic lad's struggle against the entire boarding school, with its swarm of gloomy teachers, was a very serious matter. The stern proprietor never once grew tired, disdained his own cruelty, or let Kostya out of his sight; but Kostya never relented, even for a minute. There could be no peace between him and Charlé.

Having forsaken the society in which his upbringing had taken place, Kostya grew to hate it and considered it his right to harm anybody and everybody he met. He became a little Karl Moor or Rinaldo Rinaldini;27 the most idle, angry, and desperate pupils became his faithful comrades-in-arms for his escapades and machinations.

While Kostya waged open warfare against his tutors, he did ten times more harm to his comrades and was usually embittered by the meek and humble boys who, as it happens, were the best ones in the class. I don't like having to dwell on prosaic details, but in the interest of fairness it must be said that a day rarely went by on which Kostya didn't have a fight with someone, a brawl ending in his or another boy's favor. But much more frequently he wounded his comrades through his ruses; he detested every convention of friendship and mutual obligation. If the whole class decided not to answer the teacher, he alone would reply; if the class agreed to amuse the teacher with their brilliant recitation, Kostya alone didn't know his lesson. He selected questions on exams extremely well, and his skill contributed to the general consternation. After promising to help some indolent student, Kostya would slip the most difficult question into his hands, and the trusting lad's tongue would cleave to the roof of his mouth.

And—strange to say . . . but now it doesn't seem so strange: this wild child had one strong passion that seemed entirely inappropriate to his character—a love of flowers. He could stare at a beautiful bouquet for hours at a time; outdoor flowers could induce a state of childish ecstasy in him. Everything that blossomed in the little garden at our school belonged to Kostya by right, and woe to the bold lad who ever dared pluck a flower without his permission! Kostya was always being followed by a band of desperate older schoolmates prepared to engage in battle at a single word from him. These *bravi** brandished neither stilettos nor swords, but sometimes in a dark corridor they threw themselves on their chosen victim and beat him mercilessly. Then they reported their deeds to Kostya and were beside themselves with ecstasy if they managed to win his approval.

That's the sort of person my friend Kostya was. His classmates would've beaten him to a pulp long ago, if it hadn't been for the protection of these devoted *bravi*; Charlé would have expelled him from school long ago, if the child's extraordinary beauty hadn't forced him to keep Kostya for show—wherever necessary. Besides that, his abilities were far from ordinary, especially in the natural sciences; even without studying, he could answer better than any other pupil.

I still find it extremely pleasant to analyze this strange char-

*Desperadoes.

acter and, consequently, often engage in that activity. You can just imagine how much my first friend of those years intrigued me.

Almost a month had passed since the day I first enrolled in the school. Things were going well, and my spirit was enjoying the respite. I returned home unwillingly and came back to school earlier than other boys.

Once, after a holiday, I returned to school in the evening and was planning to go to bed. Just then Kostya approached me with an extremely affectionate expression. He jumped up on the bed where I was sitting, and from there up onto my shoulders where he perched as if on an armchair. This strange behavior signified extraordinary affection on his part.

"I have a request to make of you, Aleksei," he said. Kostya, as opposed to school convention, didn't call anyone by their last name, but by their first name, sometimes adding to it some epithet that revealed his unusual, bitter powers of observation.

"Let's hear."

"Will you do it?"

"I don't know. What?"

"Promise me first."

"I don't want to."

Kostya shuddered with annoyance but restrained himself.

"Do you want to join us? The seven of us (he listed the members of his group): tomorrow we want to beat up the whole class."

"Are you crazy? There are three times as many of them."

"That doesn't matter; they're all puny. Tomorrow the history teacher won't be there. Some boys will fall asleep in class, others we'll call away. Then we'll beat up all the rest."

I was feeling both amused and uncomfortable. "Go to hell," I said. "No one's ever beaten me up like that, and I don't intend to beat up anyone."

"Well, at least keep quiet and we won't touch you."

"I won't keep quiet. It's time to stop fighting; the devil knows why you do."

"What do you mean, the devil knows why?" Kostya asked, clenching his teeth. "Yesterday one of those rogues called me names. . . . I don't know who it was—so we'll beat them all up."

"Why did he call you names?"

"He called me a naughty girl for no reason at all."

"What do I care if someone called you a naughty girl! Do whatever you want, but I'm going to warn the whole class."

"You'll do no such thing!"

"Yes, I will."

He jumped down to the floor and stamped his foot. "Just you dare!" he cried.

I turned and walked away. And indeed, the next day the whole class was ready to meet the onslaught of hostile force. To no avail did Kostya lure the strongest boys out of room, in vain did he reinforce his own *bravi* with ruffians from other classes. The attack failed and came to nothing.

For two days afterward Kostya and I didn't speak to each other. I found it terribly difficult, but didn't show it at all. I was able to control myself, a pathetic ability in a young person, but I possessed it to perfection.

On the third day in the evening I was walking through a dimly lit hall. This vaulted room with its round windows through which moonlight poured in wide stripes, with its massive columns disappearing into the distance and merging with the decorated ceiling, always made a very profound impression on me. My footsteps sounded hollow in the empty space, so I stepped more firmly and listened to the echoing sound with a strange feeling. The dim light, the serenity, the height of the Gothic room—all combined to produce an unfamiliar, pleasant kind of pensiveness. I reached the end of the hall with a feeling of regret; I wished that it had stretched far into the distance, that the moon-light would play on its shining floor forever, that the sound of my footsteps would echo even more triumphantly. . . .

Suddenly a light hanging directly in front of me started swing-ing loudly; its glass lampshade fell to the floor and the light went out. Some ferocious figures appeared as if from beneath the ground and turned up right in front of me. "Ah! So now we've caught you, you scoundrel!" shouted a dozen or so harsh voices all around me. The moon shone with extraordinary clarity. In horror I saw before me a band of the most ferocious *bravi* with their fists upraised.

In many respects I'd already come of age. Since childhood I'd regarded physical violence as a great misfortune. My late father, in spite of all his strictness, had never allowed himself to inflict corporal punishment; not knowing any childhood games, I'd never experienced even the mildest beating. You can imagine my predicament at that awful moment! But I was too embarrassed to cry out and summon anyone to my aid. I ran off to one side and stood behind one of the long tables.

"Gentlemen!" I cried to those besieging me. "Don't touch me, I'm guilty. . . ."

"It's too late!" they replied and prepared to attack from both sides.

I grabbed a stool from under the table and waved it over my head. One of the brave lads hurled himself on me. My blow didn't wound him and my weapon descended in vain: all four legs flew aside and the stool fell to the floor.

The *bravi* were astounded by my resolve. Taking advantage of their astonishment, I jumped onto the table, hopped up to the windowsill, and unlocked the frame. . . . I forgot to say that this scene took place on the third floor: a gaping abyss opened be-neath me.

Dishonor seemed far worse to me. "If you come any closer," I said, "I'll jump out of the window!"

Not believing my words, they moved forward. Not one trace of fear flashed through my mind; my one foot was getting ready to leap. . . .

"Stop, you fools!" Kostya's sonorous voice rang out from a distance. "Don't you see, he'll throw himself out. Get away, we've made up."

In half a minute not one of the rascals was left in the room. Kostya came up to me, helped me down from the windowsill, sat me on the table, and knelt down next to me.

"Forgive me, Aleksei," he said, putting his arms around my neck, his voice trembling. "I won't do it again. I'm to blame for all of this."

I let my feet down on the floor, stood up, and freed myself from the embrace of my cutthroat friend. "Get out of here," I said to him coolly.

I expected a horrible explosion but was absolutely mistaken. My first victory over Kostya entailed a triumph over the whole company. We parted in silence.

The next day Kostya was terribly sad; counter to the convention of all school quarrels, he didn't conceal his feelings. All morning he sat writhing like a sick little dog and didn't budge from his place; he didn't attach himself to anyone and didn't torment anyone. The whole class avoided him with respect, afraid to arouse the despondent tiger cub. I wasn't any happier, but during my brief time at the school, I'd already managed to learn all the local customs. I pretended to be very cheerful; I chatted and laughed, although this cheerfulness wasn't well suited to my long face.

Toward evening Kostya wanted to seek some diversion for himself. A true defender of all the oppressed—that is, of those whipped and relegated to dark rooms—he decided, with the help of direct force, to convey to a prisoner various necessities for an evening meal and a smoke. The bandits crowded around Kostya, the phalanx advanced in unanimity, but the leader abandoned his enterprise at the most interesting moment, returned to the classroom, and sat down at his place in despondent pensiveness.

I was triumphant: it seemed that Kostya would follow me, that it would be in my power to break his spirit and refashion him as I wished. I was stupid: I was unable to conceive that in such natures only one step separates love from hatred; but chance arranged everything for the best.

That night I was unable to sleep; I was tormented by melancholy and inexplicable remorse. Something told me that at the present time it wasn't Kostya who was guilty before me, but that I was guilty before him. I vaguely understood that it was dangerous to play with fire, that it was difficult to control a nature higher than one's own.

I began pacing the room. The silence in our dormitory had a beneficial effect, which was unheard-of for me. Silence in my parents' house had been more like bitter pensiveness, a momentary respite for a man destroyed by hardship.

I paused near Kostya's bed. The poor lad was crying, just as simply, as openly as he'd been grieving that morning. He was sitting on the pillow, his breathing labored, but his teeth were clenched, his eyes flashing with hostile fire.

My good side urged me on. I felt that in a quarter of an hour all would be lost; powerful bitterness would soon replace his childish grief.

"Kostya," I said, sitting down next to him. "I see that I'm to blame."

He threw himself on my neck, embraced me with his whole

body, and kissed me several times. He chatted with me for a few minutes, said that he loved me very much; we made plans to study together, and he said he wanted to work side by side with me. "Weren't you a fool for wanting to jump out of the window?" he repeated several times. "Would it have been such a great misfortune if we'd given you a beating?" In the midst of this explanation he suddenly stopped, lowered his head, and immediately fell asleep. I left him with a serene conscience, but was unable to close my own eyes all that night.

From that time on Kostya and I were inseparable. A significant change occurred in his life. He became devoted to me with all the passion of his lively, loving, childish nature. He forgot all about his wild escapades, abandoned his unshaven *bravi*, and, thanks to my efforts, grew closer to my best friends. But he could never love them; persecution and insults endured by him both for good reason and for no reason at all had embittered his sensitive soul. He was unable to cast off even his violent impulsiveness and was all the more endearing at those moments when he gave himself over to affection with tenderness and passion. A rich reserve of devotion lay hidden in his soul: up to this very day I can't forget his solicitude when I happened to be sick or depressed. He practically moved in with me, took care of me constantly, divined my every desire with incomprehensible perspicacity, fulfilled my every whim without a murmur. Sometimes, I'm ashamed to admit, I pretended to be depressed so that I could enjoy his love and caring to the fullest.

The more I regarded this strange, exceptional creature, the more I was astonished by the unlimited appeal and riches of his soul. Kostya's nature had clearly been singled out by the hand of God: he had been created for some purpose—he was fated to perform some great deed, but circumstances had destroyed his soul and not allowed it to develop. This was no child prodigy who promises much but comes to naught. Child prodigies are striking by the disproportionate development of one or another of their capabilities, while all others wither away and disappear. In Kostya his entire moral side was proportionally developed. He was fifteen years old: neither in intelligence, emotion, or ability did he outstrip his age, but at the same time he was immeasurably above all his peers.

Never in a grown man have I encountered such sensible, practical understanding of things, such active hostility to everything false, ugly, and unpleasant. Things that were futile and harmful in our studies didn't come easily to Kostya; it reached the point where he absolutely refused to study history when the monstrousness of events troubled his soul. Everything that seemed unjust to him in our school life aroused his indignation; and, because he always did just as he pleased, this indignation turned into hostility and open resistance.

In the exact and somewhat fascinating sciences his abilities were astonishing. He immediately grasped the main idea, developed it in his own way, and became attached to it with his whole soul. His sensitivities slept soundly, but physical beauty aroused in him unconscious, pagan adoration. And—strange to say—although possessing extraordinary beauty, he considered himself ugly. When we tried to disabuse him of this notion, he told us, "In your eyes a babe at the breast is the most beautiful of all." He'd give half his life to be taller, have a broad chest, possess masculine, athletic strength. Our taste had been spoiled; his struck us by its subtlety. God only knows where he came up with all of it.

But the main, most charming aspect of his soul was his profound, childlike poetic instinct, closely connected with his most insignificant actions. I know that at the mention of poetry you imagine the measured lines and nonsensical verse of "Young

Germany"[28]—rest assured: the poetry of Kostya's soul wasn't manifested in rhymes and spondees.

His poetry consisted of an unlimited, passionate love for nature, childish memories conveyed in the most ordinary words, the most guileless expressions—it was manifested in his building castles in the air that were so simple, innocent, and noble.

Kostya was a great pantheist, naturally without ever knowing what pantheism meant. Every tree, every flower was for him a living being, animated by the same life-force he shared. He placed animals on the same level as people: he could resolve to kill a mosquito only when furious at having been bitten; on the other hand, he'd have killed any person who'd bitten him with the same equanimity.

Kostya's love for nature was expressed in thousands of the most capricious, exquisite whims.

Sometimes he would make his way to the middle of the garden and lie down on the grass, looking up so as not to see the walls of the school or the chimneys of neighboring houses. Before his eyes the tops of old lime trees swayed and clouds chased one another across the dark blue sky. He would spend hours like that and referred to this pursuit as "an excursion to the countryside."

Other times he lay on the grass face down and, having selected a small clump of turf, examined it with rapt attention. He referred to this pleasure as "traveling abroad." Imperceptible irregularities seemed to be lofty mountains; among them, like palm trees, stood stalks of turf grass; clover spread its giant blossoms; and young rams, imagining themselves to be extraordinary monsters, clamored over tall mountain ranges. It was very difficult to tear Kostya away from this pursuit: at moments like these he felt happier than any naturalist who's ascended the most barren peaks in the Cordilleras.[29]

He loved flowers more than anything else on earth and treated them with great respect, never picking any, but he was fickle and inclined to flirtations. One day he'd shower praise on roses; the next, he'd walk past them with disdain and sit down next to some small bluebells. But he felt a particular affection for camellias, referring to them as Spanish women, and was always faithful to them, probably because camellias rarely came into his hands.

This sympathy for nature was the most outstanding trait of Kostya's character; but don't think that his soul's remarkable sensitivity was reflected in this alone. There wasn't one grand feeling that didn't attract his strange, childlike nature; these attachments were terribly inconstant, but the reason for their inconstancy was none other than his certitude, the precision of his intellect.

I've already told you about the terrible hostility aroused in Kostya by anything he considered unjust or stupid; it reached the point where he absolutely refused to study a subject that didn't strike him with the beauty of its exposition or the significance of its content. Little children usually like history for its accounts of wars, battles, and self-sacrifice, but Kostya couldn't stand any of it. His quick mind would refuse to function when the matter at hand concerned bloodshed arising from some trifle or heroes dying for some idea they themselves didn't even understand.

We used to study together, and I recall how difficult it was for me to get him to remember those events and ideas that were so antipathetic to his nature. There was only one way to achieve this goal: appeal to his imagination by some grandiose episode.

So that Kostya would know something about the Crusades, I was forced to crawl out of my own skin and devise various entertaining scenes for him. I had to describe Jerusalem under a burning hot sky overlooking a deep abyss. I had to portray the crusaders shackled in irons, their horses covered with golden rugs, monks with tonsured heads, pilgrims carrying long staffs.

This poetically, proportionately developed nature of his couldn't stand speculation and abstraction; all of Kostya's ideas were expressed so beautifully, so rhythmically, that they could have been used to paint a picture.

Fortunately for poor Kostya, and especially for me, we didn't spend even half a year together under Mr. Charlé's estimable roof. It was our turn to enroll in the state institution, and thanks to our own decent abilities and prior preparation, we enrolled together in one of the upper classes. I relaxed completely—I can ascribe everything decent in me to the beneficial influence of our marvelously organized system of public education. And Kostya behaved far better than he had at Charlé's: the solicitous administration at once understood the good side of his character and gradually, quietly attempted to erase all traces of the senseless Emile-like education and bitterness that, as a result of Charlé's generosity, had been conceived in my friend's childlike soul. Unfortunately, the amount of time we spent together in the state institution was also extremely limited.

But it's time to conclude this account of my schooldays. At that time Kostya meant everything to me and I was madly attached to him; up to now, of all my recollections, he alone has been preserved in my memory with a certain freshness—all others, both my former love and even my old foolishness, no longer move me in the least. Therefore, today's prolixity is forgivable. Kostya and his family played a fundamental part in my life: his role was splendid and his family did its part, as every family does.

The Third Evening

"Based on the old rule," he began, "love is essential to my story."

"You can do without it," I replied. "If you'd been in love with a Chinese princess or Saint Rosalia[30] at least, then I'd hear you out, but failing that. . . ."

"That is to say, you fear commonplaces. To my utter delight my love was so ridiculous, and it ended in so original a fashion, that I can boldly include it in the story of my life."

Kostya had a very attractive sister, older than he was by one year. He loved her with unlimited devotion, used to visit her boarding school regularly, and afterward corresponded with her and was very faithful in his letter writing.

Apparently there was a restless, unaccommodating element in the blood of all these Nadezhins; Kostya's sister, just like him, never quite settled in at her school, the only difference being that she was less hostile and merely grieved. She constantly begged her father to take her away with him to the country, but the old general would have none of it.

It must be that Russian solitude is particularly injurious when compared to others: as soon as a person moves to the country, he begins to grow stupid or do nasty things. Vera Nikolaevna's father began his rural pursuits by forming an attachment to a poor but sharp-tongued lady landowner and, after a brief liaison, made an "honest woman" of her, to use a soldier's expression.

This marriage isolated the old Spartan from all his neighbors. Apparently his new wife went against everyone's grain: the general's hospitable house became completely deserted. He became gloomier and blinder, growing more decrepit not by the day, but by the hour. His daughter's teachers were so disparaging of her abilities that he finally succumbed to her requests and took her back to the country with him, sure that he was bringing home not a daughter, but a little devil.

Kostya mourned the loss of his sister, but was soon consoled. Her letters from the country told him how happy she was, how glad to be living in tranquillity, in the fresh air with her much beloved father. Verinka[31] had only lavish praise for her stepmother and made peace, not only between her and Kostya, but even with all the neighbors.

Never did youthful innocence describe to a girlfriend the beauty of her beloved in the passionate terms in which Vera Nikolaevna constantly referred to her aging father. He meant everything to her—he was her deity and her friend; she obeyed him blindly, carefully following his every step. His gray hair, tall stature, infrequent moments of good cheer—all these inspired the young girl's passionate adoration. There are such privileged natures among old men: in spite of all their egoism and weakness, these people can inspire love in all women, from their own daughter to the cook.

But I, for one, didn't believe the young girl was really as happy as she indicated to her brother. She lived in a family; for me that was sufficient cause. All families, I reckoned, were similar to the one in which I grew up. Vera Nikolaevna was suffering; that was the only way I could imagine her.

I regarded country life with the same vulgar condescension as the most frivolous dandies residing in the capital. Intense and embittered souls usually surrender themselves enthusiastically to dreams of nature and solitude—but this was not at all the case with me. The country seemed to be a broad, empty field with collapsing ditches and yellowish mud, under an eternally gray sky with rain that never let up. On one end of the field there had to be some trees resembling bushes; at the other, a dozen or so gray huts scattered about. If I conceived of Verinka, my imagination couldn't have pictured her except against that gloomy, yellowish background; there arose in my heart a tender feeling, not in complete correspondence to the landscape described.

I'd never seen her before and therefore waited impatiently for the portrait she'd promised to send her brother. You must agree that no matter how sensibly a person is brought up, he can't fall in love with a woman without seeing her image. I was nineteen years old and not at all well disposed to anything unnatural; but there are limits to everything. At last the portrait arrived; I was in ecstasy, head over heels in love, and constantly talked to Kostya about his sister.

Kostya, however, wasn't as carried away by his sister's portrait. The scarcely perceptible melancholy countenance on this pretty girl's face couldn't be concealed from his penetrating glance. He became even more disturbed when he observed that the expression given her on the portrait was unnatural and forced. I blamed the artist, but Kostya wouldn't hear a word of it. "It means she's hidden her normal expression and, if so, she must be sad; and, if she's grieving, she's having a difficult time." There was nothing for me to say in reply to this logic, all the more so since it confirmed my own surmises.

The brief period of my education in that institution passed.

After a major examination, the main administrator approached me with an affectionate look, congratulated me on being first in the class, and concluded with a question: "Which regiment do you wish to join?"

It was quite incredible, but up to that time I hadn't even thought about my future career; at that moment the administrator's question struck me like a clap of thunder. A thousand bitter thoughts rushed into my head; I was confused and could only ask for time "to consider and confer."

One after another my comrades boldly and cheerfully called out the names of their various regiments. I stood near the window; my heart sank and envy gnawed at my insides. With every name I imagined black horses, white uniforms trimmed with gold, sabers, helmets, splendor, and good cheer . . . and I realized that none of this was made for me.

Whose heart could I gladden with my uniform? My mother was no longer alive. What fate awaited me in the world? Lack of money, loneliness, again, perhaps, an apartment in smelly Gorokhovaya Street, once more poverty and grief. What could I expect in a circle of dazzling young people, given my own awkwardness and vanity?

But another change had taken place in my soul. I didn't fall entirely to pieces when faced by misfortune; a wealth of energy arose in my heart. I understood at once that in my position I had to establish a suitable place in society for myself by means of blood, sweat, and tears.

I remembered that a month before there had been a funeral in our church for one of our former students killed in the Caucasus. In other words, there was still a place where men fought battles, killed people, struggled. Where there's death, there's life—where there's destruction, there's a path for those left behind.

I had one major distinction: I was decisive. My pathetic up-bringing hadn't succeeded in making me absolutely vulgar. I declared my intention and by that evening was already chatting with Kostya about my future plans. Kostya was still young and therefore not about to leave school. When I told him about the beauties of the Caucasus, its free and easy life, its mountains and raging rivers, his eyes shone.

"Can't I go with you?" he asked so simply, as if we were talking about a railroad voyage.

"But who'd let you?"

"I'll write to my sister; my father would be very happy. No one's prevented from going to the Caucasus as a cadet."

"No more of that, you lunatic," I said, trying to dissuade him. "In a year, if you still want to, you'll go there as an officer."

But Kostya had already taken it into his head to accompany me.

"Does the way there lead through any provinces?" he asked, without heeding my arguments.

"Through such and such province, and such and such. . . ."

"Bravo!" cried Kostya, beside himself with joy. "That means we'll call in on my father. At last I'll get to see my sister."

From that moment on, the devil himself wouldn't have been able to alter his decision. He began writing a letter, sent it off, and in a few days received permission from the old general. I concealed my pleasure, but in fact was beside myself with joy. Separation from Kostya would have meant something like death to me.

Any poor but honest family would've undertaken more prepa-ration for a trip to the country than Kostya and I did setting off to do battle in alien and troubled parts. We didn't discuss our plans or future deeds; for Kostya the next week seemed like a distant eternity, and he managed to convey this anxious view of things to me perfectly.

Following the end of school, before our departure, and all during our travels together, we lived like two heavenly birds: these were the happiest days of my life. Even to this day I can't recall my first acquaintance with our poor but generous northern nature without a feeling of sweetness. Autumn was just beginning and the weather was delightful. We traveled without stinting on time and circumstance; we stopped whenever we felt like it, staying in some places for two or three days, while rushing through others like madmen. Our attitude was so carefree that only when we'd covered half the distance did we realize that we'd neglected to bring along any heavy coats. We quickly outfitted ourselves with some loose-fitting cloaks made of animal skins, covered ourselves with them at night, and galloped on without stopping. The moon looked us cheerfully in the eye, a fresh breeze whistled past our covered cart and put us to sleep.

The time came to turn off the main road toward General Nadezhin's estate. The distance remaining was no more than thirty versts.[32] Kostya could hardly stand it; he woke me at five in the morning and we galloped along the cart-track. The coachman agreed to take us the twenty versts to the ferry; on the other side of the river we had to wait for the general's horses.

I don't recall anything more splendid than the autumn morning when we turned off the main road. The sun hadn't yet risen, the gray mist hovered over the sandy banks of the swiftly flowing river, and the dark green pine forest appeared on one side; the air was cold and the daylight struck us with its suffused whiteness. We passed huts in which morning fires had not yet been lit; the heavy sound of flails could be heard from neighboring barns; nature was becoming more alive with our every step, the surrounding landscape was becoming more and more beautiful. A sleepy peasant ferried us across the river through rising steam

»»» 162 «««

and our horses were released; but, once we got to the other side, we could see that the relay of fresh horses had not yet arrived.

In my opinion we should have waited, but for Kostya there was no worse torture than waiting for someone or something. He convinced me to proceed on foot, insisting that he remembered every crossroad. He ran on ahead, constantly racing off in different directions, and instead of one, we covered three versts, just like frisky dogs running along a road.

We got way off the path, but Kostya did remember the place very well. After walking for about two hours, we reached a tall oak grove, and from the hill on which it stood we could clearly see the manor house, a large orchard, and a church. Still, we had to cover another four versts, and Kostya was absolutely exhausted and unable to go any farther. I persuaded him to sit down and rest; he lay on the dry leaves and fell fast asleep, as he usually did. I smoked a cigar and enjoyed the view of the old orchard, the sound of which seemed to reach me—I admired the grove with its red, yellow, and green leaves resembling flowers. The sun was radiating warmth in earnest, as if suddenly remembering that it was already autumn and it was absolutely useless both for the winter and the spring crops.

Just at this moment I noticed, about twenty paces from us, an old man and a young girl making their way arduously up the gently sloping hillside. From the description, the girl's portrait, and the old man's military uniform, I guessed at once that it was Kostya's father and my heart's choice, the mysterious Vera Nikolaevna. Not wishing to startle them by our unexpected appearance, I lay down next to Kostya and watched them, covering myself with willow-bush branches.

I had imagined General Nadezhin as a stern, old complainer, so pleasant to come upon in a novel or on the stage, but so unbearable in real life. But my expectations were not borne out: the general appeared to be a most gentle, timid little old man. One could have surmised that he'd once been rather tall, but at present he was so hunched over that he seemed weak and feeble. On the other hand, it was hard to imagine a more attractive face: it radiated goodness. His expression was a little sarcastic, a little lazy, very weak, and most appropriate for an old man. His small eyes glanced affably and somewhat timidly in all directions; his completely gray hair lent his face an even more venerable appearance. With caution and graceful courtesy he rested on the arm of his kind Antigone.[33]

Once I saw Vera Nikolaevna's already familiar features, I forgot all about the old man, Kostya, and the beautiful landscape. Up to the present time I've yet to meet a woman who, in either beauty or grace, can be compared to this "noblewoman," who was raised in an institution and lived her whole life in the backwoods, almost as far away as Saratov.[34] You know my taste is impeccable, and the main thing is it's impartial.

You're not a sentimental man, and therefore you won't find it strange if I compare Verinka to a fine Arabian horse. I know of no better comparison: they both possess life, beauty, and energy. Every one of Verinka's movements bespoke her energy, her intrepid soul: she seemed to live life at a gallop; activity and speed were inherent in her every word. One had to observe the solicitude with which she led her weak old father. But it was easy to see that such an excursion was not to her liking; she wanted to scoop her father up in her arms, carry him around the garden and grove, make noise, amuse him, run, and chatter with him incessantly.

All the same, the portrait spoke the truth: during my few brief moments of observation, four times I noticed in Verinka's blue

eyes an unbearably poignant, incomprehensible trace of intense
sadness. . . .

"You've tormented me, you frivolous girl," said the general
affectionately. "So here I've come to meet him, and I bet that
terror of a boy's already at home."

"Well, then, let's head for home!" I heard Verinka's melodious
voice. "Shall we run down the mountain?"

Her gestures were so expressive that she seemed halfway
home already.

"Stop, wait, what a sprinter!" said the general, holding her by
the hand. "I'm absolutely exhausted . . . times have changed."

The daughter sat the old man down on a rock and nestled up
to him affectionately.

"It's all your fault," she said softly, "not mine. I listened to you
and this is where we've got to. . . ."

The old man's eyes shone cheerfully and his figure straightened up.

"Well, where was I?" he asked, recalling something.

Vera Nikolaevna was amused.

"Near Dresden,"[35] she said, but her father was already re-
suming his story.

"So these foolish Austrians were waiting for the cuirassiers,
but the ditch was close at hand. A very thick fog had descended,
and they forgot that all their powder had been soaked by the rain.
I stood with the battery on the edge of the ravine and saw the
cavalry galloping up, with the Austrians right there; but what
could they do? . . . even if one rifle were fired. . . . It was terrible
how the French trampled them. Sixteen battalions got confused,
attacked one another, threw down their rifles, fell into the ditch,
and no assistance could be rendered: you had to circle three
versts around. . . ."

One had to see the love on the young girl's face as she listened to the story of this bloodletting, which, in all likelihood, interested her as much as revolutions in the Japanese empire do me. But the general was carried away by his own story, his voice grew stronger, and when he came to the misfortune of his own battery, he got up off the rock and walked boldly toward the house, scarcely leaning on his attractive companion's arm.

Then I roused my comrade, let him recover, and we ran to catch up with the old man. The reunion was very merry: tears shone in the general's little eyes. He received me warmly, thanked me for my friendship with his son, and, in accordance with his innate querulousness, started scolding Kostya at once.

"If you wanted to walk home," he remarked about our latest wanderings, "why did you send for the horses? You've had the whole house up and about since early morning: such commotion, confusion. . . . Why such impatience . . . ?"

Vera Nikolaevna turned to her father in a joking manner: "Let them walk; they should get used to it," she said. "Why spoil this naughty boy? You used to walk when you were young."

The old man calmed down and looked affectionately at his son, who was already finding this reproach painful.

"What a Spartan!" cried Kostya, who'd yet to release his sister from his embrace. He began kissing her with all his might.

Rarely have I witnessed a more pleasant scene than the meeting of these two children, so head over heels in love with one another. They kept touching, laughing, singing, chattering such nonsense that I couldn't understand a word of it. . . . These two lively, graceful, eccentric creatures so resembled each other, were so delightful, that the old man softened just looking at them.

"By the way," said Kostya, turning to his sister with a tender look. "I'd like to hear a little confession from you."

Vera Nikolaevna gave a resounding laugh and looked her

brother right in the eye. "Sulk some more . . . go on," she said, kissing Kostya, laughing once again, pushing him away, and jumping aside. Kostya ran after her, and in two seconds they had gotten far away from us . . . then they made an abrupt turn and once more headed back. Verinka, out of breath, came running up first and took her father by the hand. A shadow of melancholy flashed across her face and disappeared once again.

"And here's Marya Ivanovna," said the general, turning to me.

The tense figure of a tall, thin woman was heading straight toward us; she was dressed with inappropriate elegance and a terrible lack of taste. But the latter elicited a somewhat painful, gloomy feeling, rather than laughter. The stepmother's dress, like costumes of theatrical villains, struck my eyes with its bright juxtaposition of black and red; these sinister colors cast a dark shadow on the face of the general's wife, which, even without that, was not very attractive.

Paying attention neither to me nor to Kostya, this woman went straight up to the general, who'd grown absolutely quiet and very withdrawn.

"Will this never end, Nikolai Aleksandrych?" she asked, turning to her husband with a most impertinent tone. "This is the third day you've gone traipsing off to meet him, creating disturbances! And again you're wearing only a jacket! Whom are you planning to surprise? It's all your fault, madame."

Vera Nikolaevna bit her lip, walked quickly over to her stepmother, arranged her shawl, and whispered something into her ear. All the woman's rage seemed to disappear; she nodded slightly to her stepdaughter, bowed to me, then greeted Kostya and kissed him.

He fixed his bright eyes on his stepmother's and didn't take them off her even as she kissed him. Curiosity, solicitude, and incomprehension were all reflected in his frank gaze: the inexperienced boy vaguely understood that his stepmother meant a great deal in their family life and that it was essential to get to know her before he could question Verinka.

After the initial inquiries, Kostya lifted his gaze from his stepmother, looked at his father and sister, and then began to think.

But I was more experienced than Kostya, knew all about family life, and had seen a number of wicked women in my time. I surmised a great deal from the stepmother's black, unpleasantly bright eyes, her strong, brusque voice, and her irritating blush, so out of keeping with her sallow complexion.

"And so," Marya Ivanovna asked me, continuing the conversation, "you abandoned Petersburg, life in the capital, luxury?"

I replied that since splendor and luxury weren't available to me, I'd left Petersburg without regret.

The house wasn't far away and we all began walking faster. I escorted Marya Ivanovna; wanting to scrutinize this woman, I talked about theaters and "salons" in which I'd never shown my face. The general began a conversation with the gardener and fell behind us; Kostya and Verinka brought up the rear and were arguing. My sensitive ear caught the following exchanges:

"But she's a scarecrow!" said Kostya. "No matter, I'm head over heels in love with her." "She's tormenting you!" "Why do you think that?" "I'll interrogate her myself." "You'll insult me by doing so." "Then you tell me." "Enough of that: what a capricious boy you are!"

I doubled my pace and initiated a conversation with the general's wife. She spoke about depravity, insubordination among the peasants, and old man Nadezhin's unforgivable weakness. Verinka, exchanging remarks with Kostya, listened in on our conversation with difficulty.

The poor girl's situation seemed to resemble that of the proud pauper to whose table a wealthy and whimsical friend has invited himself for dinner. In vain does the beggar treat him to expensive cigars, in vain does he double his solicitude and tell lies regardless of the consequences—he can't conceal his poverty and embarrassment, can't adorn his pathetic apartment, can't pull the wool over his guest's penetrating gaze.

It was clear that in the general's household all was not well; it was apparent that Vera Nikolaevna had experienced considerable grief. But it was hard to discern the details, especially for Kostya. Verinka managed the entire household; the stepmother, apparently, only knew how to rave about the capital and the aristocracy. But that wasn't much: as soon as an argument was about to erupt, as soon as the general's wife prepared to abuse her poor husband, as soon as Kostya began trying to learn something, Vera Nikolaevna would arrive on the scene instantly. Her appearance was like that of a guardian angel: everyone would fall silent, start smiling, and tranquillity would return.

I admired the young girl passionately and in fact was able to understand her more quickly than anyone else. I even grasped the essential meaning of one circumstance that produced an unpleasant impression on Kostya. The general's entire house was arranged in a rather luxurious way, not in accordance with the owner's real income. The furniture was magnificent, the garden elegantly laid out, and all the servants wore frock coats and white gloves. Such decorum prevailed that Marya Ivanovna herself, upon entering the house, quieted down and said very little, afraid to contradict the fashionable surroundings. This luxury constituted a burden for the stepmother.

Dinner and the evening passed quietly and cheerfully. The general's wife clearly revered her stepson, who was a nice young man indeed, a *mignon** much beloved by forty-year-old women.

*Favorite.

Kostya seemed to forget his own warning about the stepmother; he joked with her, teased her, jumped up from the table, pestered Verinka, sat on his father's lap, pulled his mustache, drank wine with him, called in all the servants, exchanged kisses with each one, sent for his old wet nurse, and brought the whole household to a point of absolute ecstasy. Verinka couldn't get enough of her brother; the stepmother gave free rein to her husband—only the old man regarded Kostya with some lack of understanding and seemed to be surprised at the absence of ceremony in his Emile-like behavior.

When night came, we were escorted to a small wing of the house, the windows of which, lit by the moon, barely emerged from behind some huge dahlias. The floor, doors, and windowsills of our room were hewn of plain wood and astonished us by their coquettish neatness. Bouquets of dahlias and asters stood near the windows; a fire crackled in the fireplace and cheerfully lit the entire room.

I sat down by the fire and became lost in thought. My comrade's family reminded me of many painful moments in my own life. Soon these reminiscences faded and Verinka's image rose before me in all its wonderful, fascinating appeal. On the first day of our acquaintance this girl had engendered an inexplicable feeling of hostility in me; this feeling, although it didn't actually strengthen my love, nevertheless lent it a strange, unnatural, somber character.

All the while Kostya sat on the arm of my chair and, as he was accustomed to doing, placed his face against my chest and embraced me with fitful intensity.

"Kostya, my child, what's the matter?" I asked, fearing this unexpected burst of emotion.

"Aleksei," he said with difficulty, "you've seen my sister. . . .

For God's sake, what's wrong with her? Was I telling you the truth?"

I tried to comfort him.

"What's gotten into your head?" I said calmly. "She's a little bored: who wouldn't be, living in the country?"

"No, no," Kostya replied. "It doesn't matter that she's in the country. Baron Retzel has been courting her; he's a lieutenant, wealthy and handsome. She's refused him point-blank. Aleksei, she's ill and going to die soon."

Grief led to an attack of hysteria. I brought him some water and helped him recover; I dismissed the idea of his sister's illness. I knew she wasn't physically ill.

"But what's wrong with her?" Kostya asked me once again. "Why has she grown so thin and why's she so sad all the time?"

"What can I tell you? It seems to me she doesn't get along very well with your stepmother."

"Not get along? What do you mean, not get along? Who dares not get along with Verinka? Why doesn't she have it out with our stepmother, why doesn't she throw her out, run away from her? Drive her away from my father?"

How could I answer these questions? Kostya didn't know much about family life; this strange child didn't even suspect the existence of hundreds of fatal dramas that are played out, not with shouts or thunder, but with intense grief. My mouth wouldn't dare relate such tragic tales.

But Kostya started to cry again; slight shudders began to shake his limbs.

"Aleksei," he said through tears, "help me . . . teach me. I haven't lived among people . . . I've seen so little of women . . . they only kissed me and rocked me in their arms. . . . I love them, but I don't understand them. I love my stepmother, but

I'm afraid of her. . . . My friend, I don't know what's happening all around me . . . I don't understand this life. I'm afraid for my sister; Verinka's having a hard time . . . very hard. . . . Explain it to me, you've lived with your relatives, you have a sister, you love Verinka . . . explain it to me, all of it. . . ."

My heart swelled. The terrible wail of this pure, innocent soul shook my insides. Tears that hadn't flowed for some time welled up in my eyes, and for the first time in my life another person's grief aroused genuine compassion in me with no hostile admixture. In the whole world only Kostya could display as much misery in my presence as he wanted: I couldn't ever be angry at him.

Vera Nikolaevna's sonorous voice roused me from my painful embarrassment.

"Now then, Kostya," she cried from the garden, "have you changed your mind about taking a stroll, you sleepyhead?"

Kostya forgot all about our conversation. "Coming, Vera, right away!" he cried, smiling through his tears. He ran to the stairs, opened the door, bounded down all ten steps, and went running after his sister. One could hear their appalling shouts, noise, and laughter: holding hands, they ran down the steep path, made their way right to the river, and disappeared into the evening mist hovering in uneven patches over the swampy outskirts.

The river was dammed up there and formed something like a broad lake about fifty paces from the wing of the house. The noise of falling water reached my ears; the old lime trees, leaning down over the water, dropped their leaves, which were turning yellow earlier than usual. At times one could catch a glimpse of Verinka's bright mantilla among the trees.

For a long time I sat near the window and gazed in that direction. The bright, moonlit, dark blue night somehow looked me sadly in the eye; I didn't feel like sleeping, but everything became gloomier and gloomier. Kostya returned in an hour, completely exhausted, got undressed immediately, and threw himself into bed.

"That confounded girl! She didn't tell me a thing . . . ," he muttered as he was falling asleep.

»»» «««

The Fourth Evening

The day after the conversation I've described I met Aleksei Dmitrich on Nevsky Prospect. It turned out that neither of us had slept the night before: I'd been playing cards, while my friend kept tossing from side to side, disturbing his own serene composure with recollections of days gone by. As a result of this circumstance, we decided to afford each other a pleasure appropriate to Aleksei Dmitrich's taste.

Having dined in a most gastronomic manner, we headed back to his apartment, locked all the doors, ordered the shutters closed, lay down to sleep, and slept until eleven o'clock that evening.

I awoke and was horrified to hear the clock chiming. The room was illuminated by a red fire in the warm stove and my friend was sitting near the fire, smoking with the enjoyment of a man who'd learned to smoke in the fresh air, in rain and bad weather.

"Hey, most esteemed sir!" I shouted, drawing my armchair closer to the fire. "Continue your adventures—stories told in the darkness are somehow always more candid and more interesting. Why didn't you wake me? You only claim to sleep for a long time."

The story continued:

Whether it was Kostya who'd so upset me that evening, or whether my fatigue was to blame, nevertheless I had such nasty dreams all night that I can't even relate them here. I got out of bed around eight o'clock, dressed, and wanted to wake Kostya, but the general's butler conveyed Vera Nikolaevna's request not to disturb her brother before he woke up himself.

I began to wander around the garden and near the house. Both there and in the courtyard many house servants were busy with their morning tasks. I kept encountering the quiet, frightened faces of women, sometimes covered with bruises; they exchanged angry words with each other and uttered phrases such as "*akhti-khti*, to live a life . . . " or "o-o-oho, life, our life," utterances that abound in a Russian's vocabulary during both bad times and good.

Occasionally these women expressed themselves more definitively. "Hey, what a wicked woman!" "Oh, woman, you woman!" uttered in a biting tone, described the stepmother's impact on her subjects and cast some light on the general's familial and household affairs.

Some twenty paces from me, near the house, the mistress's irritated voice could be heard thundering: it rose to a high C and then scattered like small shot. Marya Ivanovna, her head leaning out the window, wearing rather flimsy apparel, was reprimanding a crowd of peasants gathered underneath. Her speech was interspersed with expressions that, though not exactly indecent, were certainly inappropriate in the aristocratic circles that the angry general's wife so loved to describe.

This is what was happening. The evening before, there had been a patronal festival, which, in olden times, had given the peasants the right to ignore the corvée[36] for three days straight and drink beer to their heart's content. This privilege had been revoked by the stepmother, but the peasants, meek and obedient when confronted with all other oppressions, always protested when it came time for their one patronal festival during the year. On this occasion, having lodged their complaint before the young gentleman's arrival, they dispatched their elders to ask for Vera Nikolaevna's intercession. The unfortunate delegation didn't find the young lady at home, but did encounter the mistress of the house, who greeted them in her own fashion. The poor peasants stood there scratching the backs of their heads, twisting their necks, and maintaining their timid silence. My appearance saved them from any further disaster; judging from the woman's raised voice, her verbal abuse was soon to be followed by other, more energetic measures. But upon seeing me, Marya Ivanovna was ashamed of her morning negligé, and, to the great relief of the poor delegation, her wrinkled cap and dirty tunic soon disappeared from the window.

Without replacing their hats, the delegation set off on its way home and at a bend in the road met Verinka, who was just coming out of the garden. She stopped the peasants and spoke several words to them. It was obvious that the young woman's words were very comforting because the old men began bowing deeply and kissing her little hand; they headed off in different directions with cheerful grins on their faces.

"You get up so early, Vera Nikolaevna," I said, approaching her. She rested her elbow on my arm and we went back into the garden.

"I must scold you in earnest, Aleksei Dmitrich," she said rather drily. "What nonsense did you tell Kostya about me? All evening he tormented me with his questions. Why did you take it into your head that I don't get along with my mother?"

"Wouldn't it be better to ask why your stepmother doesn't

get along with you?" I replied, emphasizing the word step-mother.

"I know you used to live in a family and you may even have suffered there. But why say things to Kostya that he doesn't understand?"

I wanted to justify myself and conveyed the content of the conversation we'd had in our wing of the house. Tears welled up in her eyes and then disappeared.

"Kostya's an angel," she said pensively. "There's never been such a wonderful child on this earth. But our life's not as he would like it, and he's letting himself in for much grief. . . ."

"It's easy to deal with him," I said. "Only his eyes are so sharp-sighted. That unfortunate portrait of you occasioned his gloomy thoughts; behave a little more coolly, look more cheerful, and he'll forget all about it."

Verinka blushed and tossed her head.

"What's that you say?" she asked angrily. "I'm not going to disguise my expression for an eccentric child! Thank heaven I'm not at boarding school anymore . . . no one can order me to look more cheerful . . . there's an end to my patience! I have enough to worry about!"

She grew frightened at her irritable response, one that ex-plained her situation to me more than she had intended.

We strolled around the garden for a long time and talked about our concerns but—you'll have to excuse me—I'm getting dis-tracted by Kostya and Verinka, while I intend to remain in the shadows.

About an hour and a half later we went back to the old man and settled down to have tea in his room. The stepmother, appar-ently, had already succeeded in abusing her husband because the general was in a very bad mood. Accustomed to his regular life, he was annoyed with Kostya, who, having exhausted himself the previous evening, was still asleep. Finally, in spite of Verinka's requests, he sent his butler in to wake his son and summon him to appear and have tea.

But at that very moment Kostya came running into the room with much noise and cheerful laughter, lively, fresh, wild as ever. Not a trace of yesterday's grief could be seen in his eyes. Without paying any attention to his stern father or his remarks, he greeted everyone, teased each and every one of us, ran around the house, and sat down to tea near the table. But he didn't want to sit anywhere except on Verinka's lap. In all the commotion they somehow got caught on the table, it started to shake, the cups clattered, and the heavy samovar nearly tumbled onto the floor. The general was furious.

"Enough of this, Konstantin!" he cried harshly, banging his fist on the table. "Sit still; what a terror you are! Hey, you haven't been beaten enough; that's it, that's upbringing nowadays!"

"And . . . and I won't listen to you!" Kostya shouted back at him, continuing to carry on with his sister. "See, what a complainer he is! And, so angry! Sit down, Vera. . . ."

The general was absolutely staggered by this Emile-like display of informality. For some time it had gone against his grain that Kostya addressed him in such a familiar way. There might have been an unpleasant scene if the stepmother hadn't interceded on Kostya's behalf. At her first words the old man was appeased and fell silent.

Kostya didn't give his sister any peace. "Why do you have such a slim waist?" he asked her. "It's not at all becoming. Hey, what skinny shoulders you have! Why's that? What does it mean?"

At these last words Kostya jumped up from his armchair and stood on the floor directly opposite his stepmother.

"What's this I've been told," he said quickly, "something to the effect that you don't get along well with Vera? If you don't get along with her, it must be that you alone are to blame."

The general blanched, Vera Nikolaevna blanched, the stepmother blanched and cast a malicious, satanic look at the poor girl. Kostya alone noticed nothing and continued speaking.

"You probably scold her all the time and criticize her behavior! Vera and I are spoiled children; no one dares scold us . . . no one dares criticize us . . . that's what. Well, don't be angry."

I expected a terrible squabble, but, to everyone's great relief, the matter was peacefully resolved. In the last day and a half Kostya had acquired such power over his stepmother that she remained silent during his questioning and then replied meekly and sensibly. Vera Nikolaevna was trembling; as a result I could see what the stepmother was capable of in moments of anger. Kostya wouldn't have let go of her for one moment, I could bear witness to that.

By making various jokes at Kostya's expense, I succeeded in turning the matter around and changing the subject. But the previous harmony could no longer be restored among us. The general was clearly annoyed at Kostya, the stepmother was on the lookout for some convenient opportunity to repay Verinka's audacity, Vera Nikolaevna was unintentionally angry at me and felt that Kostya's continued presence in their household would lead to endless difficulties. Kostya himself became pensive on two further occasions and at dinner got angry at everyone, even picking constant quarrels with me and his sister.

After dinner the general retired for a nap and the stepmother declared that she had to finish reading some books sent her from Petersburg—that is, in other words, to occupy herself for three hours. The sun had set in full splendor, an evening breeze had arisen and begun to rustle the drying leaves; Vera Nikolaevna, Kostya, and I headed out into the garden.

At first we chatted cheerfully, then Kostya fell to thinking once again and became gloomier and gloomier, as never before.

"Listen, Sister," he said at last, jumping up from the bench where we'd been sitting all in a row. "Somehow or other this has to stop! The devil take me if I can understand anything of your affairs. Father, you, and Stepmother all live so very badly. Father's sunk so low, and you've grown so very thin. Let's start with you at least; looking at your portrait, I know I'm not mistaken. I have seen grief; I've been oppressed, ill-treated, tormented. But I knew who was tormenting me. . . . I despised and knew whom to despise . . . whom to avenge. . . ."

Vera Nikolaevna looked timidly at Kostya, who at this moment was no longer a child.

"Tell me, Vera," he said gently, "who's tormenting you? Why have you grown so thin, why are you so often angry, why are you grieving?"

Vera Nikolaevna looked at him with surprise and burst out laughing.

"Where does all this come from?" she asked. "Can one really grieve here?"

"Yes. You see I'm grieving."

"Nonsense, you're pretending. As if you didn't love our garden? As if these old lime trees weren't to your liking? Look at the wonderful evening, the fine trees, the pleasant autumn. . . ."

"Your autumn is nasty. Is it cheerful to look at trees that'll die in a month?"

"But they'll be reborn next spring. . . ."

"I don't like that rebirth. If there is rebirth, then there was death. And death's a nasty thing."

I'd never seen Kostya so angry. Vera Nikolaevna smiled and then led us down to the little stream, which we crossed on a small raft. Near the opposite pier stood a mound overgrown with old pine trees. Neither wind nor cold dared invade the area shaded by these trees. The sand beneath them was dry, soft, and comfortable for sitting. We lay down underneath the pines.

"Here's immortality for you!" Verinka said in jest. "Isn't it nice here?"

Kostya looked more cheerful.

"It's so nice," he said, "that I'd seriously like to stay here with you. You go on alone, Aleksei; I'll send along some certificate and settle here with my father. It's too early for me to fight battles."

This time it was Verinka who blanched. But I was positively delighted. I'd been tormented by my conscience for some time for dragging this weak child with me to unwholesome and dangerous lands, for not making greater efforts to dissuade him from his desire to pursue military adventures.

"But how will you do it?" Vera Nikolaevna asked.

"Very simply, I won't go, and that's that."

"You must behave differently," I said. "Tomorrow I'll take it upon myself to speak with the general. Even a blind man can see all too well that at your age and with your health it's too early for you to roam the face of the earth. A doctor will provide you with a document testifying to your illness, and then, perhaps, without having to leave home, you can request a transfer into one of the regiments stationed here."

My plan was approved. I felt sad, but my conscience required me to do it; besides, Kostya's presence seemed essential for the family.

Just then, from the other side of the stream, we heard His

Excellency's voice. He was calling Kostya to help him cross over to our side. Kostya ran toward his father, while his sister moved even closer toward me.

"Aleksei Dmitrich," she said in a trembling voice, "dissuade my brother. There's no reason for him to stay here. . . ."

I looked at her with surprise.

"That's very odd! Are you hoping he'll be killed in the Caucasus?"

Her whole body shuddered.

"He won't be killed, that I know," she declared firmly. "God didn't create him to perish in his youth. . . ."

"That's fine in books, but not in life," I objected. "Why shouldn't he stay here with you?"

"My God! My God!" Verinka uttered with some effort. "He'll be much unhappier here. . . . I won't be able to endure it. . . ."

"I don't think so. What appears to you as sorrow may not really be that. Together you'll be able to overcome all misfortune," I added in jest.

"For heaven's sake, dissuade him."

"I can't guarantee it: I understand the necessity and agree with him."

"Nevertheless, he'll go, I tell you!"

Her eyes flared, just as Kostya's did when he got angry.

"I don't know," I replied coolly. "I'll do what I can."

Early the next morning I was in the garden pondering my words and my plan of attack on old man Nadezhin's paternal feelings. I soon encountered him with his inseparable Antigone.

The old man listened to me with an absentminded expression as I described Kostya's health and his situation. He would absolutely not allow him to remain there in the country. In vain did I try to persuade him; he behaved as if he were deaf: he appeared to have grown completely decrepit in one night. Only when I emphasized Kostya's youth did he reply, "At the age of thirteen I sailed in galleys against the Swedes."

Then he related the endless story of his first campaign.

I didn't give a damn about the Swedes or the galleys and looked at Vera Nikolaevna. She was paler than usual, but didn't say a word during my entire conversation with her father.

The old man settled down on a bench, finished his story, and became thoughtful. I went up to his daughter.

"I feel sorry for Kostya," I said to her. "You caused a quarrel between him and his father. He won't leave here."

She looked at me boldly.

"Perhaps you didn't hear?"

"What makes you think Kostya will obey his father?"

Verinka looked at me in surprise.

"You've forgotten," I went on, "that your brother isn't ten years old and that he's terribly stubborn. Remember his upbringing . . . you think he'll obey your weak father when dozens of teachers were unable to oppose his smallest whim?"

She became thoughtful and smiled faintly.

"Count on me," she said. "It'll all come out for his own good."

The general was starting to doze and we walked toward the house. I was surprised by this young girl who, not content to deal just with her own worries, engaged in battle with her best friend without worrying about any difficulties. . . . Near the wing of the house we met Kostya, and all three of us sat down on the dry grass.

"My goodness, you look so pretty today!" he said to his sister. "I'm sure you spent two hours getting dressed. Let me give you a kiss."

Verinka wouldn't allow it and sat down behind Kostya so he couldn't turn his head toward her pretty little lips.

"Kostya," she said, putting her hands on his shoulders, "Papa doesn't want you to stay here. We asked him, but to no avail. . . ."

"I'll stay nevertheless," Kostya said softly.

Vera Nikolaevna realized that it was impossible to argue with him.

"My friend," she said, leaning closer to his face, "take pity on the old man . . . I give you my word, he himself will summon you home in a year. . . ."

Kostya wanted to embrace his sister once more, but she quickly turned away with charming coquetry.

"There's no reason to worry about me, my friend," she said, continuing to flirt with her brother. "I'm happy, I tell you. . . . Why do you insist on quarreling with father? Listen to me, my darling. . . ."

She reached for Kostya's shoulder and drew his head down into her lap. Her brown curls covered her brother's eyes, and her little face was bent over his.

Kostya raised his head once more, but his sister avoided his kiss yet again.

Verinka embraced Kostya more tightly and his head rested against her chest. This splendid grouping of two children was easily the equal of Canova's *Amor and Psyche*.[37]

Kostya weakened and submitted. The little pagan, confronted by his sister's coquetry, crumbled into dust before such beauty.

"All right," he said, pressing his head against his sister's chest, "I'll leave. But listen: tell me the whole truth, honest to God, about your life with Father and Stepmother. Most of all, I want to know why your face is so sad. . . ."

Verinka leaned over to her brother and kissed him.

"When you've lived to be my age," she said in jest, "you'll feel sad, too. You're still a little boy."

"Nonsense, nonsense!" cried Kostya. "You just want to bewitch me, you sly girl. I don't want to kiss you; I'm like Joseph . . . I won't listen to you; I'll leave my cloak in your hands. . . ."[38]

He wanted to lift himself up, but glanced at Verinka's face and once more fell back into her embrace.

She leaned over her brother again and this time didn't take her lips away from his face.

"In a year everything will be arranged," she said, interspersing these words with warm kisses. "I give you my word: it's all nonsense, my little secret . . . you'll find out all about it when you come home for your first vacation . . . let Aleksei Dmitrich be a witness. . . ."

She looked at me in embarrassment and once more leaned down to her brother's face.

"Just as you say, Vera," said Kostya in a weak voice, "but be careful that nothing bad happens. . . ."

Within a month we were in Stavropol,[39] and that spring the expeditions began in earnest.

Here Aleksei Dmitrich entered into purely strategic details and even unfolded a map of the Caucasus; I listened very carefully, but couldn't restrain myself and yawned. My host smiled and immediately curtailed his military considerations and transported me to some godforsaken battlefield. Only from the name of the forest was I able, albeit approximately, to determine the location of my friend's heroic deeds. Since I'd long forgotten my military service, I can't convey his account very skillfully; I apologize in advance and in any case will try to cut these scenes short.

The farther we made our way into the forest, the more unwillingness and timidity appeared among us. Smoke had already hidden the narrow spaces between the trees; at times bullets shrieked past me and struck the thick trunk of a larch with an unpleasant thud. Indeed, my position was not altogether advantageous for my first debut: I had to push my way through the thicket, afraid to lose sight of my scattered detachment; in addition, I had to keep an eye on Kostya, whose military proclivities had begun to trouble me in earnest. At first he went along rather serenely and reserved his ammunition, dragging his awkward old flintlock with considerable effort; but after seeing his first wounded man, he became very angry and kept firing at random, in full confidence that every one of his shots would inflict terrible destruction on the enemies' ranks. He kept running up to me asking questions: "Will we be fighting soon? Where are those Circassian beasts?"[40]

But the trees began to thin out and soon a small meadow opened before us; a shallow ravine overgrown with bushes cut straight across it. Two or three shots could be heard from the opposite forest wall, then everything was silent. An open space, some fifty paces in all, separated us from the enemy, but there was no way to cross it other than under enemy fire. One slain mountaineer lay on the edge of the ravine and, counter to the rules of his fellow countrymen, he hadn't been picked up. A shaggy noncommissioned officer in our regiment went up to the body. Only one shot rang out from the enemy's side, and the poor chasseur fell down dead on top of the corpse. Our line halted and hid behind the trees, waiting for further orders.

Our company commander had suffered shell shock at the very beginning of the campaign, and the line commander was giving orders on the other flank, so the fate of hundreds of men rested with me. I'm not a coward, but I was inexperienced: I knew each one of Napoleon's campaigns like the palm of my hand and could recount all the stages of the battle at Leipzig,[41] but all this information was inappropriate for the present occasion. I realized, however, that until we received new orders we should halt near the edge of the forest and not set foot on the meadow, where they could shoot at us as if we were grouse.

Having given that order, I emerged from the forest first, successfully made my way up to a high rock and, hiding behind it, tried to determine the enemy's position. But Kostya's patience gave out: he couldn't understand that war isn't an incessant, ecstatic march to attack, but rather an exhausting period of waiting, punctuated occasionally by moments of brief wild skirmishes. Discipline went against my friend's grain: this unbearable child made his way alone out of the forest and, without paying any attention to the bullets whizzing past us, began inciting me to new exploits.

I grew absolutely furious, wanted to chase him away, but suddenly Kostya cried out, turned pale, and grabbed his left arm. His uniform was torn at the shoulder and blood was gushing from the opening. I felt calmer; the wound wasn't serious.

But now no one could control Kostya: his insane impulsiveness manifested itself in a fatal manner. Seeing his own blood, his whole body shuddered; he screamed, clenched his teeth, tore himself from my arms, and rushed in the direction from which smoke was still visible from the last shots fired. In a moment or two he'd run twenty paces, but at the same time four mountaineers in tattered beshmets[42] emerged from behind a bush, seized the poor lad, and dragged him off to the forest, from which another two dozen or so bold fellows appeared, as if wishing to snatch away his diminutive booty.

I forgot everything on earth, lunged forward, and took command of an assault. In half a minute we routed the whole enemy band; in the scuffle I shoved the largest of the Circassians aside and grabbed poor Kostya from his temporarily loosened grip. Kostya was unable to stand on his own feet and pointed to his chest; I lifted him up, tossed him over my left shoulder, and only then saw what a careless thing I'd done to my subordinates.

Hundreds of rifles were pointing at us from bushes near the

ravine, above the ravine, and from the forest opposite. Shots rang out like a drumroll. Gathering into a tight group, we made our way into the forest, but a huge number of the enemy were heading straight toward us.

I was overcome by some insane anguish. I wanted to vanish into thin air, to die, but the bullets didn't touch me. Our line didn't suffer significant losses; after collecting our wounded, we made our way into the depths of the forest, but I remained behind the first trees at the edge. The enemy was still pressing forward: way out in front of all the others, the one Murid[43] whom I'd so easily thrust aside was running straight toward me. The whole scene lasted only two or three minutes, but as long as I live it'll remain fresh in my memory. As long as I live I'll never forget the sallow expression of that obese horseman, his enormous nose hanging down like a shaft-bow over his bristly, almost blue mustache. He came right at me, although he could've shot both me and Kostya without risking a skirmish: he clearly wanted to capture my friend alive.

Only someone who, to his own misfortune, has engaged in hand-to-hand combat knows how a man's strength can increase if he sees no possible escape from danger. My head strained forward, my chest tensed and expanded, my left arm, which was supporting Kostya's body, felt not the least bit of fatigue. Waving my weapon, I rushed forward, my right side protected by the trunk of a fallen larch that had long since scattered its needles on the damp earth. On the left side the thicket stood like a wall— the enraged Circassian came toward me head-on; the saber in his hand, brandished on the right, attested to his diabolical strength.

It was impossible either to attack him or to repulse his blows: I swung my arm and our sabers met with incredible force. Our lives depended on the strength of the steel, but my saber was wretched, made of thick iron. It saved me. My blow landed a little above the hilt of his; the Muslim warrior's slender steel saber rang out and broke into pieces.

His whole body curved like a snake; he dug his heels into the ground, jumped backward, and grabbed his dagger, large as a broadsword. But my jump was just as sure. The moment my legs hit the ground, my weapon struck the Murid's unprotected shoulder and tore into the center of his chest. He fell as if struck by lightning. I don't recall whether even a hundredth of the energy that surged within me that moment was ever to appear again. With inconceivable clarity my eyes saw everything that happened on both sides of me and penetrated far into the thicket; my head was brimful of thoughts, but they were clear and not at all confused. In my hands I felt a great, feverish strength, and I awaited a new attack in complete composure. But the entire crowd of the enemy disappeared to the right without paying me the least attention. I was cut off and separated from my detachment.

Gradually my brutal, agitated state of mind subsided: Kostya began to moan and twist on my shoulder; once again all my thoughts were directed to my poor friend, and I began running without really knowing in what direction.

The battle had yet to end; at times shots resonated near me and bullets cut through branches on both sides. Kostya, afraid of falling, held on to my neck so tightly that it was hard for me to breathe. God only knows how I made my way through the thick growth of trees and managed not to pierce our heads a thousand times on twigs as thick as boards. Branches slashed across my eyes painfully, shots rang out shrilly and resoundingly on both sides—something terrible, wildly poetic, was contained in the twilight of that dense forest, in those shots, in the enemy's wild, dissonant voices.

Thus I ran for a long, long time and finally wandered into the deepest backwoods. Everything was quiet all around; no human traces could be seen, even though trees were sparse and burnt stumps stood everywhere, the result of a recent fire. I caught my breath and proceeded more slowly, glancing occasionally at my poor companion. He was pale and cried out whenever an awkward movement disturbed his wound; he clung to me with all the strength of a young creature who values his life. He knew how difficult it was for me to manage and sporadically tried to smile and encourage me. Blood slowly dripped from his chest and shoulder; soon he lost consciousness.

Suddenly, not far from us there resounded a terrible exchange of gunfire and I heard people shouting. For some time I'd been hearing noises and muffled speech on one side. Hoping to begin some new stage, I headed boldly toward the shots, constantly shoving the bushes aside with my hand, jumping over bony skeletons of fallen, scorched trees. Every so often I glanced at Kostya and listened to his breathing; every minute seemed like a year. Almost another hour passed; we finally reached the place where a skirmish was in progress. A narrow road broken by tall rocks and large, interwoven roots of trees, had been occupied by several hundred troops of a certain militia. A company of cavalrymen stood behind. There were no mountaineers to be seen anywhere, neither retreat nor assault; meanwhile an exchange of fire was in full swing, and dozens of dead men were sprawling in the middle of the road. Along both sides of the detachment stood the eternal, inevitable forest, overhung with gunpowder smoke swaying lazily, like fog amid a wooded swamp.

Here I witnessed one of those disastrous scenes that often occur in military actions taken in broken terrain against a deceitful and hardened enemy. The small detachment in question was sent to circle around a winding and little-known road; in the middle of its path it encountered an unexpected obstacle. Ahead the road seemed to be blocked by large bushes, behind which fires flickered and shots were being fired. But an experienced eye could discern that these were not bushes but huge trees, cut down and positioned in such a way that their strong branches stuck straight up. The enemy was concealed behind these tree trunks and was defending this green fortress, known to our heroes of the Caucasus as an "obstruction."

A small column on the right side endured even more. Under cover of the forest, mountaineers fired shots at their own discretion. In vain did our marksmen try to drive them into the open: as soon as the attack subsided, the enemy appeared once again in its previous place. Several brave men ran along the road firing at the chasseurs' tail. The detachment was in obvious danger, but held its ground, prepared to expend its last efforts against the enormous, superior strength of the enemy.

Suddenly a joyful cry arose from bands of chasseurs; all heads turned to the rear; reinforcements were coming to the rescue.

All along the road to my right two new battalions were advancing, winding like a long serpent, flashing hundreds of bayonets. Men marched serenely, in as orderly a fashion as the uneven road would permit, without slowing or hurrying their pace. Out in front, on a dark bay, rode a dashing young lieutenant dressed in a fashionable uniform; rocking lazily in his saddle, squinting his eyes, he looked at his own troops, the enemy, and the obstruction, which, it seemed, was burning and smoking, so heated was its defenders' fire.

At a time of danger subordinates conceive an incomprehensible sympathy for the man whose command can result in victory, end in defeat, or escape from death. . . . I eagerly scrutinized the lieutenant's cold, pale face, and, indeed, his alert expression, his serene bearing in the saddle, and his most relaxed gaze promised both victory and success.

He drew even with me and rose up in his stirrups: "Get down!" he cried, hardly opening his mouth.

But his voice was loud and clear. The whole detachment standing between the obstruction and the new battalions threw itself to the ground. The lieutenant turned his head back, waved his arm, and galloped forward; eight columns of men extending along the edges of the road followed their commander.

The obstruction was surrounded on three sides and captured after a brief, though desperate, defense. The mountaineers paid dearly for their first few moments of success: they were driven back into the forest and took terrible losses. During their chaotic flight hundreds of them met their deaths from our sharpshooters' bayonets.

All during the skirmish the young lieutenant never drew his saber from its sheath, didn't allow himself even one ecstatic gesture, though it certainly would have been permissible in such a case. He reined in his horse at the obstruction and observed the course of the action, rocking in his saddle as before, nibbling the glove on his left hand. A cloud of smoke hanging over the site of the battle dispersed at times and revealed, in all its noble beauty, the meditative figure of the detachment's commander.

And—marvel at the strangeness of human nature—I myself, not at all a warlike person, an enemy of battle scenes and destructive motives, while gazing at this total stranger to me, forgot all the horror of my own situation. A passionate, unconscious sympathy, the result of a disturbing day and thousands of new sensations, took root in my heart. I could hardly catch my breath; without worrying about anything, I stood there under the gunfire and couldn't tear my eyes away from this fascinating lieutenant.

Having exhausted all my strength, not seeking anything resembling assistance, still carrying Kostya in my arms, I entered the forest where the bullets had yet to reach and carefully laid him on the soft grass. He was unconscious, the flow of blood had caused his chest to stick to my shoulder, and it took some considerable effort to disentangle my burden. It was impossible to assess the size and depth of his wound.

The sun had already set and the bright pink color of the sky shone through the leaves hanging over us. The air was cooling rapidly, and it revived Kostya: color reappeared in his face; he sighed heavily and opened his eyes with the thoughtful look of a child waking up in a strange place. The pain in his chest made itself felt at once; he cried out and reached for the bandage I'd hastily improvised. The horrible fever of southern climes began to torment him; we had nothing except my short jacket.

"Well, is it very painful?" I asked Kostya, trying to warm his cold hands.

But he didn't hear my question or respond to my kindness. First he tossed and raved, then came to again, got angry at me with his customary impulsiveness, complained about his pain and the cold—then called to his sister, gave commands, and imagined he was still fighting a battle. These bellicose outbursts, so incompatible with his previous indifference to military scenes, moved me most of all.

The firing had died down some time before; I was certain that we were close to our own detachment. It seemed that white soldiers' caps could be glimpsed fleetingly not far off in the distance. I wanted to stand up, but lacked strength—wanted to cry out, but lacked strength. I had been feeling tired before, while still standing, but the last brief moments of rest, as usually happens, weakened me once and for all. My whole body felt as if it were being stuck with needles; my feet wouldn't budge and my knees ached terribly; my left arm had fallen asleep and felt as if it were two miles long; the trees, stumps, and thick grass all danced before my eyes. In my exhaustion, close to losing consciousness, I leaned over Kostya, instinctively pressed against him, and was just about to fall asleep.

At that moment a small, thin hand was lowered onto my shoulder and someone's loud but extremely pleasant voice began speaking to me in French. With effort I turned my head, and before me stood that young lieutenant I just described.

"Come over here quickly," he said. "*Soyez le bienvenu, monsieur.** Your detachment is far from here, very far, so you'll spend the night here with us."

He noticed my fatigue, leaned over, took Kostya in his arms, and helped me stand.

"Poor child!" he said, more with annoyance than pity, as he regarded my friend. "When will these boys stop butting in and interfering with us? . . . "

We returned to the bivouac—I could scarcely move my legs. The commander summoned one of his officers and handed me and my heavy burden over to him.

"Come see me tomorrow," he said, bidding me a polite farewell. "I saw you both in Stavropol and remember you well. My name is Retzell and I'm the commander of such and such regiment."

Upon hearing this man's name, so renowned for his vagaries and bravery, I wanted to make some respectful gesture and almost fell off my feet.

I don't recall who took me by the arm, led me to the campfire,

*Welcome, sir.

poured a glass of vodka into me, and offered me some tea. Immediately afterward I fell fast asleep.

The next day I awoke very late. I experienced a strange weakness in all my limbs, my eyes constantly opened and stuck together again, my reason wandered lazily and stubbornly refused to undertake its usual work. My sleep was so sound that I'd heard neither the exchange of fire nor the uproar that had occurred during the night. The mountaineers didn't leave us in peace; they regrouped in the forest and toward morning attacked the advance guards. Fortunately, a change of guard was occurring just at that time, so a double complement of pickets met the attack. Baron Retzell, as the officers near me related, was first to appear at the skirmish and as usual rode under the enemy's bullets, repulsed the attackers, and drove them back into the forest. Then, without praising or condemning his subordinates, he rode away, after ordering his entire detachment to get some rest.

My neighbors concluded their conversation with enthusiastic praise for Retzell; then one of them looked at me and declared his lighthearted uncertainty as to whether I was still alive.

I was only half awake and listening to their speech in a state of oblivion. The officers' words arose clearly in my imagination, without touching my faculty of reason, and appeared before me as some kind of dream, as usually happens when one is half asleep. First I saw a group of Lezghians[44] with long noses, then the slim figure of the young lieutenant stood before me with his long black mustache and a cold, theatrical expression on his face. For a moment I was absolutely convinced that everything I heard was a dream: the officers began recounting the dead and wounded, and I made a great effort to rouse myself. The following possibility even flashed through my mind: I wondered if

I'd read too much Marlinksy[45] the night before, and perhaps that was the reason I was having such improbable dreams.

Suddenly I jumped up like a madman, but there was no madness; on the contrary, the fog clouding my head dispersed for a moment and I realized at once where I was, who I was, and in that same moment recalled the past, understood the present, and peered into the future. One of the officers had uttered the name of my regiment and Kostya's surname.

I stood up; my fatigue had passed. Within half a minute I'd fastened my jacket and was already a hundred paces away from my astonished neighbors. My heart was hardly beating; some instinct led me on. I stood in front of the tent occupied by the commander of the detachment; two medics were going in—it was probably that circumstance that directed my journey. Before my eyes infrequent trees and stacked rifles engaged in a terrible dance, while the tent seemed to grow bigger and began to resemble an Egyptian pyramid, or else it became smaller and receded entirely into the distance, as if I were looking at it through the wrong end of a looking glass.

"*Entrez donc, monsieur,*"* I heard the sound of Baron Retzell's pleasant voice from inside the tent. "We've been waiting for you all morning; the poor little fellow wanted to come have a look at you himself . . . *le pauvre petit.*"†

I entered a small tent furnished with eccentric elegance. Kostya was lying on a bed that the lieutenant had given up for him, and two doctors bustled about him solicitously. A fatal blush played on his face, the symptom of fever, inflammation, or infection. He had changed tremendously during the night and now resembled an eight-year-old child. Never before in anyone's face

*Come in, sir.
†The poor little fellow.

had I ever seen such changes; notwithstanding all this, God only knows why, I guessed that this change was a sign of approaching death. Kostya gave me his hand—it was hot as fire, and he pulled me down and kissed me. . . .

On the edge of the bed sat the owner of the tent, the commander of the detachment, already known to you; he was entertaining Kostya, showing him various splendid items, including, by the way, three medals removed from his own uniform. The poor lad held his chest occasionally, wept quite openly, or got angry with the doctors who were quietly ministering to him; sometimes he became calm, took Retzell by the hand, and began joking or arguing with him.

Baron Retzell was a brilliant representative of that previous younger generation that had lived life to the fullest, very cheerfully at that, had revered Byron, and had played at disenchantment while receiving an annual income of some fifty thousand rubles. In society such people were somewhat vulgar, or at least boring, but during a war their disenchantment was a useful and effective instrument. The baron's life was like an endless theatrical production. While still a young lad he would gallop ahead of his platoon of cuirassiers, constantly spurring on his already overheated charger; as a grown man he loved to participate in assaults on the enemy, halting under fire, never getting excited, and standing there silently as a gloomy philosopher, a cold observer of the general brawl.

But at the same time he behaved extremely well during the affair and inspired the passionate amazement of his subordinates. Always drenched in perfume, always dressed in uniform, he rode very poorly, and at every possible opportunity threw his legs over one side, never dispatched his troops in vain, and watched coldly and grimly as their front ranks came under fire. If his adjutants galloped up to him with hurried orders, he listened to them serenely, paid them compliments, and issued commands lazily; yet his entire regiment, and I, sinner that I am, I, first of all, would have crawled out of my own skin to please the baron and to distinguish myself in his eyes.

He was about forty years old but looked much younger; he was very handsome, his manners very aristocratic, even too polite. I served two years under his command, felt close to him, but still couldn't make out the man's character very well.

"*Allez donc, mon colonel,*"* Kostya said to him. "I don't need anything, not a thing, not one thing! My chest hurts so much, more than anyone in the world has ever known . . . it's so painful. . . ."

"I know, I know," Retzell replied in jest.

"You're fooling me . . . ," said Kostya, staring intently into the lieutenant's eyes, in which this time there shone some genuine, warm sympathy.

"We'll send you on leave," the baron continued. "Your father will revive all the customs of the old days; he'll dance with joy when he sees you. Have you fallen in love with anyone special?"

"I'm in love with my sister," Kostya replied innocently, smiling at the thought of Verinka.

"You'll see how delighted your sister will be! She'll start carrying you around in her arms. People will begin talking about you and writing about you in the newspapers, and so they should."

"I don't know, so help me God," said Kostya, turning to me, "when I succeeded in doing such things?"

The baron coughed slightly, glancing at me.

"What do you mean, when?" he replied, not letting me utter a word. "The attack by your line decided the whole affair, and you were out ahead of everyone. Then, even though you retreated,

*That will do, Colonel.

we advanced and defeated them. The whole campaign is over; I don't think the war will go on much longer. Rest assured, I don't take such pains for anyone in vain, and if I do, no one ever refuses me."

Kostya smiled again and was absolutely delighted to hear about his own heroic deeds. He was even dissatisfied that the war had ended just as he was embarking on a military career.

"However," he said thoughtfully, "it's time for you all to stop fighting."

I guessed what was happening. In my impatience I got off the bed and led the medic to the corner, the one who was fussing over the cupping-glass[46] with some lotion.

"Tell me, is there really no hope?" I asked, scarcely breathing.

"The wounds themselves are superficial," said the doctor, "and I was feeling very relieved . . . but at his age any wound can be fatal."

"God is merciful," he continued, noticing that I was about to collapse.

"Which means . . . ?"

He realized that it was impossible to deceive me.

"He'll die this evening."

I ran out to get a breath of air. The sun was already moving toward the forest; there was no time to analyze or reflect; all that remained was for me to do everything for Kostya that I possibly could so he would die peacefully, to cheer him up and console him during his last moments.

A few paces away from me a thick larch towered above the sparse trees, its heavy branches almost reaching the ground. The view from it was delightful: not far off the forest grew dark; right in front of me began the gently sloping ascent to some mountain, and millions of colorful flowers adorned the meadow occupied by our detachment.

Absolute lightheartedness and cheerfulness characterized all our men who'd spent the previous day under fire. Groups of chasseurs, colorful militiamen, and cossacks wandered merrily around the bright green meadow flooded with light.

This life and movement, the sun and beauty of nature, inspired my passionate sympathy. It seemed a shame to grieve about Kostya and do nothing to provide him with at least one last moment of joy.

In general I'm slow to appreciate the beauty of nature, but by this time I'd actually become like Kostya. I gathered a few soldiers, sent them off in different directions with orders which they found rather strange to understand. Within five minutes mounds of flowers had been collected and placed under the tall larch, rifle barrels were stuffed with wild roses, sheaves of flowers were fastened together and tossed over the broad branches of the old tree.

Our commander stuck his head out of the tent and understood my idea at once. Kostya was asleep or, more likely, unconscious; we lifted him up quietly, along with his bed, and placed it under the larch, between mounds of wildflowers. We sat down next to him, looked at him, and waited in silence. Before sunset the entire bivouac became animated; life itself, merry conversation, was in full swing not far from us.

Kostya woke up, clapped his hands, laughed, touched the flowers, asked their names, and wanted to get out of bed, constantly calling me and the baron up to the mountain that, according to the mirage, seemed not more than a hundred paces away from us. With difficulty we persuaded him to wait a little while; he was so happy, so cheerful, that even the iron baron couldn't restrain himself and moved to one side, wiping his forehead.

Indeed, the scene around us was splendid. The last rays of the sun cast a violet light on the whole slope of the mountain, the branches of the tree under which we sat intersected and overhung them, like bunches of pure gold. The flowers shone no less than rubies and sapphires, the terrible forest looked so inviting! All its black trees led upward, and one's eye could follow the illuminated patches for some distance.

"My goodness, it's so nice here!" said Kostya, beside himself with rapture. "I'll stay here to sleep, wake me early tomorrow morning. I'd like to live here; all of this, mountain and forest, I'd make it into a park. I'd drive you and the regiment out of here, *vous autres exterminateurs!*"*

This was directed at Baron Retzell, who'd drawn near again and was sitting quietly at the head of Kostya's bed.

"He hasn't guessed," said the baron, continuing this generous comedy. "I'll stay here with my regiment. The war, of course, has ended entirely; they'll let us settle here since we defended this place. A palatial building will stretch the length of the whole field, we'll till the earth, live well, and the whole Caucasus will become an enormous garden. We'll give you a little place of your own on the very top of the mountain from which you'll see everything in the distance extremely well."

Kostya believed it all. I won't begin to recount every one of the soothing words in Retzell's lullaby to amuse the poor lad. The baron understood very well human nature's credulity in the face of death, and consequently his words possessed a higher, sacred meaning at the dying child's bedside; but they would sound banal and ridiculous in the context of an ordinary story. It grew darker and darker; for no reason at all the idea of death crept into

*You destroyers, you!

Kostya's mind. He presented Retzell with a miniature portrait of his sister. "And as for you," he said to me, "I urge you to provide yourself with the original."

"If I die," he continued, "describe our conversation to Verinka; she loves you very much. But the main thing is, find out why she's grown so thin of late. I see she has something painful weighing on her soul; find out what it is and help her. Oh, I'm afraid of our stepmother; I'm afraid of that family!"

Darkness filled the environs immediately, but the night was unusually warm. Measured footsteps could be heard in the distance, the stamping became stronger, rifles and white swords flashed before us. A certain battalion, setting off on a dangerous reconnaissance mission, passed by its own regimental commander. The baron moved off to one side and sat on top of a fallen tree.

The even pace of a thousand men could be heard indistinctly and triumphantly in the darkness. In reply to a greeting from their beloved commander, the soldiers raised a ferocious cry.

The baron took the cigar from his mouth.

"The second battalion loves to make an uproar," he said distinctly and abruptly. "It's time to calm down; you're not going off to a dance."

Whether Kostya heard these words or his pain had intensified, he began to moan and toss in all directions. "Again the war, more killing each other!" he said, without responding to our attempts to console him. We tried to distract him, give him flowers, but he wouldn't take them and asked for camellias. Taking advantage of the darkness, we handed him some poppies and wild roses; he grabbed them and raised them to his lips, but the thin petals couldn't withstand his feverish movements; they broke and dropped off. Kostya guessed they weren't camellias and got angry at us; we wanted to carry him back into the tent, but he suddenly became very calm. The moon rose from behind the forest; stars, three times more of them than in Petersburg, shone in the dark blue sky, and the entire landscape appeared to us in a different light, with new, solemn beauty.

"It's become nice again, it's cheerful once more!" cried Kostya; he glanced up, looked around, and sank back on his pillows. Those were his last words: he died without suffering, without anguish, in the midst of this joyful sensation. We had done what we could.

"Next time I'll tell you the conclusion of my story."

The Fifth Evening

"And so," said Aleksei Dmitrich, "two years after my appearance in the Caucasus, I once again found it necessary to travel the familiar path from Stavropol to N.[47] and was already debating how I might turn off the main road and visit General Nadezhin's estate."

Perhaps the reader has noticed that my interlocutor didn't maintain a strict sequence in his story. On this occasion a jump of two years ahead is so impermissible that I'm obliged to summarize the events that occurred in the interval.

Aleksei Dmitrich's military struggle with the recalcitrant mountaineers did not go unrewarded, as befits every good deed. In response to a request by his new commander, Baron Retzell, over the course of two years our hero received a promotion for excellence and a decoration. After depriving him of his best friend, fate was attempting to make up for its bad manners. Aleksei Dmitrich's distant relation, a retired person, was so carried away by my friend's exploits that before his death he left him a decent estate not far from Petersburg. A hundred and fifty Finns[48] embodied for Aleksei Dmitrich the ideal of blessed independence, golden mediocrity, and tranquillity.

After one very long and boring exchange of fire, Baron Retzell rode up to our friend. Aleksei Dmitrich saluted him with respect.

"You know," said the baron, "you've been with us long enough. I don't want you to get wounded in battle. Now you have a chance to live in Petersburg."

As a result of this advice, Aleksei Dmitrich decided to return home. I'll continue in his own words.

It was necessary to leave in the morning, even though I knew that the night before my departure would do me no good. How well I sleep when my spirit is completely at peace; but that night I was far from such a blissful state.

Neither the muddy thaw nor my exhaustion could keep me at home: at midnight I went out to roam the crooked streets of the little town where the headquarters of my regiment were situated. I regretted having to part with places where I'd traveled for over two years in order to go to Petersburg, toward which I'd always felt an incomprehensible aversion. I also felt sorry for my subordinates, whom I'd gotten used to, in whom I'd observed considerable devotion, much strange, careless, sarcastic generosity that constitutes the distinguishing characteristic of the Russian soldier. I didn't feel too sorry about the officers: maybe they were not for me; perhaps my unaccommodating character alienates my comrades.

In particular, I regretted parting from my commander, Baron Retzell, to whom I was obligated for so much and to whom, since the first day of our acquaintance, I felt a strange attachment. There seemed to be no reason to love him so fervently: the baron could be an excellent general, perhaps even a government minister, but never a friend. God help them, these people who are so splendid in battle or on expeditions! Retzell was a proud and capricious man; his whims were sometimes inexplicable, especially during times of inactivity. He often locked himself up in his quarters for days at a time, and if anyone came in to see him on business, he greeted him drily and made rude remarks. And so on and so forth.

But we had much in common. We both shunned our comrades, we both were in love with the same girl, if one could suppose that the baron's wooing of Vera Nikolaevna had as its reason more than senseless caprice. As a result of such circumstances, I wandered through town and wound up near the lieutenant's quarters.

I wanted to knock, but imagining that any inappropriate tenderness might amuse Retzell, I was about to turn away when the door of his little house opened and, with sluggish steps, the master himself came in my direction.

"Ah! you're roaming," he said, as if surprised to meet me.

He took me by the arm and we set off around the deserted place, stepping in the mud with our high boots, as if onto a carpet.

"I'm glad, very glad you're leaving," the baron continued. "You'll be a bit bored at first, but then you'll thank me. You know, you should take up some specialty, read military works, torment yourself, annoy yourself for a while, seize upon so many pursuits that you'll have no time to think. It would be a good idea if you settled in the country and collected your thoughts. But there's one terrible thing: getting mixed up with your esteemed neighbors, incurring some misfortune, and deciding to get married."

The genuine sympathy with which these words were spoken indicated that the baron understood my character and was conjecturing about my past life.

"You see, Aleksei Dmitrich," he continued, trying to give his voice a cold intonation, "you're a strange man. You haven't lived much at all, and you don't want to live. All your life you've been preparing for something, but you're not at all ready. You need to be careful, to see people less often, to understand yourself better. If I return to Petersburg, I'll have a nice place there and will try to get to the bottom of you. By the way, concerning Petersburg; you'll be there soon, and I have one urgent matter."

I said that I still had to make one stop along the way. The baron looked at me thoughtfully. "Not to the old general?" he asked. I replied in the affirmative.

"Not to marry Kostya's sister?"

"Yes, if I can."

"Listen, Aleksei Dmitrich, don't go there. If you value yourself, find ways to avoid visiting that estate. . . ."

"God only knows," I said, "if I can do that."

The baron sat me down on a bench and seated himself next to me.

"Did something happen there?" I asked with impatience.

"Worse than if it had happened," he said in reply. "Nothing happened. Can anything happen? Believe me, there's some destiny on earth that makes everything worse. I'm prepared to bet my life that old man will outlive and destroy your fiancée. . . . If she survives them, it would be an unbelievable miracle, contradicting the general law. . . . "

There was something harsh, even terrible, in such an original set of convictions. Having made this *profession de foi,** the baron continued his speech with sincere, profound concern:

"Do you know what I feel for that girl? I hate her. Judge for yourself and you'll see that I'm right. What's her life, her actions, if not the embodiment of some capricious, uncalled-for self-sacrifice? . . . My rule is this: unnecessary virtue is no better than vice, senseless virtue arouses enmity. . . . As for me, I can both love and hate, and be at peace. But you're a very young man,

*Statement of faith.

extremely distressed, and you're susceptible . . . why, you even love me, God knows what for.

"You're in love with this girl. You can encounter obstinacy, self-sacrifice . . . oh, what self-sacrifice! . . . and leave her with a broken heart. What's even worse, you can stay with her, settle down, and perish in the maelstrom of family. . . .

"You see, Aleksei Dmitrich, family is something, perhaps, that's well respected, but not really suitable for the likes of you and me. Look at the terrible, unnatural multiplicity of this machine and you'll agree that if there's only one screw out of place . . . woe to the entire machine, and woe to him who approaches it. . . . Vera Nikolaevna's family is one of the most unharmonious.

"I'm harping on this painful string for your own good. Don't become involved with family; try to live all alone until your soul becomes stronger. Then you can act or be a spectator in life, but until then, take care of yourself. Forgive such long-winded advice and my ruthless repetition: remember, Aleksei Dmitrich, don't get involved with family thoughtlessly."

We sat for a long time talking like this; our farewell was somewhat strange—two people who loved each other very much and who, for some ridiculous reason, were afraid to acknowledge that they were sorry to be heading off in opposite directions. Several times I tried to take my final leave, but each time the baron kept me there, saying that the night was so fine, even though the mud came up to our knees and a piercing wind surrounded us on all sides.

"It's very cold indeed," he said at last, wrapping himself up in his overcoat. "That's what it means to sleep after dinner and loiter about all night until dawn. Good-bye, Aleksei Dmitrich."

We shook hands. "I'd like to see you in Petersburg," said the baron, "but I doubt I'll make it there. For some reason I'm too lucky these days, all bullets pass me by; perhaps one will sting me."

After this riposte he went back to his quarters and locked the door. I was surprised by this strange man and felt very sad. Then it seemed that his window opened and he looked out after me; not wanting to embarrass him, I hastened my steps and returned home, pondering our conversation. There's no need to admit that I didn't heed Retzell's advice; I turned off the main road and headed straight for General Nadezhin's estate.

Apparently fate itself wanted to arrange my affairs for the worst in order to confirm the baron's thesis. To listen to him and go on to Petersburg without stopping along the way wouldn't have required much effort on my part. It may be that I was in love, or imagined that I was; it may be that I was young, willful, stubborn, and wanted to see the object of my passion; but it would've been easy to demolish that love, if I'd recovered in time. My feeling for Vera Nikolaevna wasn't proper, natural passion. It had been conceived in my imagination, not in my heart; my brief stay in the old general's house not only didn't bring me any closer to this girl, but shrouded her image in mystery, not at all disposed to tenderness.

Moreover, Vera Nikolaevna's family circumstances and be-havior couldn't help but make a bad impression on my irritable character. Together with love, a feeling of hostility toward the young girl developed in me. The affair didn't end for any good reason: who, if not Vera Nikolaevna, as a result of her family fanaticism, had driven Kostya to that place where he had to lose his life? The thought of whose grief poisoned my poor friend's last minutes on earth?

And so I was in such a state of moral vacillation, in which, apparently, it's so easy to decide intelligent matters—in truth, though, it only appeared to be so. Nevertheless, I went on and on, and approached the familiar place and inquired everywhere about Vera Nikolaevna and her family. The news was not altogether cheering: the old man had become completely decrepit; moreover, he'd fallen entirely under the stepmother's power. His attachment to her had increased; he was distressed if she went away from him and fawned on her with all the devotion of which old men are capable. The stepmother, who, it turned out, had some money of her own hitherto unknown, had assumed the management of the household and earned from all her neighbors the esteemed sobriquet of Baba-Yaga.[49] Vera Nikolaevna hadn't gotten married, although dozens of suitors had wooed her. The general's estate had fallen into disrepair in spite of the mistress's cruel administration: rumors circulated to the effect that the stepmother was afraid to go out of the house; it was constantly reported that the peasants intended to do her some harm. As a result of these suspicions, she oppressed them even more.

I drove up to the general's house with gloomy impatience. The weather corresponded precisely to my mood and seemed to bode worse for the future. Thick clouds hung over snow-covered fields; the bare oak grove where I had first seen the old man and his daughter appeared on my left; this grove seemed not even to be standing on a hill—there was so much snow lying beneath it. The familiar old garden stretched along both sides of the road; bare branches rustled and knocked against each other, a flock of crows croaked on top of some tall lime trees, and a depressing half-light was quietly descending over these peaks.

The gates were locked, everything around the house was deserted, the previous splendor had completely disappeared. "No doubt the reins have been taken off the stepmother," I thought. "Have they been, or was there no need for that? . . ." It was difficult to get a response to my knocking; the old housekeeper opened the gates, tearfully recalled her child Konstantin Niko-laich, and then ran in to announce me.

The stepmother was out visiting the neighbors. I quietly en-tered the room where the general was sitting at a game of soli-taire. I didn't notice any change in him; his face reflected weari-ness, some dissatisfaction, and anxious expectation. He was simply bored without Marya Ivanovna.

Vera Nikolaevna sat next to her father, surrounded by books and pictures, which she was showing him to relieve his painful separation from his esteemed partner. She was pleasantly sur-prised when she saw me, but my face soon reminded her of Kostya; she was about to cry, but quickly regained control of herself and indulged in small talk.

She had changed considerably and was a mere shadow of her former self. You may perhaps have seen a beloved person who's endured a painful illness. Isn't it horrible to behold suffering in a face not made to suffer, to search for tender attractiveness in features where such desolation has occurred! Of course, if love survives, it won't hesitate to assert its rights, taking an interest in exhaustion and finding beauty even in deathly pallor; neverthe-less, the experiencing of this struggle is painful. Such were my feelings at seeing Vera Nikolaevna.

She had grown thin, her chest had sunk, but her eyes had become bigger, the thinness of her face conveyed energy to her gentle features, although this energy was deceptive, unreason-able. Instead of the grief formerly mirrored in her face, now there was only hopeless despondency; instead of the previous boldness in her eyes, there shone only an irritable readiness to endure everything, without retreating one step from her goal, to sacrifice both herself and others to the object she'd set for her-self.

The old man was the first to reminisce about Kostya, and he did so rather coldly. With pleasure he recalled how much Marya Ivanovna had liked his son, and he regarded Verinka rather caustically, as if to say, "You're the only one who can't get along with her." Afterward he started mumbling all sorts of nonsense.

Vera Nikolaevna seemed to share the old man's thoughts and agreed with him wholeheartedly, although at times tears glistened under her long eyelashes. Knowing how to please her father, she began to interrogate me about my own exploits and the Caucasus. The general grew livelier and entered the conversation with warmth and willingness; he criticized the disposition of his local superiors and tried to learn about the latest expeditions down to the last detail. Talk about military events afforded him great joy, and it was interesting to see how this decrepit old wreck of a man came to life as soon as we touched on some episode involving bloodshed.

But one circumstance both startled and astonished me. The general related several military scenes from his own youth. During this part of his tale he wasn't addressing Verinka, as had usually happened in the past, even though she was listening to these stories with the same love and attentiveness. There was no doubt whatever about it: the old man didn't love his daughter any more; the wicked stepmother had achieved her goal. But Verinka's behavior hadn't changed in the least: she was just as affectionate toward her father, looked after him in the same way, but without hope, without any expectation of gratitude.

We parted late; my mouth was tired from all the talk, and my heart was heavy. Vera Nikolaevna and I left the general's room together. She paused in the next room and took me warmly by the hand.

"Thank you, Aleksei Dmitrich," she said cheerfully. "I haven't seen Papa so happy in a long time. Stay here a while with us, if you're not in a hurry. You've cheered him up; he's so bored on his own."

Her voice trembled; I could hear bitter tears in it.

"I have so much to tell you—let's talk about him, about Kostya. . . ."

I took her two hands and kissed them. She was neither offended nor angry; she seemed not even to notice what I was doing.

"Let's *reminisce* about Kostya, but let's *talk about you*," I said, emphasizing the last word.

She looked at me attentively, bit her lip, shook her head, and returned to her room.

Once again I was back in the wing of the house where on my first visit Kostya and I had spent the night and talked at length about Verinka and her stepmother. However, I don't have such a weakness for reminiscence and didn't have much time to dwell on my former comrade. A multitude of sensations were rising within me, and all of them concerned the present.

In the first place, I was feeling sad. The room was cold, a snowstorm was blowing outside, and dogs were howling in the distance, sensing the approach of a wolf. Bare trees swayed and creaked under the windows; a human voice was nowhere to be heard. All these gloomy surroundings closely corresponded to the scene I'd witnessed!

This pitiful, lonely old man had lost his son and was consoling himself with bellicose pronouncements; a girl had sacrificed herself to provide temporary support to this decrepit shell of a man who didn't value her sacrifice; and above all, there was the thought of that peevish, dreadfully malicious woman who poisoned everything she touched.

Verinka seemed tall and noble to me. Her actions were beyond all praise; but her motive was unreasonable and aroused not so much sympathy as annoyance, tending toward hatred. In Vera Nikolaevna's tired eyes, pale face, and trembling lips I read the whole story of her terrible struggle, an unceasing, useless struggle that was confused, trivial, shameful, and at the same time demanded inordinate spiritual strength. In what did this struggle consist? Some heroic self-sacrifice, a passion to conceal and relieve her family's distress, and an unnecessary devotion to a vain, cold old man to whom a young creature, full of life, was so attached, like healthy ivy to a half-rotted tree. And where did this devotion lead? If Vera Nikolaevna had been able to wrench her father away from this wretched woman's control, if she could have made him happy—no one would have dared condemn her. But there was no hope; she was left to destroy herself, her energy, beauty, and youth . . . everything that a person has no right to destroy.

"Women, women!" I thought with indignation. "Who taught you to assume the prerogative of self-sacrifice, who forced you to die for that prerogative?"

And when I imagined once more the scene the poor girl had acted upon, when I imagined her family's pathetic life, recalled our last conversation, full of stifled tears and torments, my heart began to beat and pound painfully, bile rose in my throat, and I clenched my teeth in irritation and bitterness. An instinctive feeling cautioned me, advised me not to submit to love, pushed me away from Vera Nikolaevna. With full clarity I realized that to love such a girl meant to court misfortune, to destroy both myself and her; that there was insufficient spiritual strength in both of us to overcome the circumstances that entangled us—I understood all this, yet I loved her nonetheless.

But man is a worthless being, therefore it's not difficult to understand that all these rather sensible ideas didn't make me the least bit smarter. The next day, even before I saw Vera Nikolaevna, I'd already managed to forget all these dark thoughts, all Retzell's warnings, and my own speculations; I'd become a complete Lindor or Aminta.[50] I was twenty-three years old; consequently, I sighed in a most indecent manner, dreamt about my first kiss and the reciprocity of feelings; in conversations with Vera Nikolaevna I became embarrassed and confused. It was a good thing that, given her character, uncertainty couldn't torment me for long or completely intensify my love.

Vera Nikolaevna was in love with me and conveyed her feelings without beating around the bush. I was almost the only man she'd seen in the last two years; my friendship for Kostya had previously won her favor. She appreciated many things about me; my inborn idleness was to her liking (women admire that failing); but my passionate outbursts aroused little sympathy in her. For Vera Nikolaevna, love for a young man was by no means the goal of her entire life; for her the feeling of love was like an *appetizer*, nothing more. The whole loving part of her nature was directed toward her aged father; all her energy was devoted to a struggle against anything that could distress or disturb him.

Of course, she blushed upon hearing my kindnesses; her heart beat faster at the sound of my ardent confessions, but this occurred more as a result of her inexperience, the novelty of the situation, than for any other reason. One word from her father, one hint about the absent stepmother, and she would stop listening to me and reply in an absentminded way.

But once involved in this amorous game, I was incapable of turning back; I was attracted more and more by this girl's beauty, the puritanical purity of her soul, the unnatural maturity of her intelligence. She seemed to be a majestic creature, an exceptional one; in times of religious fanaticism, I thought, she would have been a Joan of Arc; in times of political fanaticism, she'd have been a new Madame Roland or Charlotte Corday.[51] But at the present time she could only perish as a victim of family fanaticism.

I'd already spent three days at the general's estate, and in all that time not one of us had left the house. The terrible snowstorm hadn't diminished and had piled up such snowdrifts that the view of the neighboring fields changed every morning. Both garden and road were covered with snow, and it was impossible to expect the stepmother's speedy return. Everyone in the house began to breathe more easily; Verinka had noticeably filled out a bit during these last three days.

Only the old man grieved visibly over the stepmother; he didn't dare be annoyed at her absence. Gradually, however, he too fell under his daughter's influence; she expended all her effort, all her tenderness, to console him and cheer him up. We played cards with him, related military tales, induced him to tell stories and then listened to them with rapt attention. In the evening he loved for us to read aloud from books from his library, which consisted entirely of old Russian writers and translations of Voltaire done in the 1780s. It was pleasant to hear Verinka struggle over those wooden verses from Ozerov[52] and other poets, very respected ones, but completely unsuitable for reading aloud nowadays. After struggling over a tragedy or some solemn ode, Verinka would open *Zadig* or *The Babylonian Princess*[53] and read them smoothly, serenely, without stumbling over any stupid, barbaric translations or cynical remarks made by the mischievous old man of Ferney.[54] The old man laughed to the point of exhaustion, admiring the most insignificant parts, sometimes trying to snatch the book away from his daughter, saying, "You're too young to read such things." But the reading continued. Verinka didn't really care: to afford her father pleasure she wouldn't have refused to read even *Faublas*[55] or *Marquis G.*[56] aloud to all those assembled. The general wouldn't allow any contemporary books to be read to him under any circumstances.

On the fourth day after my arrival, the snowstorm ended and the weather grew calmer. The frost hardened the mountains of snow and, before setting, the sun shone through leaden clouds and filled the white fields with unbearable brilliance. After a late breakfast the general fell asleep sitting in his armchair. Verinka left the room and returned a minute later in a warm coat.

"Let's go," she said, taking my arm affectionately. "Let's go say some prayers for Kostya."

This familiar, unconstrained contact aroused my blood. I was like a sixteen-year-old boy melting in the soothing embrace of a thirteen-year-old girl.

We proceeded along cleared paths. I wasn't wearing an overcoat but felt quite warm. It reached the point where I can't even recall what we talked about.

We moved forward at a brisk pace. Vera Nikolaevna fluttered about between snowdrifts like a little bird, supporting me when my feet broke through the frozen crust of snow. Soon we were walking along a smooth, clear path. There was the familiar little stream; the old ferryboat was barely visible on one side; in front of us stood a tall, semicircular fence, beyond which rose the green tops of old pine trees.

We went through the gate into the enclosure, climbed up a beautiful staircase, and ended up on sandy ground under some old pine trees whose branches hung down above us. Not one trace of snow was visible either on the ground or in the trees; one would have thought it was summertime—that's how alive and joyful this green clump of immortal trees appeared. Several flowers from the greenhouse had recently been picked and strewn on the ground; their pervasive fragrance seemed all the more noticeable, even more intoxicating, in the cold, rarefied air.

On this same ground, some two years ago, Vera Nikolaevna had teased her brother and persuaded him to take pity on their father and go off to serve in the army. . . .

Straight ahead of us there stood a little stone chapel decorated in dark colors. We went in; a small stove was lit and many candles were burning in front of the icons. Inside, opposite the door, stood a rough-hewn marble statue of an angel. Under the angel's feet lay a black marble gravestone.

I didn't feel any special tenderness; I could only imagine how much trouble and effort it must have cost the poor girl to build this whole memorial, to procure this crudely fashioned angel from so far away. On the other hand, Vera Nikolaevna was absolutely convinced that the angel resembled Kostya, like two peas in a pod. I couldn't keep from smiling as I agreed with her.

Verinka slowly leaned forward, bowing gracefully from the waist, and quietly dropped to her knees on the cold gravestone and began to pray, easily and peacefully. Gradually her prayers became more passionate, and tears streamed from her bright eyes; weak but convulsive sobs could be heard occasionally, and the young girl's slender frame swayed painfully. The sobs became stronger and the tears no longer fell just on Verinka's cheeks; she bent all the way over, cried out, clasped the left side of her chest, and laid her warm head on the angel's pedestal, her dark curls spilling over onto the white stone.

And what do you think I did all during this sacred, holy prayer? I stood in the corner, clenching my teeth and digging my nails into my palms until they bled. Tears, grief, and the poor girl's prayer kindled the usual feelings of hostility in me. My entire history with Verinka turns on these transitions, which are so difficult to describe. In her grief and tears shed over the past I could see her inability to deal with her present life. I realized that a woman who could surrender so extremely to her misery was powerless in the face of reality. I wanted to disturb Verinka's pure prayer, destroy the beauty of her joyful recollections, tell her that the figure of the angel had been made by a pathetic sculptor and didn't resemble Kostya in the least and that Kostya himself had been more like a little devil than an angel.

When we left the chapel, my grotesque disposition vanished entirely. It seemed that Vera Nikolaevna was no longer crying, no longer praying. She was peaceful, even a little abrupt, and no trace of tears could be seen in her eyes. Once again I became a happy young man in love and collected all my composure for a definitive declaration.

"Vera Nikolaevna," I began, supporting her as we descended the hill, "you're so clever that with you there's no way to employ romantic phrases. Any 'sympathy of hearts,' any 'bubbling up of passions' melts and vanishes before your bright gaze. I will speak to you very simply. I love you very much. Tell me just as plainly: do you love me, do you wish to become my wife . . . no, even that's too high-flown, do you want to marry me?"

She smiled affectionately, looked at me boldly, and blushed a little. In that blush there appeared not only simple embarrassment but even a little affection.

"You've mourned here long enough," I continued. "We'll go to Petersburg, perhaps; at first our life will be difficult, but I swear to you, you won't have to endure squalid poverty. I have considerable income and my friends are rather powerful. . . ."

"I love you. I love you very much," Verinka said, interrupting me. "But I won't leave here, I won't leave my father alone."

I was silent for a little while and then resumed the conversation.

"I respect your father deeply," I said, "but I must tell you frankly, I'm jealous of him. Your affection as a daughter is so strong that it leaves you no time to think about a future husband."

She dropped her eyes.

"You're not speaking honestly," she said. "I see you're not afraid of my father. . . ."

"No, I'm not afraid of your father, but of that terrible, exhausting struggle you endure on his behalf. I understand your life; I'm surprised by you. I see where your energies are directed, for what sacred goal they're exerted and wasted. But at the same time I want your love. That love isn't possible under the present circumstances. A choice stands before you: love or struggle, a husband or your father.

"Don't think," I continued in a humorous tone, to soften my emotional tirade, "that I'm reproaching you for being cold. In my eyes you're a kind of Napoleon; your struggle with family life is worth all his major campaigns. Before his battles the French emperor was probably not very affectionate with women: you're in the same situation. In your eyes I can read an account not only of Marengo, Wagram, perhaps, not only of Waterloo. . . ."[57]

Vera Nikolaevna flared up. I had touched her weak point.

"In that case," she said quickly, "what do you want from me? If I agree to go, if I decide to leave him all alone with. . . ."

She stopped suddenly. I was surprised by her self-control; I lost all restraint and effaced myself in front of this wonderful, exceptional woman. My composure was gone; I shuddered, I was losing my mind, I almost fell on my knees in front of her.

"If that's necessary," I said passionately, "if my requests don't win you over, I'm resigned to anything. I'll stay here with you. I'll forget my dislike of family quarrels, the difficulty of my own childhood, and I'll sacrifice myself entirely for your father. I'll wait years for your love. I'll protect you, love you without any hope of reciprocal love, and woe unto him who dares offend you, who even thinks of disturbing the object of your affection, who doesn't bow down and worship your actions. . . ."

"My friend," she said gently, "your threats won't help in this matter."

These few words altered my entire approach. I understood the insignificance of my childish temper, but my love wasn't diminished in the least.

"Please," I said, "if necessary I'm ready to remain silent, prepared to endure everything, settle down with you and become the most tight-lipped member of your household. It won't take much effort for me to leave the civil service. I promise to obey you in all things and act in accordance with your wishes."

I knew all too well that I was bringing disaster on myself, but at that moment passion was sweeping me away.

Vera Nikolaevna smiled and looked at me with her former affability.

"That's just what's needed," she said. "But I won't give you my word. Before agreeing, I must explain my position in as much detail as possible. Then, if you still haven't changed your mind. . . ."

"Speak, tell me right now," I said, encouraging her, trembling with impatience.

We were only a few steps away from the house; I was in a total sweat, although a cold wind had arisen at twilight and was blowing steadily on us. But Verinka was cold and hurried home.

"There's no time, no time," she said, smiling in reply to my urging. "It's time for dinner; Father's had his nap, and after dinner we'll sit down to play cards."

"My God! When on earth will I ever get your answer?"

"It's impossible today. But," she said, taking pity on me, "wait until this evening. After supper go back to your wing of the house, and in half an hour, after I've put Papa to bed, I'll wait for you in my room. Come through the side door, quietly, without taking any special precautions. . . ."

"I understand," I replied. "Any secret is an insult to you."

"Exactly," she said amicably.

We entered the room. Verinka sat down in front of me in a lighthearted way and soon went off to change her clothes.

Both dinner and all the time afterward seemed intolerably long, in spite of the fact that my impatience had lost its feverish aspect.

"It must be that she loves me," I said to myself. "It must mean that we'll live together. This evening she'll tell me all about her life, she'll abuse her stepmother and then give me her word. Perhaps I'll even excite her then, perhaps she'll press herself against my chest and kiss me."

Reflecting in such a way, I felt ready to dance around the room; happiness seemed so feasible, so easy to achieve.

We had supper later than usual. Around midnight I said goodnight to the general and returned to my wing. I passed the time there very pleasantly, waiting until the whole house went to sleep. I smoked a cigar after lighting it from both ends, drank five glasses of water, and sang arias the likes of which no one's ever heard. I was still unable to pass more than a quarter of an hour. A painful premonition had stolen into my soul, even though quite a muddle was present there already. I was unable to wait any longer; without putting on my coat, wearing only a jacket and cap, I rushed out into the garden, from there to the side staircase, and then into Vera Nikolaevna's room.

The moon was shining brightly and cordially; the frosty air was still.

That was the most horrible night of my entire life. If I had had to endure two such nights, I'd certainly have become decrepit, or even died prematurely. To understand the full horror of this extremely ordinary story, you would have to be in my skin or to have been brought up the way I was.

The whole house was asleep, but Vera Nikolaevna wasn't in her room. From behind the partially closed door to the general's study there came both light and the sound of a voice. She was reading aloud, probably to her father. I sat down quietly on the sofa and examined the young girl's room with great interest.

At first glance the room didn't make a very pleasant impression on a coldhearted visitor; but I was in love, and everywhere there appeared delicate, womanly charm, although Vera Nikolaevna's lofty room more closely resembled a hermit's retreat or the study of someone engaged in serious intellectual work. There was not one feminine touch; not one magnificent item disturbed the cold, ascetic quality of the room. Severe furniture was arranged in an unoriginal, unattractive way, and a few pictures were hung on the walls. But even the selection of these pictures was astonishing, if not in their workmanship, then in their subjects. They were all landscapes, but each one struck me by its elegance; looking at them carefully, one could see how the soul itself flew so far, far away . . . to the summit of snow-covered alpine mountains, to flower-strewn shores of Italian lakes. . . .

Vera Nikolaevna loved nature just like her brother; looking at these pictures relieved her tormented soul and provided her with strength for the difficult struggle. In my exalted state of mind, I didn't miss the chance to compare her to the giant who struggled against Hercules. Although he gradually grew weak in the first skirmish, each time the giant touched his "fertile mother earth," his strength was replenished and the endless combat was resumed again and again.[58]

I quietly stole toward the door and sat on a chair next to it. From there I could see the general, sitting in an armchair, and his daughter who, in a pleasant though somewhat tired voice, was finishing one of Voltaire's novels begun the day before. The old man listened with reverent excitement and frequently expressed his pleasure.

"Hee, hee, hee!" he cried occasionally. "Oh, that Voltaire is a wizard! What won't he say next? Look what he's gone and done! He's got right to the heart of the matter! . . . Go on, keep reading!"

The old man started laughing again and looked around timidly, as if afraid that someone might overhear his liberal thoughts. Verinka was delighted, though not really understanding the point: she raised her eyes from the book and smiled slyly at the old man, the way a young mother smiles at the incomprehensible innocence of her child. The reading continued.

"And you, you most ignoble Freron, from the Jesuit school, driven out for. . . ."[59]

"Well, enough, enough!" the old man cried, interrupting her and taking the book away from his daughter. "Go to sleep, you're too young to read this sort of thing."

Indeed, Verinka was too young to read that sort of thing: she didn't understand one word of it. She looked at the clock and the door of her room.

"Good night, Papa," she said gently, approaching her father.

Her father made the sign of the cross over her, kissed her, and grew tender.

"Good night, my pussycat," he said affectionately. "Thank you, I've felt very happy today . . . I myself don't know why."

Vera Nikolaevna was rewarded in full and pressed herself affectionately against her father, who was unable to guess why he was feeling so happy that day. She gave her father her arm to lead him to his bedroom, but the door of the study opened by itself. Before them stood the stepmother. Having returned from her brief trip, this woman had already managed to upset the entire household, scare the sleeping servants, and, it seemed, was now waiting impatiently for a chance to disturb the serenity of her husband and stepdaughter.

I recognized this nasty woman: her gaunt, unpleasant face hadn't changed in the least, her black gypsy eyes darted around as before and seemed to scatter sparks. She was dressed like a typical landowning mistress: a brightly colored warm coat and a kerchief with a green hood accentuated the repulsive expression of her face.

He who hasn't lived in the backwoods and has known only women of the capital will have difficulty understanding the extent to which an idle life and the habit of commanding others can disfigure any energetic female character. Spite was both an illness and a consolation for the stepmother; her sickly blush and the constant trembling in her voice indicated how adversely this habit of raging and tormenting other people had affected her; on the other hand, two or three days of tranquillity could completely exhaust this woman. She was a pernicious creature, incorrigible in the highest degree, who aroused not only revulsion but also pity.

"Lock up those servants who went with me!" she cried in the other room. "They'll have something to remember me by, those monsters!"

Such a beginning promised no good. The old man was about to rejoice upon seeing his wife, but didn't dare speak to her after hearing these first words. Vera Nikolaevna went up to her stepmother and inquired after her health and the state of the road.

"The road was fine," said the stepmother, sitting down in an armchair and shaking her head triumphantly. "May God grant health to all your servants!"

She fell silent. Verinka gave her a curious look.

"I know what they say, I know what they want," continued the stepmother. "But no, clearly, God didn't betray their wicked mistress."

She stopped again, fell silent, and then said, "The road was fine, may God grant you health."

Without any more questions, Verinka moved away from her, but the old man anxiously began asking what was wrong. After tormenting him a while, the stepmother explained how some monstrous people had arranged to kill her, had overturned her cart on an even stretch of road, but, for some strange reason, took no further measures.

A light blush appeared on Verinka's face.

"Mama," she said, approaching the general's wife, "leave this matter to me; I shall find out what happened. I'm convinced you're mistaken."

"Mistaken!" the stepmother cried, bursting into bitter laughter. "How can you make sense of it? They all like you! The angel noblewoman . . . why should they tell you? As for those servants of ours—why they're all good people whose patience has simply been exhausted! And that stepmother is such a wicked woman, that stepmother's an old Baba-Yaga; down with her, that old woman. . . ."

Vera Nikolaevna rang for the servants at once. "Release the people who came back with Mama," she said to the footman who entered.

Marya Ivanovna jumped up from the chair and stood facing her stepdaughter . . . she was gasping for breath and couldn't utter a single word.

"I tell you," said Vera Nikolaevna firmly, "those people are not to blame. You bring disaster on yourself; while I'm alive you won't touch a single one of them."

"Aha! It's always like this!" cried the stepmother with diabolical sarcasm. But she was unable to go on; she encountered the bright, steadfast, powerful gaze of her stepdaughter. This look reminded her of Kostya; the stepmother shriveled, retreated before this gaze, just as Kostya's morose persecutors had before him.

Oh, if only Verinka could have been as steadfast and imposing for even a day, for an hour, as she was at that moment! She would have vanquished her enemy and rescued her father from that vile woman's yoke. But this effort weakened her; she put her hand to her head and sank quietly onto a chair.

But the general spoiled the whole scene. He realized that the stepmother had been defeated and wanted to reassure her. "Of course they're not to blame," he said, for no reason at all.

Marya Ivanovna was indefatigable in battle. She realized that by insulting the old man she could retaliate against her stepdaughter, and she fell upon her poor husband.

I'm relating a true story—not a novel or a tale. There's no need to convey all the words of the actors, especially if the recollection causes me pain. And there's little interest in repeating the words used by the enraged woman to torment her aged husband. Vera Nikolaevna took her father by the arm; he, apparently, was trying to defend himself, though very weakly. She led him toward the door without paying any attention to her stepmother's disgraceful cries.

The stepdaughter's indifference maddened Marya Ivanovna, and in a frenzy she threw herself between the father and his daughter. It was terrible to see her at this moment: some demonic force was reflected in her face.

"Why are you embracing? Where are you going?" she asked the old man, then Vera Nikolaevna.

"Let's go to sleep, Papa," Verinka said quietly, resting her tired head on the general's shoulder.

"Aha!" bawled the virago, "Old songs, old tales! You've started it and there's nothing to hide. That's the way you'll overcome your old stepmother! Where do I live? Why hasn't God taken me away so I won't have to witness this?" She moved quickly from rage to outbursts of bitter despair. This woman was astonishing; she believed her own ridiculous fabrications, she wailed with a pure heart; her convulsive sobbing could be heard clearly throughout the room.

Vera Nikolaevna met this new, disgraceful attack with contempt. In all probability, the stepmother had never before resorted to this last, shameful tactic. At first the old man shuddered, straightened up, turned his head quickly, but instead of abuse, he heard only wailing and sobbing, and sank down again. In vain did his daughter try to lead him away from this painful scene; he wasn't listening to her anymore. He withdrew the hand that his astonished daughter was holding and, upon hearing these new wails and cries, quickly moved away from his daughter without looking at her and approached the armchair where the enraged woman was sitting; he leaned down and began to console her with the most affectionate, humiliating phrases. Both he and his wife were repulsive at this moment.

Vera Nikolaevna stood alone in the corner of the room, her head drooping, her arms motionless. I had more or less predicted this moment when earlier that morning I'd compared her in jest to Napoleon. This bitter scene was a Waterloo for this unfortunate girl. In her eyes her father, to whom she'd sacrificed her entire life, had abandoned her; and at the same, most terrible moment, he'd bowed down before this woman who didn't even deserve to be called a woman. The poor child was vanquished.

The stepmother wasn't finished yet: she didn't reply to her husband's submissive assurances and continued to wail, cry, and complain about her fate. It was difficult to imagine a nastier, viler, more contemptible scene on earth. My heart was broken, my throat was choked with unbearable bitterness, I was feeling ill. But when the shrew's wailing and crying intensified, when from various corners servants' faces began to appear, when I saw fear, joy, and curiosity on all these faces . . . I could contain myself no longer. Like a madman I rushed for the stairs by which I'd entered Verinka's room, plunged down them, ran out into the garden, and fell down on the frozen snow.

I felt the onset of some incomprehensible illness; my heart was rent asunder. Violent vomiting relieved my physical distress, but nothing in the world could alleviate my spiritual torment.

To understand these torments, I ask you to recall my childhood and upbringing; I don't plan to say any more about it. A healthy person can endure a wound, but if you stab a wounded man with a dagger in a place that's still not healed, the onset of gangrene is inevitable.

A radical upheaval occurred in my soul. I could be surprised by Verinka, but I could no longer love her. Like a tender blossom that has taken root on scanty soil, my love could no longer withstand a storm such as it had to endure. I lacked the strength to save Verinka: a man of my years, my character, was unable to rescue her, unable to accept ruination along with her. And that's not all; not only did my love vanish, but a hostile feeling, which this girl had aroused in me from our first meeting, began to develop, to intensify without reason or cause, to assume colossal proportions and stifle within me all traces of love, friendship, and compassion. All during that awful, terrible night I dreamt of the gloomy figure of Retzell, and his horrible words resounded clearly in my ears: "Unnecessary virtue is no better than vice. . . ." I didn't want to dwell on the idea that even in a woman's futile self-sacrifice there might be some sacred, sublime merit—that would have encouraged faith in the possibility of pure motives on this earth. . . .

The next morning the servants knocked and knocked on my door to wake me and then left me in bed; my sleep was more like a faint. I awoke late and my head was quite clear; having endured sickness many times as a child, I easily guessed that at the present time I was suffering from the first symptoms of some grave illness; the ends of my fingers were cold and I felt pressure in one side; the water with which I washed glided across my skin and produced an excessive chill. In addition to all my grief, there was a new worry—I didn't want to fall ill in this accursed house where I was already so obligated. I availed myself of the first opportunity to leave: three days before, I'd received from Petersburg news of my brother's illness. After giving the order to pack my belongings and bring round the horses, I overcame my agitation, went in to see the general, and found the entire household gathered in complete silence. I thanked them for their hospitality, informed them of the unexpected news, and announced the necessity of my leaving for Petersburg that very day.

You may be amazed at the strangeness of human nature, but do not hasten to condemn me: I suffered badly all during this gloomy conversation; meanwhile, I looked at Vera Nikolaevna with malice. I didn't soften even one of the blows struck by my words; I didn't shorten my speech, even though my heart was breaking, didn't take my eyes off her pale face, even though no last sparks of love shone through the hostile, shameful disposition of my soul. Tormented, beaten down, I made my way back at last to the wing of the house, hurried the servants, sent for the horses, and with horror realized that such preparations took an unusually long time, as is the custom in Holy Rus.[60]

I couldn't sit still; thoughts and recollections began stifling me as soon as I took up my peaceful position. The strongest cigars didn't cloud my head at all: their bitter smoke seemed mild and tasteless. Having walked around the room in all directions hundreds of times, I ran outside and, without knowing what I was doing, rushed quickly along the garden paths, which were so well cleared they resembled ditches.

God knows how it was that I wound up at that chapel on the little hill you know so well. It was warm and snowing lightly; I stopped at the locked gate and stood there looking at the monument that Vera Nikolaevna had built to her brother. The thought of Kostya somewhat relieved my spiritual agitation: in all my life I'd met only one being whose influence on me was so beneficial, who repaid me with neither hostility nor bitterness. I thought about Kostya for some time, and it seemed that I wept and, as it were, bid farewell to him once again; for a while sad remembrances of the past dispersed all thought of the disastrous present. Kostya was helping me even from beyond the grave.

After a little while I looked to the right, and once again the blood rushed to my heart, the former chaos began fermenting in my head. A few steps away from me, leaning against the old spruce tree, stood Vera Nikolaevna, holding a bouquet of hothouse flowers in her hand. She seemed not to notice me and was looking in the other direction.

By this time I no longer loved her, but I still wanted to save Verinka, my Kostya's sister. My ardent compassion was similar to love. And who wouldn't have felt the same, looking at her at this moment?

Graceful and slender, she seemed not to be touching the tree against which her whole body was pressed. Her eyes looked tired, but stared just as boldly; the reflection from the snow fell on her face; the hollowness of her cheeks seemed even more noticeable than before, her gaunt chest was sadly conspicuous, the hollows between her eyes and the corners of her lips looked so cheerless on her face.

My God! As long as I live I'll never forget the lackluster,

melancholy atmosphere of that scene. It was twilight; leaden gray darkness was descending slowly from above; it seemed to be enveloping the treetops with its massive cover, and the trees seemed to be suffering, as if bowing under this metallic burden, as if grumbling against the oppressive twilight and mournfully dropping clumps of snow on us from its branches. I went up to Verinka, took her hand, kissed it for a long, long time, and was unable to utter a word.

"Farewell, Aleksei Dmitrich," she said softly. "I don't blame you, I'm glad for you. . . ."

"My friend," I said, "collect your thoughts, come to your senses, save yourself. There's still time, take pity on yourself; you have no right to bring about your own ruin. Give me your word, let's leave this maelstrom together. . . ."

She shook her head quietly. I hadn't expressed all my thoughts to her and therefore still had hope.

"I'm not demanding you sacrifice your father. . . . Bring him with you, I will love him. Abandon this woman, leave your estate to her, take this poor old man out of her hands. It would be better to cause one severe shock to his system than to continue such a life."

"My father has grown accustomed to his life . . . he's content with it. A severe shock would kill him. Farewell, my friend . . . wait for me . . . even better, forget all about me."

I went up even closer to her, embraced her. I have no idea how my heart survived such an ordeal. . . .

"For the last time I'm asking you," I said. "Save yourself, decide, leave here. . . ."

I moved away from her and continued kissing her hand.

"Aleksei Dmitrich," she said through her tears, "forgive me once again. I see I've done you much harm. Leave here at once, I'll pray for you. . . . I'll stay here; my place is here."

The last spark of pity died in my soul. I pushed Vera Niko-laevna's thin hand away so fast that it crunched a little. She looked mournfully at her pale, skinny fingers and didn't say a word.

"Damn," I said, gasping and losing all sense of decorum, "damn your fanaticism and your destructive, senseless self-sacrifice! Damn the whole idea of family that so oppressed my childhood and now threatens to destroy my youth!"

She looked at me thoughtfully and smiled gently, the way martyrs used to smile in days of old when they regarded the instruments of their own execution.

"God be with you," I said somewhat more serenely. "Stay here then, be happy; I despise you."

I turned aside and walked a considerable distance without looking back. It made no sense for me not to look back in that direction: in my mind that familiar scene, bordered with over-grown spruces, stood out with astonishing clarity. And there, under one of those trees, stood the slender figure of a young girl, and sadly, without thinking, that girl was looking at the thin fingers of her right hand. From that time to this, in exactly the same way, with the same gesture, the single object of my unre-quited love presents itself to my imagination. I see her so clearly that it seems I could count the veins on her open hand; and behind her I see that sad, leaden background of the scene, made even darker by clumps of gray, constantly falling snow.

When I returned to the wing of the house, the horses were ready. Forgetting half my belongings, I jumped into the sledge and gave the order to set out at once. At every station I felt that illness was overtaking me; I aroused myself, put snow on my head, drank vodka, and thus traveled a hundred and fifty versts without rest. At the sixth station I gave the order to stop, found night's lodging, and decided to rest. In the morning it turned out that I had an attack of jaundice; I endured it rather calmly and spent six weeks absolutely alone.

"That's the first part of my story. I won't relate the second part now: I'm terribly fed up with analyzing myself and all those around me. Last week I decided to retire and settle down in the country for a while. There I have everything that a man dreams of in moments of evil affliction and spiritual exhaustion: a little house with green shutters, a collection of weapons, a dusty library, and other pastoral appurtenances. I confess, I don't expect very much from this seclusion at the age of twenty-five, but then again, why not try it? *Le repos—c'est Dieu** said your favorite writer."[61]

*Rest is God.

»»» NOTES «««

INTRODUCTION

1. V. G. Belinsky, *Polnoe sobranie sochinenii* (Leningrad, 1956), 10:347.

2. Ibid., 12:444.

3. Ibid., 12:467. The letter continues the comparison by referring to Alexander Herzen's story "The Thieving Magpie" (1848), a dialogue between a Slavophile and a Westernizer about why Russia had failed to produce any outstanding women in the arts.

4. See Alexander Herzen, *Who Is To Blame?* trans. Michael R. Katz (Ithaca, N.Y.: Cornell University Press, 1984).

5. The annual sum paid to landowners by serfs who farmed an estate.

6. Samuel Richardson's *Clarissa Harlowe* (1747–48) and Jean-Jacques Rousseau's *Julie, ou La Nouvelle Héloïse* (1761).

7. A novel by D. V. Grigorovich, published in *The Contemporary* in 1847, which portrays Russian peasants with compassion.

8. F. M. Dostoevsky, *Polnoe sobranie sochinenii* (Leningrad, 1975), 13:10.

9. L. N. Tolstoy, *Sobranie sochinenii* (Moscow, 1965), 18:86.

10. Derek Offord, *The First Russian Liberals* (Cambridge: Cambridge University Press, 1985), 152.

11. See N. G. Chernyshevsky, *What Is To Be Done?* trans. Michael R. Katz (Ithaca, N.Y.: Cornell University Press, 1989).

POLINKA SAKS

1. From the comic masterpiece by François Rabelais entitled *The Lives, Heroic Deeds and Sayings of Gargantua and His Son Pantagruel*

(1533–67). Pantagruel's world is one in which no restrictions on sensual exploration are tolerated.

2. A popular dance of the time.

3. From Rossini's opera *Otello* (1816), as performed by an Italian troupe in Petersburg.

4. "The Color Black" and "The Young Girl with Black Eyes" were two popular songs of the period.

5. A clear distinction is drawn between nature and nurture, with the onus of Polinka's problem laid firmly on her upbringing.

6. See the Introduction. Sand's most popular novels were *Indiana* (1832), *Valentine* (1832), and *Jacques* (1834).

7. Cecilia was a virgin martyr in second- or third-century Rome; she is considered the patroness of music.

8. This assortment shows Saks's interest in scientific observation and materialism.

9. Quitrent was a system in which peasants farmed the land and paid the landowner an annual sum. Lowering the quitrent was an indication of liberal views.

10. The ancient Greek god of marriage.

11. An island near St. Petersburg in the delta of the Neva where many wealthy Russians had their dachas or summer cottages.

12. A town near ancient Rome (now called Tivoli) where Horace's villa was located. He used to sing the praises of Falernian wine.

13. Legendary city of a South American Indian chief ("the gilded one"), a place of gold and wealth sought by the Spanish conquistadors.

14. Clarissa is the idealized heroine in Samuel Richardson's epistolary novel *Clarissa Harlowe* (1747–48); Julie, the idealized heroine of Rousseau's epistolary novel *Julie, ou la Nouvelle Héloïse* (1761).

15. Fashionable spas in Germany.

16. Rabelais's legendary hero visited the oracle of the "holy bottle," who uttered the prophecy, "Drink."

17. The heroine is called by a variety of French and Russian names and nicknames.

18. The French artist Jean Granville became popular at the end of the 1820s for his caricatures on social and political themes.

19. The Nobles' Assembly was an organization of nobles established in 1766 to examine and resolve questions that affected the nobility as a class and was the center of high society for the gentry.

20. In aristocratic society only French and Italian theater productions were viewed as high culture; Russian theater was seen as a form of plebeian entertainment.

21. In mythology, Psyche, the personification of the human soul, was loved by Eros (Amor) but forbidden to look at him. She disobeyed, and he abandoned her; but after a series of trials she became immortal and was reunited with him forever.

22. An inexact quotation from Pushkin's lyric "Fyodor and Elena" in the cycle entitled "Songs of the Western Slavs" (1834).

23. The Russian convention is to omit place-names, but because the town of Pskov is indicated in Druzhinin's rough draft, it has been included here. Pskov is one of the oldest Russian cities, dating from the tenth century, and is located near the southern end of Lake Peipus and the Estonian border.

24. In Greek mythology, the many-headed dog with a mane and a tail of snakes that guards the entrance to Hades.

25. A social system with the family as its basic unit. The word derives from a religious sect called the Family of Love that arose in Holland in 1556.

26. The novel was written in 1837.

27. A line from Pushkin's lyric entitled "The Nineteenth of October" (1825).

28. The pseudonym of Aleksandr Bestuzhev (1797–1837), a romantic writer, poet, and Decembrist.

29. The Sistine Madonna is the best-known painting by the Italian Renaissance painter Raphael (1483–1520).

30. Spanish judges and policemen. Here the term is applied ironically to Russian officials.

31. Russian convention leaves the name unspecified.

32. "Fra poco" (Wait a bit) is an aria from Gaetano Donizetti's most popular opera, *Lucia di Lammermoor* (1835); "Stabat mater" (There stood the grieving mother), one of the few sequences still sung in the Catholic mass, was set by various composers, including Pergolesi (1729) and Rossini (1842).

33. Sites of German universities frequented by Russian intellectuals during the nineteenth century.

34. An inexact quotation from N. Polevoi's translation of *Hamlet*, probably the line "Man delights not me," from Hamlet's conversation with Rosencrantz and Guildenstern in act 2, scene 2, line 320.

35. V. A. Karatygin (1802–53) was the principal tragedian of the Aleksandrinsky Theater in Petersburg from its opening in 1832. He played the lead in a production of *Hamlet* in 1837.

36. This idea was to receive fuller treatment in N. G. Chernyshevsky's novel *What Is To Be Done?* (1863), in which the author develops a system of human relations based on "rational egoism."

37. Hero of the famous novel of vengeance with the same title (1845) by Alexandre Dumas *père*.

38. Hero of the novel with the same title (1834) by George Sand.

39. Based on Pushkin's lyric "The Black Shawl" (1820).

40. The source of this reference is unknown.

41. Pierre Jean de Béranger (1780–1857) was a French lyric poet whose songs expressed republican and Bonapartist ideas.

42. A fortress and prison at the confluence of Lake Ladoga and the Neva.

43. Brave knights from medieval French epics.

44. An edict of April 2, 1842, allowed landowners to "emancipate" peasants without land.

THE STORY OF ALEKSEI DMITRICH

1. Neptune was the Roman god of the sea; the reference should be to Morpheus, god of dreams and sleep.

2. *Village of Gorse*, a play written in 1846 by the French dramatist Melchior-Frédéric Soulié (1800–47).

3. A popular comedy first performed in 1832, written by the prolific Russian playwright Prince A. A. Shakhovskoi (1777–1846).

4. Now the Maly Theater on the Square of the Arts in St. Petersburg.

5. *Tired and Heavy*: no such work has been discovered. The title is most likely the author's humorous invention.

6. The name of the hero, a cool, detached "superfluous man," in M. Yu. Lermontov's novel, *A Hero of Our Time* (1840).

7. The source of these quotations has not been identified.

8. A particular fondness for family life.

9. The theater in question is the Bolshoi in St. Petersburg, located on Theater Square, where the Opera Studio of the Conservatory now stands.

10. A hero in Russian folkore.

11. An old city in south central European Russia.

12. The hero of Jean-Jacques Rousseau's novel *Emile* (1762), a didactic work arguing that education consists not in the imparting of knowledge but in drawing out what is already inherent in the child.

13. A mercenary soldier in western Europe from the fifteenth to seventeenth centuries.

14. The regency of Philippe II, duc d'Orléans, in France (1715–23), was a period of extreme licentiousness.

15. A reference to the lyric "To Burtsov" (1804) by the "hussar poet" and memoirist Denis Davydov (1784–1839).

16. Children from noble families of modest means hoped to be placed in educational institutions at state expense; sometimes they had to wait years for a vacancy.

17. A Russian translation of Voltaire's *Candide* (1759) was first published in St. Petersburg in 1769. Russian translations of Goethe's novel *Die Leiden des jungen Werthers* (1774) began appearing in 1781 and were initially entitled *The Passions of Young Werther*. The novel *Die Leiden der Ortenbergischen Familie*, by the popular German dramatist August von

Kotzebue (1761–1819), was published in 1785 and translated into Russian in 1802 and 1823.

18. This work is unknown.

19. A Russian translation of the mystical work by Karl von Eckartshausen (1752–1803), *Zahlenlehre der Natur* [A key to the mysteries of nature] (1794), was published in 1804.

20. The year of Napoleon's invasion of Russia. The Frenchman is fictitious, and there was no such school in Petersburg.

21. A fortification near the village of Shevardino, built by the Russian army not far from Borodino; a bloody battle took place there on August 24, 1812.

22. "These blue uniforms, worn out by victory," is an inaccurate quotation from a lyric, "Old uniforms, old galloons" (1814), by the French poet Pierre Béranger.

23. Site of a fierce battle near Vienna on July 5–6, 1809, between Napoleon and the Austrian army.

24. Site of Napoleon's greatest victory in Moravia on December 2, 1805, when he defeated the combined forces of the Austrian and Russian armies.

25. Frederick II (1712–86) was king of Prussia (1740–86) and one of the great military generals of all time. The palace in question is Sans Souci, his chief residence in Potsdam.

26. Baron Henri de Jomini (1779–1869) was an officer in Napoleon's army who in 1813 decided to join the Russian side and became a general and aide-de-camp to the tsar. He wrote a number of works on the history of warfare.

27. Karl Moor was the hero of Schiller's first play in verse, *Die Räuber* [The robbers] (1781); Rinaldo Rinaldini was the hero of a picaresque novel by the German author Christian August Vulpius (1762–1827), *Rinaldo Rinaldini* (1797).

28. A group of German writers in the 1830s who opposed the traditions of romanticism and the cult of Goethe.

29. The general name for the chain of mountains stretching from

northern Alaska to Nicaragua, including the Rocky Mountains and the Sierra Madre.

30. According to tradition, Saint Rosalia was born in Palermo and is the patron saint of Sicily.

31. A diminutive form of the girl's name Vera.

32. A unit of length measuring 3,500 feet.

33. Oedipus's solicitous daughter in Greek legend, who was thus portrayed by Sophocles.

34. A city located on the right bank of the Volga river.

35. The general is describing a major battle fought by the Austrian, Prussian, and Russian armies against Napoleon in August 1813 near Dresden.

36. Before emancipation all cultivation of estates in Russia was carried on under the system of either corvée or quitrent. Under the former, serfs were obligated to provide certain services for the landlord.

37. A sculpture by the Italian artist Antonio Canova (1757–1822).

38. In Genesis 39:1–12, Joseph rejects the amorous advances of Potiphar's wife and flees her house, leaving her holding his robe.

39. A city in southeast Russia. Founded in 1777 as a fortress, it became an important base for the Russian conquest of the Caucasus.

40. A Muslim people speaking North Caucasian dialects.

41. The battle of Leipzig (also known as the Battle of Nations), fought on October 16–19, 1813, was a decisive victory of Austrian, Russian, and Prussian forces over Napoleon.

42. A kind of quilted coat.

43. A follower of Muridism, a reactionary sect of Muslims obliged to obey the rules of a sheikh or imam. The sect was characterized by a fanatical hatred of foreigners.

44. One of the hardy Caucasian mountain peoples of Dagestan.

45. The pseudonym of Aleksandr Bestuzhev (1797–1837), a Russian novelist and poet who wrote popular romantic tales in a Byronic style. *Ammalat Bek*, his best novel, was set in the Caucasus.

46. In medicine, a cup applied to the surface of the skin to draw blood through or to it by creating a partial vacuum.

47. The Russian convention for omitting the actual place-name.

48. Much of the peasant population around St. Petersburg was of Finnish origin.

49. The name of the wicked witch in Russian folktales.

50. Lindor: a Spanish lover with a guitar; Aminta: the young hero in love in Torquato Tasso's pastoral drama *Aminta* (1573).

51. Madame Roland (1754–93) was a political figure associated with the Girondists in the French Revolution. Charlotte Corday (1768–93), also a sympathizer of the Girondists, assassinated Jean Paul Marat (1743–93), one of the supporters of the Jacobins. Both women were guillotined.

52. V. A. Ozerov (1769–1816) was a Russian dramatist who wrote historical tragedies in French classical form.

53. Two "philosophical romances" written by Voltaire in 1747 and 1768, respectively.

54. The name of the estate purchased by Voltaire in 1758 to escape persecution by the French authorities and where he lived until 1778.

55. *Les Amours du Chevalier de Faublas* (1789–90), an amorous novel written by Jean-Baptiste Louvet de Couvray (1760–97), translated into Russian twice in the late eighteenth to early nineteenth centuries.

56. A series of novels by French writer and cleric Antoine François Prévost d'Exiles (1697–1763), known as Abbé Prévost, under the general title *Memoires et aventures d'un homme de qualité* (1728–32). A Russian translation called *The Adventures of Marquis G.* was published in Petersburg in 1793.

57. Three battles fought by Napoleon listed in succession: the French defeated the Austrian army at a battle near the Italian village of Marengo on June 14, 1800; Wagram, in lower Austria, was the site of one of Napoleon's most brilliant victories over the Austrians in July 1809; and Napoleon was finally defeated by the British and Prussian forces at Waterloo in June 1815.

58. The myth of Antaeus, a giant who became stronger each time he

touched his mother, Gaea, the earth. He killed everyone with whom he fought until Hercules overcame him by lifting him into the air.

59. An approximate quotation from the conclusion of Voltaire's story "The Babylonian Princess."

60. The old name by which the land was known in medieval times.

61. An inexact citation from a French fable by Jean de La Fontaine (1668–94), "The man who chases after fate and the man who waits for it in bed." Here, and in his diary for 1848, Druzhinin mistakenly ascribes the quotation to George Sand.

Selected BIBLIOGRAPHY

Belinsky, V. G. "A Survey of Russian Literature in 1847." In Belinsky, Chernyshevsky, and Dobrolyubov, *Selected Criticism*, ed. Ralph Matlaw. Bloomington: Indiana University Press, 1976, pp. 33–82.

Brojde, Anmartin-Michal. "Druzhinin's View of American Life and Literature." *Canadian-American Slavic Studies* 10, no. 3 (Fall 1976): 382–99.

Klenin, Emily. "On the Ideological Sources of *Cto delat'?*: Sand, Druž-inin, Leroux." *Zeitschrift für slaviche philologie* 51, no. 2: 367–407.

Offord, Derek. *The First Russian Liberals*. Cambridge, Eng.: Cambridge University Press, 1985, pp. 144–74.

Stites, Richard. *The Women's Liberation Movement in Russia: Feminism, Nihilism, and Bolshevism*, 1860–1930. Princeton, N.J.: Princeton University Press, 1978, pp. 3–25.

Walicki, Andrzej. *A History of Russian Thought from the Enlightenment to Marxism*. Stanford, Calif.: Stanford University Press, 1979, pp. 115–51.